Mary

Lance Clarke

Mary

This is a work of fiction. Names and characters relate to deceased relatives but in all instances the story is completely a product of the author's imagination and any resemblance to actual events or personal characters, living or dead, is entirely coincidental.

The catalogue record for this book is available from the British Library

Cover image: Shutterstock
Cover design and typesetting: Lance Clarke
Published by Manor Cottage Books
ISBN: 9798564891431

Other Books by Lance Clarke

Horizons I
Horizons II
Not of Sound Mind
Balkan Tears
Cruel Harvest
30 Days

Acknowledgements

My hearty thanks go to Judith Leask of Just Right Editing who helped me to get the manuscript in shape - also to my partner and muse Diane who takes all the flak when mistakes are discovered.

Dedication

To my mother

Hitler is doing what centuries of English history have not accomplished – he is breaking down the class structure of England.

Attributed to an American journalist.
September 1940 - the beginning of the Blitz.

Mary

1

The front door to the rectory slammed so hard the architrave shuddered in response. Mary stomped down the path swinging her arms defiantly. The garden gate was open with its rusted lever permanently raised as if in submission. She flounced through it and headed to the open doors of a large wooden garage. Her beloved Enfield motorcycle stood at the back, and she smiled at its shiny black paintwork, and the chrome forks and handlebars that gleamed in beams of light piercing the gloom. It was her refuge; it never argued with her, did exactly what she wanted and never let her down. Her mood softened.

Outside, Mary pulled on her leather cycle helmet, letting her red hair hang loose, and secured the chinstrap. The minute hand on her watch approached ten o'clock. Breathing deeply, she steadied herself. She waited.

Ready, steady – go.

The Enfield jerked forward like an excited stallion with a mind of its own, but Mary was unconcerned, she would tame it. The rectory's shingle driveway was short. Small stones flew in all directions when the tread on the rear tyre bit into the ground. Soon she was charging along the country road to the small market town of Ottery St Mary. The corners were dangerously narrow, and she had to keep her wits about her, steering carefully, braking at the right moment then accelerating fast. The excitement was just what she needed, the noise, the vibration, and the rushing air in her face.

Another angry confrontation with her aunt Agatha earlier that morning infuriated her. What an utter snob her aunt was about the few friends she had – who cared what their fathers did for living?

Ride on, ride on, think only of the ride!

Alongside, to her left, she saw small clouds on the horizon driven by a lively breeze; two of them had broken free of the others and were doing their best to make a race of it.

'Catch me if you can, boys!' she yelled.

Today of all days she had to beat the record, and determinedly gritted her teeth.

After exiting a tight corner, which slowed her speed, a long stretch of road came into view. To the right she saw a field with farm hands loading bundles of cut grass onto a wagon, its horse idly swishing its tail. Now was the time to accelerate. The men stopped work, leaned on their pitchforks, and looked up as the motorcycle roared past them, its throaty exhaust announcing her presence in the quiet Devon countryside. They waved their hats and whistled; undeterred, her gaze remained fixed on the road ahead.

Within two hundred yards of a sharp bend, she glimpsed a Spitfire circling over the trees to her left. It crossed the road in front of her, flying low and now quite close, and the pilot waved. A brave man, living a real life – that was it, a real life. Seconds later her concentration was back on the corner looming in front of her and she braked at the last minute, getting the very last bit out of the straight-line speed.

On she rode, head down, body arched, screaming with excitement. Motoring round the long bend, she leaned heavily to the left and strained to keep the handlebars steady on the dishevelled patches of gritty surface. A ragged hole appeared in front of her, but she was going too fast to avoid it and the front wheel dipped into it and jerked to the right, bouncing her towards the untended hedgerow. Where the hell did that come from?

Her heart beat madly as she stood on the footrests to stop herself going over the top. The motorcycle jumped into the air then yawed left and right, but she wrestled it straight again. 'Wo, beast,' she spluttered. On she went, intoxicated by her success.

Brambles and small branches threatened to rip her woollen jacket and a bunch of leaves flapped at her face as if stroking her onwards. The road levelled and she twisted the throttle on her handgrip, and the motorcycle lurched forward again.

At last, she saw the Bull public house and skidded to a halt flinging the motorcycle against the pub sign and running to the pub door to touch it. Only then could she allow herself to look at her watch: eight minutes and ten seconds after ten. She had beaten her record by a giant thirty seconds. That put the day right.

Exhausted, she allowed her heartbeat to settle, then removed her sweaty goggles and thin leather helmet, pulled her hair above her head, and wiggled her back to loosen it, it felt good. She raised her right hand triumphantly and twirled her goggles around her fingers.

Jack Galloway, the publican, looked up as Mary came through the door and waved. He was a tall man, with a ruddy face and muscled arms, honed from lifting barrels of ale onto wooden blocks. His white shirt was flecked with traces of spilled beer.

A year ago, just after her twentieth birthday, Mary marched resolutely into the public bar and ordered a glass of ale. She recalled the atmosphere that followed. Centuries of male culture frowned upon a woman entering a public house, let alone this room, the male customer looked up silently. Mary smiled politely at Jack's attempted compromise as he pointed to the lounge bar. She ignored it, turned, and grabbed a man's glass on her right and drank its contents, then calmly put the empty glass down, apologised and offered to buy him two in return.

No one said a word, seconds later the man put his head back, burst out laughing and readily accepted. The older men looked up from their dominos and shove ha'penny and joined in with banter.

One shouted, 'You got a lively one 'ere, Jack. Give her ale.'

This show of character from a young woman won over the customers and Jack had nowhere else to go – now she was a regular. After that she was a firm favourite, albeit the only woman ever to use the hallowed sawdust-floored public bar.

The glass in Jack's hand sparkled as he dried it and he smiled at her. 'Beat your record yet?'

'Funny you should ask, as a matter of fact, by thirty seconds. That deserves a gill or two of your best.'

Jack took up a glass, turned and poured ale slowly from a nearby wooden barrel. He looked over his shoulder, half-smiling. 'May I guess that you've had another tiff with 'erself?'

'Yup, something like that.'

Handing the glass to Mary he tilted his head forward. 'If she knew that I served you ale she would damn my soul.'

'I know, but luckily you lost it decades ago, so no worries there, then.'

He laughed loudly at the response, she always had an answer for everything.

Mary gazed out of the half-open door at her motorcycle leaning against the pub sign as though it were resting and out of breath. It meant everything to her, but its real value was that riding a motorcycle was not something prim young ladies were expected to do. But it was not just this challenge to conventional behaviour that she liked, but the chance to master riding techniques and learn about motorcycle components. Importantly, it was her antidote to boredom.

The Bull was Mary's haven, where she could relax and be herself. She would not let her aunt stifle or control her and was damned if she would be cowed.

To an aged retiree, Devon would be idyllic – but to Mary, sent there from her home in London to recuperate after bouts of rheumatic and scarlet fever, it felt like rejection. After almost two long years away there was no sign of a return to join her siblings, and letters had become infrequent. Now the war clouded everything – it was something almost everyone was actively involved in – except her.

Mary sipped a glass of ale and chatted with Jack about motorcycles, soaking up his knowledge about carburettors – her Enfield had problems that needed solving. He quickly identified her problem.

'You're a gem, Jack, I don't know what I would do without you.'

'Just keep giving me your cash for ale, that'll do nicely,' he said, smiling broadly as he waved a dishcloth over the surface of the bar.

A low hum from outside the window broke their conversation and Mary rushed to see what it was. Pulling the flimsy net curtains to one side she rubbed the dust off the grubby window. There it was again, in the middle of the bright blue sky – the Spitfire. It whirled and circled like a captive bird let out of a cage, enjoying the freedom to rise and fall, whirl and glide – perfectly free and with no constraints.

2

The atmosphere in the rectory was leaden and silent, except for the monotonous, deep tick, tick, of the grandfather clock in the red tiled hallway. Mary sat awkwardly on a carved wooden chair in the study trying to control her emotions by examining one of her fingernails still stained from cleaning the carburettor on her Enfield.

Aunt Agatha stood looking out of the window, her bony frame, ramrod straight, illuminated by the afternoon light, giving it an eerie appearance. She was dressed in a black woollen skirt and wore a three-quarter length grey gardening jacket over a dark green pullover. In one hand she held a walking stick and in the other her battered wide-brimmed gardening hat. Her magnetism filled the room, even the air felt prickly.

Mary waited to be confronted by Agatha's usual tight-lipped expression and wondered if she ever smiled - perhaps God forbade it? She knew the form off by heart: her aunt would turn slowly, and place her stick and hat won the table, she would raise her head, stare at her, and fold her arms. Then the silence would be broken. Battle would commence.

It didn't take long.

'So, where were you earlier today?'

'Why?'

'Don't be insolent. Never mind why, where were you?'

'If you must know I went for a quiet ride on my motorcycle. It's such a nice day.'

Agatha stiffened and scowled. 'You're lying, and I don't like lies. The verger was shopping in the village and saw you. He said you went into the Bull public house. Apparently, you skidded to a halt after driving that dreadful machine at a mad speed. I have no doubt you were in one of your silly moods after our discussion over breakfast.'

Mary fumed, it was an argument not a discussion and pretty one-sided at that.

'I don't know what you mean. The verger must be mistaken. A slow ride into the village and a glass of lemonade is surely not a crime. I'm surprised he saw anything, he's so short-sighted I'm sure he couldn't even recognise a picture of the King.'

Agatha slammed her hand on the table. 'Don't be rude and don't lie to me. He looked through the window and saw you - drinking ale. What do you think you are, a farm hand?'

Mary went to stand up.

'Sit down.'

'No.'

Agatha's face reddened.

'Then I'll see to it that your father's allowance is forfeited forthwith. I'm fed up with your insolence. Your uncle and I have given you room and board here for many years and all you do is throw it back in our faces. I'm going to write to your father. Lord knows, in these troubled times he has enough stress to deal with without having to sort out an errant daughter.'

Mary ran her hands through her hair and regretted her incautious comments about the verger and tried to avoid more discomfort.

'I'm sure you mean well, Aunt Agatha, but you watch my every move and I'm totally isolated from the community. You don't want me to meet younger people, I'm dragged to church, and you question my every request. Frankly, I don't want to be controlled. I want a life of my own.'

Agatha's face was a mask without emotion. After a short pause she smirked, 'I think you had better go, now, if you please.'

Mary shrugged her shoulders and walked into the hallway. She accepted this unwarranted scolding, just another in her life at the rectory. As she passed a window by the front door, she saw a small truck exiting the gates. Something caught her eye - bile rose in her throat, and she looked on in disbelief. On the back of the truck was her beloved motorcycle tethered upright, the handlebars jerking left and right as the vehicle moved making it look like a wild animal trying to get loose from bondage.

She screamed, 'No!'

Bursting through the door she ran outside and chased the truck shouting, 'Come back, that's mine!'

It drove on and she was left stunned, her heart beating wildly. She stormed back to remonstrate with her aunt.

'You are truly an evil person. I hate you. Why would you do that? You know how much that motorcycle means to me.'

Agatha was unmoved. Straightening her back she clasped her hands in front of her and leaned her face towards Mary. 'The infatuation of material things is evil, young lady. You would do well to deal with your nature and discipline, rather than wasting your time on such pursuits. It's for your own good.'

Mary stomped upstairs her eyes brimming with tears. Her body was consumed with anger that threatened to burst out of her chest. She slammed her bedroom door and threw herself face down onto her bed.

This really was the very worst thing her aunt had done to her. It effectively imprisoned her in the rectory, unable to travel far – she'd rather her aunt poked her eyes out.

She punched the mattress furiously. 'I hate you. I hate you,' she cried and buried her face into the pillow.

Bright sunlight flickered through the branches of a large yew tree at the back of the rectory and Mary sat with her uncle, Raymond, on the dry ground around its base. The canopy provided coolness against the heat of the late Spring sunshine. The surrounding countryside, with rolling green fields, rows of new vegetables reaching for the sunshine and apple orchards in blossom, formed a pallet of colour below the bright blue sky. But even this failed to provide the balm needed to reduce her distress. Mary was still furious about the injustice of her aunt's action. Her uncle was a gentle man, who lived in the rectory with his sister, Agatha, and was so much better at rolling with the fire.

Raymond's grey hair flapped in the light breeze and his blue eyes twinkled as he sought to calm his favourite niece. He took off his wire-framed glasses and pulled out a handkerchief from his waistcoat pocket. After cleaning the lenses, he put them on, looked at her fondly and touched her shoulder. 'Don't take on so. It's only a motorcycle!'

Mary glared at him, the force of which made him instantly lean away from her. A wild stare from a formidable young woman was no match for this mild man.

'You just don't understand, uncle. That motorcycle was the only thing that I owned which gave me freedom to get away from this mausoleum. It was my salvation, I could clean it, repair it, and now it's gone.'

'But it was only on loan and could have been reclaimed at any time, couldn't it?'

'Oh heck, yes, but we both know that's highly unlikely. It's thanks to that parish councillor, Colonel - what's his name?'

'John Field, yes, a nice man indeed.'

Mary smiled as she reflected. 'After church one day we talked about isolation, and I prattled on about my need for a bit of excitement, and he winked at me in a rather conspiratorial way. Out of the blue, he turned up here with the motorcycle and caught Aunt Agatha out by recounting that her own husband, uncle Leonard, had owned one when he was young, and it was only right and fitting that I should be given the chance too.'

Raymond laughed. 'Oh, do I remember that. Her face was riven with uncertainty as she thanked him for his kind gift, but before she could decline the offer, he proclaimed her most considerate and handed you the keys. He manipulated her beautifully – not many men can do that.'

Mary put her hands between her knees and shrugged her shoulders. 'I spent months riding around the fields learning to ride the beast, as my scarred shins will testify.'

Raymond gave her a hug. 'That's you all over, you never give up, Mary.'

She leaned against his cool bony body that smelled of sweet aftershave. What a lifeline he was for her with his good humour and support when she needed it most. He was a good man, kind and thoughtful. She looked up at him.

'What about the games we used to play when I was younger? I'm not sure which of us was the child. The best was knocking at the front door and hiding in the bushes, watching Agatha stride out and look around angrily but finding no one there. It was so funny.'

'Yes,' he said, grinning broadly, I think I should've been a bit more grown up, but then who wants to grow up?'

Mary jabbed him in the chest.

'But my best move was when you were a teenager and I prised you away from the house to join the local amateur dramatic society. Agatha tentatively agreed, as it was time for the Christmas pantomime, and she probably thought her church friends would take kindly to it and it would enhance her status. Then you continued in the other productions, after they spoke so highly of your talents. That was a coup I was particularly proud of.'

Mary felt calmer talking about amusing past events but couldn't dispel the sense of injustice. She stood up suddenly.

'Uncle Raymond, I simply must get home to London. I'm fit and well and have been for years – I can't understand why Papa hasn't called for me to return. I need space to make a life for myself and not have to endure someone else doing it for me. I'm better than all this, I know I am.'

Raymond pursed his lips. 'Well now, there's rather a lot going on right now and think on, most young people are leaving London for the country. You're better off here what with all those bombs being dropped. As for your father, he's struggling to get more books published – it can't be easy in this financial climate. Then there's other duties he may have because of the war.'

Mary fizzed at the platitudes. 'For goodness sake, uncle, he's a writer and a poet, that's hardly of use to Winston Churchill. He's not even an air raid warden. I'm his daughter and I need him.'

She felt guilty for saying that. Her anger still hadn't drained away, and she put her head in her hands. 'I want to go to Papa, but I can't because I'm broke.' She stood up and banged her foot against the ground. 'To hell with it, I'm going to London, even if I must walk there. You'll see.'

Raymond winced. He had often observed the headstrong Mary, and when said she would do something, then it was highly likely that she would.

'Excuse me for a moment, my dear. Don't go away, I won't be long.' Without looking back, he walked briskly into the rectory, and she heard him clump up the stairs.

Mary gazed forlornly at the gate through which her beloved motorcycle had been taken and looked up when Raymond returned ten minutes later. He sat down and addressed her seriously keeping his voice low.

'Listen to me, Mary. I've had a life, military, civilian, managing, planning and all that stuff. I've been a bit of a chump and made mistakes, too many in fact, and will have to live with them.' He stopped as if he had innocently called them up and was now trying to push them back in their box, then gathered himself. 'But this is not one of them. Please take this and don't argue.'

He handed her an envelope.

'I can only afford twenty-five pounds, it's all I have. I want you to have it. Use it to get to London, buy clothes, spend it as you like. Depart this place and then, Mary, follow your heart. Don't be worn down by the words of others, know your own mind and cherish it.'

Mary took the envelope with trembling hands. 'Uncle Raymond, thank you so much, but I can't take this.'

'Yes, you can. Now then, there's no time for sentiment, we need a plan. There's a pushbike behind the garage, get up early tomorrow and ride to Exeter railway station – it will take you about an hour and fifteen minutes, but you'll have to peddle hard. It will be dark, but sunrise is at about ten minutes to six. At seven o'clock there's a fast train to London Paddington. Buy a ticket and go. You rarely get up before seven thirty to eight o'clock, so you'll not be missed until the train is well on its way. To make sure, you, and I mean you, not me, will let down the tyres on your uncle's car, just in case a search party is organised, so build in enough time to do that. I'll loosen the telephone wire so that possible calls to our neighbours for assistance cannot be made. By the time all the chaos is sorted out you'll be having lunch with your papa.' He smiled like a genial general that has just sorted out an important mission that avoids casualties.

'I don't know what to say.'

'Say nothing. It's a long time since I've done anything remotely brilliant and positive.'

Mary touched his shoulder gently.

'I'm so very grateful,' she said. Her nerves were dancing a jig. This was her moment - *London, here I come.*

The morning was cloudless, and the sky was beginning to lighten as Mary crept downstairs and out of the kitchen door. The mist in the fields gave everything a magical glow. Her anger forgotten, she focused clearly as she made her way silently towards the garage. Putting her small suitcase to one side, she went to her uncle's car and bent down to let the air out of all the tyres. The top of the first valve was difficult to unscrew because of ingrained dirt but eventually gave in, and she used a screwdriver to release the pressure; as the air hissed, she giggled. Revenge is best served cold, they say, and wished she could see Aunt Agatha's face. At last, the positions were reversed - she was in control.

When this part of the mission was complete, she located the pushbike, secured her case tightly to the carrier above the rear wheel, and pedalled slowly down the driveway. Halfway along, she became anxious at the loud crunching of the cycle on the gravel, stopped and kept perfectly still. All was quiet and a minute later she judged it safe to continue. Nevertheless, it felt eerie, almost as though the rectory was pulling at her; she half-expected a wild shout from a bedroom window – thankfully, none came.

The ride to the railway station took as long as Raymond had estimated but she hardly noticed. Her mind raced with the need to get there, get on the train, and get to London. She was warm and slightly out of breath when she arrived. After removing her suitcase, she put the pushbike behind the ticket office and went inside.

The place was draughty and cold, and the untreated dusty floorboards creaked as she approached the counter. She wrote a note for her uncle, pinned it to the noticeboard and hoped he would be able to retrieve the bicycle later. The man at the window was chubby, ruddy-faced and wore an ill-fitting railway hat that looked as though it would slide off his head if he coughed.

'And what can I do for you young lady?'

'Single to London please,' and she put a five-pound note on the counter.

He looked surprised at the banknote. 'First class, second or third?'

Mary stuttered, 'Oh, second, sorry.'

He handed her the change and ticket and nodded towards a door to the rear of the office. 'Up the stairs and across the bridge to the other side. The train will be here in ten minutes or so. There's a kiosk and you can get yourself a cuppa if you want.'

Mary took the change and ticket, almost dropping them in her rush. If only the train was there, right now, ready to go. She felt a mixture of nervousness and excitement and knew that she would only feel safe when seated and on her way.

But a cuppa sounded like a good idea.

The London-bound express pulled away from the platform, large puffs of smoke belching from the chimney and steam hissing from the engine. She was thrilled to be on her way. The train got up to running speed and soon the hypnotic sound of the wheels clicking along the track's fishplates made her relax and her nerves calmed. The sun burned off the morning mist, and the rolling green fields with their dry-stone walls and coppices made pleasing scenery. She felt like waving to the cows as they stood idly chewing their cud and staring at the charging locomotive.

It was time to leave the storms behind, to forget her frequent long spells away from home and recapture a family life. So much time had passed. Above all, she would need her father's advice about getting a job. As the train sped onwards, she imagined that the steam trailing behind resembled loosened coils of tension, disappearing as she left Devon.

Her eyes roamed around the carriage and settled on the only other passenger who sat across from her, a young man, about her age, dressed in a beige double-breasted suit, white shirt, and brightly coloured tie. He wore a neatly trimmed, pencil-thin moustache. His hair was dark and slicked back with brilliantine, she recognised the scent because one of the church wardens used it and she didn't care for it.

He pulled out a cigarette packet.

'I'd rather you didn't' she said abruptly.

'Oh?' he replied with a crooked smile. 'Want one?'

'I don't smoke.'

'Don't, or never tried?'

'Well, actually...'

'Look, take one. Go on. Give it a try. Everyone smokes, it's all the rage. If you don't like it, I'll throw it away, no loss to me.'

He held the packet towards her, tantalisingly. She had indeed seen lots of people smoking in the pub and in films, it always looked so stylish. Perhaps now was not the time to be the odd one out. It was time to try new things.

'All right. Thank you. I will try one. But if I don't like it, I'll stop.'

'Deal. That's my girl. Now then, pop it in your mouth and when I light it suck in the smoke and take it right into your lungs, don't hesitate. You'll cough at first, everyone does, but after that it'll be okay.'

With a deft flick of his wrist, he opened his Zippo lighter, thumbed the spark wheel, and put the flame towards the cigarette which wobbled in her trembling lips. As predicted, she coughed at first, but determined as ever she continued with more drags and was soon experiencing the hit that nicotine gives the lungs – that feeling of a cool spiky wind filling her chest and making her head fuzzy.

He showed her how to hold the cigarette and what to do with the ash. She looked at her faint reflection in the carriage window and laughed to herself as she instinctively posed like the famous actress, Marlene Dietrich.

The man sat back and regarded her slyly.

'What do you do for work?' she said, trying to avoid his roaming gaze, as she straightened her skirt.

'I'm a travelling salesman - ladies clothing,' he said, adding with leery look, 'my popular line to my mates in the pub is that I travel in ladies' underwear.'

He gave a rasping laugh.

Mary couldn't see the joke.

'And you?'

'I don't work, yet that is. I'm going to stay with my father in London, Fentiman Road, Vauxhall, do you know it?'

'No, can't say that I do. Bermondsey, yes, Fentiman Road, no.'

Mary missed the veiled sarcasm.

'He's a writer of books on horticulture and gardening in general, he also writes poems. He sent copies to most politicians as well as the King who thanked him in a letter.'

He feigned interest. 'Well, well, lovely old job. Clever chap.' He dragged deeply on his cigarette and blew the smoke making large circles. When he smoked it looked unsophisticated, quite unlike how it was depicted by famous actors in films.

After a while, the conversation became stilted, he talked about his job selling clothes and before that, food, but fidgeted and seemed preoccupied. He leaned forward, and looked straight at her.

'Well now, I taught you to smoke, how about that, eh?'

Mary nodded naively, not knowing how to respond.

'So, I wonder what else I can teach you?'

'I'm not sure what you mean?'

As the words fell from her lips her stomach churned as he smirked.

'Oh, come on. You're very pretty and you can't be that innocent.' He got up and sat beside her and put his hand on her knee. She tried to move away but he held it tight. He pressed his body against her, it was muscled and firm and she felt his hot breath on her neck. Her stomach churned and she used all her strength to untangle herself from his grip.

She sat up straight and faced him. 'Please, don't do that.'

He leaned back and laughed. 'Now there's spirit, I like it. But that's not very nice. After me teaching you to smoke so you can join the grown-ups. This is just another bit to your education – where's your gratitude?'

Mary wriggled as he put his arm around her shoulder again. As his face closed in on hers, she angrily brought her fist up and hit his jaw.

He reeled back and looked at her threateningly. 'I can see you need to be taught a lesson, my girl.' He stood up and raised his clenched hand, then the door to the carriage opened with a thud.

A soldier filled the doorway, his fists closed as if ready for a fight. He breathed heavily and looked angry. Mary noticed how big he was.

'Hey, you. That's no way to treat a lady. Now pick up your things and get out.'

'What's it got to do with...?'

He didn't finish. The soldier grabbed his collar. 'Out, now, or I'll be forced to give you a good beating.'

The man picked up his coat, hat, and briefcase and snarled, 'Go on then soldier, she's all yours. Officers' meat!'

Without warning, the soldier punched him on the nose making it bleed profusely. Then he grabbed the man by his jacket lapels and threw him into the corridor.

He closed the door, turned to Mary, and said softly. 'I'm so sorry for the violence but he really shouldn't have talked to you like that. My name is Giles Masterson, captain, Royal Engineers. I was passing when I saw him grab your knee. Bit of a cad, wasn't he?'

'Yes, you could say that. Thank you so much for rescuing me.'

'It's a pleasure. But I saw your punch – frankly, I'm not sure who scored most, you or me. May I sit down?'

Mary laughed and felt better for it.

'Yes, of course, please do.'

His old-worldly good manners charmed her. He was good-looking and had the most sparkling blue eyes she had ever seen. He settled back then turned to her.

'I need to say something, and I hope you don't think I'm trying to be a big brother. Times are tough these days and it can be quite challenging for a young woman on her own, especially in London. Keep your wits about you and don't trust anyone until you get to know them properly. Sorry, but it has to be said.'

Mary felt safe with him, but more than that, she felt equal. Although he was giving her good advice on personal safety, he was talking to her on the same level. That was something new to her.

'I think I've a lot to learn, Giles. My name's Mary Henslow by the way.'

'Nice to meet you, Mary.' He paused for a moment, ran his hands though his fair hair and looked thoughtful. 'Now I do feel sad. I'm joining a regiment tonight and we expect to be off to North Africa in the next few weeks. Were it not for that, I would certainly be approaching your father for permission to take you out.'

Mary blushed. 'And, kind sir, I must tell you that I would be prodding him to say yes!'

For the remainder of the journey, they talked and laughed as though they had been friends for years. He was a little older than her and had a disjointed family life. He was put into boarding school after his father accepted a post in the Diplomatic Corps in India and only reunited with his parents during holidays. Mary soaked up his lively conversation as he drew her out of herself.

'What about you, where have you come from and where are you going?'

'Oh, it's all too complicated to discuss really. Put simply, I've abandoned a boring life in a rectory in Devon and I'm going back home to be with my family and get a job. Home is Fentiman Road, Vauxhall.'

Giles listened carefully and deftly teased out facts such as Aunt Agatha's eccentricities, and that her father was an author and poet. Mary was afraid that he would press her for more information, but he didn't.

Time passed quickly and she felt a tinge of disappointment when the train arrived at Paddington. Giles took her suitcase and escorted her to the taxi rank. He politely touched his cap. 'I must report to the Railway Transport Officer at the military desk.' Then with a regretful expression added, 'I suppose this is goodbye?'

'Yes,' Mary replied unsteadily, she wanted more of his company but didn't know how to express it. 'Goodbye, you never know, we may meet again.'

'I do hope so,' he replied warmly.

They briefly touched hands and she watched as he walked slowly away. He looked over his shoulder and smiled. A shrill whistle blew, and a mixture of steam and smoke enveloped him. It was like a prince disappearing in one of her village pantomimes. The image would stay with her – so would that brief touch. It was odd – such a short meeting and yet she felt so attracted; now the joy was draining out of her.

Regaining her purpose, she turned and joined the taxi queue. It shortened in no time and Mary was grateful for that. The whole area was buzzing with people, many of whom were in uniform. They jostled and bumped into each other, but strangely no one got upset.

Finally, a taxi stopped, and the driver shouted, 'Where to, luv?'

'Fentiman Road, Vauxhall, please.'

'Hop in.'

Mary put her bag into the cab first then got in and sat down heavily. Her face was beaming, and she felt excited. It was so good to be on her way home. She would settle in, take stock of her situation, and set about finding a job. She couldn't wait to see the look on papa's face.

Here I come, Papa!

Nora Henslow folded an intercepted letter carefully then placed it with others in a bundle held together by an elastic band. She opened a small drawer in her secretaire and put them inside, then locked it. The sun was just rising, and a shard of light pierced the dusty air and lit up her pale face - she irritably moved away from it, stopped and stared into space.

That girl always has an answer for everything, she is my daughter, but will always be a thorn in my side. It was for her own good that Mary should settle down, find herself a husband and have babies. God knows, I've had enough to put up with in this family, when all I want is respect and to be left alone to enjoy my later years. I deserve it – I want it!

Reading the month-old letter, addressed to her husband, Thomas, had angered her. *Dear Papa,* no mention of her. *Papa* was everything to everyone: an army veteran from the First World War, ex-clergyman, writer on horticulture and a poet. She huffed and clenched her hands. Talent is all very well, but only good management of resources brings in much needed finance to keep a household going. That was what she was good at and congratulated herself.

Flipping open her compact, she peered at her reflection in the mirror as she applied her lipstick. Powder filled the crow's-feet cracks around her eyes. It was so unfair, men and women aged on different tracks, quite apart from the pressure of multiple pregnancies, which irked her. Nevertheless, she was determined to look and dress well.

Today, she would see friends in her club for a game of bridge, a gin or two and a light snack. Each of them had a 'spouse' issue and usually aired the challenges and outcomes to the amusement of all. Kindred spirits and kindred strategies. As she contemplated the morning ahead, she heard a floorboard creak.

In the doorway stood her husband, Thomas, his face lumpy with early morning folds, fiddling awkwardly with his collar-stud, as he did most mornings. As he coughed his chest rattled.

'Here, let me,' she said, brushing his hand away with a gesture that was halfway between helpful and irritable.

He twitched as the skin on his throat was pinched.

'Thank you, dear. Bridge today?'

'Yes, that's right. And for you, a meeting with your literary agent, Gregory - remember?'

'Ah, yes, of course,' he replied, disingenuously.

Nora raised a knowing eyebrow. Gregory was one of the few agents left who had funds to spare and needed nailing down. Thomas touched his nose with his finger inferring he was in control then strode down to breakfast.

Nora straightened her skirt and reached for her jacket. Thomas was still a handsome man, even in his sixties. She was long since over the sadness of a past hurtful event and the steps that she had taken to survive. But that was what life was about - surviving and surviving well.

Regaling him from time to time with the contents of non-existent phone calls from Agatha regarding Mary's life in Devon was necessary, and she felt no guilt. His infatuation with *little miss feisty,* was too much. *Mary this, Mary that.* Being let down by him had been a pattern she was used to, but being sidelined in her own home was more than she could take.

The front door to Fentiman Road slammed shut as Thomas left the house. Twenty minutes later, Nora left. During the interval neither spoke to each other.

The first thing Mary noticed as she stood outside 123, Fentiman Road was its faded Victorian façade. She didn't remember it being so scruffy. Six large steps, slightly worn in the middle, led up to a dark blue front door, in the middle of which was a brass doorknocker in the shape of a lion's head. She had no key and felt silly having to knock at her own front door, and a moment later it slowly opened.

'My goodness,' said a lady in a starched white apron. It was Mrs Annie Knight, the family housekeeper, short and slim, a beaming face below grey hair in a bun. 'This is such a surprise, we haven't seen you for ages, Mary. I wasn't expecting you.'

'Well, Mrs K, it was kind of on the spur of the moment.'

Mrs Knight gave her a gentle hug and they both turned and walked through the hallway. Mary wanted to reach out and touch familiar things as if the feel of them would revitalise her.

'Your mother's upstairs. Have a care, she's in one of her moods – if you don't mind me saying.'

She was right.

Mary's mother sat upright flicking through papers on her small writing desk in her study. When she saw Mary, her face flattened. A blush of pink began to form under her ears and her eyes stabbed at her.

'What on earth are you doing here?'

'Mother, at least say, hello!'

Her mother retraced her steps. 'Yes, of course, Mary. It's just a surprise. You just turn up out of the blue, that's all. Now perhaps you can explain?'

Mary had the sense to realise that it was too much to expect her mother to greet her with open arms even under normal visitations. She gathered her wits and decided to give a straight answer.

'I'm here because I hate the seclusion of the rectory, and I hate Aunt Agatha's pious unworldly discipline that tries to flatten me daily to her will. There's more, but I think that may be enough for now.'

There was a long silence, then her mother forced a smile, straightened, and said purposefully, 'Why don't you go to your room, and we'll talk about it when your father gets back from his agent.'

She turned back to her papers as if nothing had happened.

Mary went upstairs to her room – it was not quite 'her' room, rather, it was one used by her brothers as they transited from university to military service, via Fentiman Road. For the moment it was hers and at least she was home from Devon. She hadn't expected a grand welcome from her mother, but a hug would have been nice.

She was tired after the day's events and decided to lay on the bed for a short snooze. Her rest was disturbed when a vision of Aunt Agatha appeared, pursuing her down the rectory driveway, shouting and reaching for her, getting closer and closer. She woke up with a start and heard the unmistakable sound of two girls arguing. It was her sisters Hazel and Mavis.

'No, I did not, did not, did not...!'

Hazel's strident voice retorted, 'You did, don't tell fibs, you spied on me and Roger, you're weird.'

'That's so mean. It was just chance I saw you both,' then she spat out, 'kissing!'

By now Mary was at the door to the laundry room and saw the look on Hazel's face as she tried to silence Mavis.

'For goodness' sake, shush! You know that mother will go berserk if she finds out.'

Mavis looked smug. 'Then you'll have to be good to me from now on.'

'Don't hold your breath,' said Hazel and she stomped out.

Mavis briefly glanced at her. 'Oh, hello, Mary.' Then she too was gone.

Mary shrugged and quietly walked to Hazel's room. The fragrance of perfumes hung in the air.

Hazel looked up sulkily. 'Hi there, sorry about that, our younger sibling can be such a pain. This is a surprise. Why are you here?'

'When we have time, I'll tell you more. But for now, let's leave it - it was bad enough explaining to mother.'

Hazel squealed. 'I bet that was fun.'

'So, how's London been since I was last here?'

'It's a bit strange really - especially the bloody bombs. Lots of buildings have that hideous tape on the windows, but Papa won't have it. He says a bit of tape is not going to save anybody. He's adamant that the government won't drive him out of London. So, here we jolly well are. It's not so bad, I've had dozens of boyfriends, my dear you wouldn't believe the choice a girl has in the city these days. That little wretch of a sister of ours caught me kissing my latest, Roger. You'll like him.'

'Well, Hazel, I can see that Mr Hitler's antics haven't stopped you from enjoying yourself. You have boyfriends and I have, well 'had,' an Enfield motorcycle.'

'Ugh, a motorcycle. Give me a decent car driven by a handsome chap any day - but each to their own, eh?'

'Yes, that's about it I suppose. Well, I'd better unpack what little I brought with me from Devon.'

Hazel turned away without a word and set about examining her lipsticks and make up.

Sitting on her bed Mary recalled what life had been like when her sisters were small, it had been so much more peaceful. After a while she felt a presence, looked up and saw the tall imposing figure of her father. He had the bearing of an ex-military man. A faint aroma of tobacco smoke was in the air. His face opened into a broad smile, and he bent down and kissed her lightly on the forehead.

'Well, my sweet, you never fail to surprise me.'

She huffed and reached out for his hand, holding it tightly to her cheek.

He put on a pretend-angry expression, let go of her and theatrically splayed his hands from his sides. 'Your mother is furious, but don't take it to heart. She's never been that good at being put on a spot. We also have rather irritating bills to clear today, perhaps one or two extra bottles of Scotch stretched the budget,' he said, pulling a silly face. 'The moment for explanations is therefore not quite right.'

She took advantage of the light mood. 'So, I'm here and I want a job, I really want to work. Where do I start?'

Her father looked surprised and raised his eyebrows. 'To do what exactly?'

'I don't know,' she blurted and felt silly for saying it. 'Oh, don't look at me like that, Papa. I just want to be independent. I'm a very capable, you know.'

Her father sat on her bed and regarded her with a smile. 'My dear girl, when you work you are hardly independent, let me assure you of that. You'll have a boss and will need to do as you're told,' adding with a hint of irony, 'for you that might be a tad difficult!'

He put his hands together as if in prayer, his thumbs turning like mini-windmill blades.

'Mary. It's confusing. We've been getting reports from Agatha that you were well settled. We even got hints that you were becoming romantically attached to the new parson and that wedding bells were a possibility.'

Mary exploded. 'What? No way, no way whatsoever. He's got nothing about him, and I have no feelings for him at all. In fact, he's utterly boring.' She was breathless and red in the face. 'I can't think why Aunt Agatha said that. As for being settled, I'm here for reasons I don't want to discuss now, but I'm anything but settled. Papa, I want a life.'

Her father was taken aback at her anger. 'Oh dear, I'm sorry to upset you, but I'm only telling you what we've been told. Look, about work,' he paused and looked awkward, 'the fact is that you've had a very sound private education on the literary front, but the rest has, I'm sorry to say, been rather overlooked. That's my fault I suppose. You see, I, or should I say, we, thought that you and your sisters would marry well, to a man in the city, or church. The war has made things a little more challenging.'

Mary was surprised and baulked at his scenario for her future, but put it to one side and said urgently, 'But you must know of an avenue into work. If not, then perhaps I could join up?'

He straightened his back and raised his chin. 'My goodness don't do that, that's not for you, Mary. You would have to enter low, and goodness knows who you would end up mixing with. Twelve months into service and you would be dropping your aitches and taking on the emerging socialist drivel currently gaining traction.

Quite apart from that, the people I talk to consider this war to be something we should never have got ourselves into and if we cannot win it by force there must be another avenue to bring it all to an end. Watch this space, as the Americans say in their films.' He tapped his nose knowingly.

Mary was deflated but didn't want to show it. She didn't like what he was saying and was confused.

Her father took her hand, 'Let's just see what turns up. But best of all, let's just find you a good man, preferably a rich one!' He laughed in a hollow, insincere way.

He kissed her head like he used to do when she was a little girl and then got up.

'You had better settle in and then I suppose we should talk. I don't really know when or how – never was good at such things. Later perhaps?'

'Yes, Papa, later will do. It's so good to see you - can I have a hug?'

'Of course, my pleasure, dear.'

He held her and she felt protected in his arms. Arms that cosseted her, away from the ire of her mother when she was young. Arms that wrapped her in a loving carapace. Arms that she missed so much. They parted and she felt sad, she wanted more of his company.

Mary was disappointed. Papa made light of her getting a job, without having a proper conversation about her needs or even trying to give her help or advice. This wasn't like him and reasoned that he must be busy or under stress with his work. Yes, that was it, busy. Nevertheless, she desperately wanted to get him focused on her aim to get into work, without the interruption of dealing with why she left Devon, namely Aunt Agatha's actions. It would not be easy.

He must surely have a well-placed contact or two and she was determined to squeeze an introduction out of him - it was just a matter of time.

The evening meal was a trial of endurance and guarded emotions. The girls tried to keep their animosity to themselves but barely succeeded; Mavis's face telegraphed menace that held her sister's secret. Her mother politely went through the mechanics of serving dinner, but failed to address Mary's return, almost as if she had not been away and there was nothing to discuss - but of course there was.

Mrs Knight put the plates in front of everyone and then placed the serving dishes on the table before leaving. Her mother served Papa first and then turned to the girls.

'Rabbit?'

Hazel and Mavis grimaced. Mary said enthusiastically, 'Yummy, we ate a lot of rabbit in Devon.'

Her mother gave her an icy stare, long enough to be awkward. Mary squirmed, the meaning telegraphed, but the words remained unsaid.

'Potatoes,' said her mother and everyone accepted them without response.

Mary knew that it was likely to be difficult, arriving home unannounced and having to explain why, but hadn't quite expected the rather dysfunctional atmosphere, each family member seemingly living in their own bubble. Even Papa was in another world, detached and glancing at a small notebook, content to address her mother with platitudes such as, 'very tasty rabbit dear.'

Everyone drifted away from the table and went to their rooms. Her mother and father went to the lounge to discuss important business – Mary mused that it was probably about Papa's Scotch order.

His hug now seemed a thousand miles away.

Though Mary was glad to be home, the challenges were enormous. Things were not quite panning out the way she expected, but then what had she really expected? It was exhausting trying to gain attention, but she steadfastly resolved that it was simply a waiting game. For now, she needed to escape her sisters' squabbling, and her mother's indifference – they had never had a tender relationship, but it still hurt. She missed the laughter and innocence of childhood, now damaged by the sharp fingers of puberty. Excuses or not, it was painfully irritating after the solitude of the rectory, and she needed a break and decided to go for a walk.

Mrs Knight saw her approach the front door. 'Mary don't forget your gas mask, there's a spare one on the last peg on the rack. Can't have you being told off by the wardens now, can we?'

'Thanks, Mrs K, us country folk need looking after.' She put on her raincoat, grabbed a gas mask container and left the house.

Fentiman Road was quiet, and she ambled along, peeking into the trees that lined the avenue to see if she could spot the birds that, despite Mr Hitler's attention over the last year or so, might have opted to stay and sing for the neighbourhood. The air smelled of sulphur after a short shower. She aimlessly scuffed the pavement with her shoes and noticed the number of cigarette butts discarded carelessly. It never used to look like that. The streets were eerily quiet, a lot of houses were boarded up, whilst others looked lived in, judging by the enormous blackout curtains that hung lazily along the edges of the windows.

A small group of men and women passed, wearing dark blue overalls covered in thick grey dust, and their faces pallid and exhausted. Haversacks, tin helmets, and gas masks clinked as they walked. They looked up at her and managed weary smiles.

As she walked round the corner, she came up short.

'Giles!'

He stood there in his army uniform, smart, upright, and beaming.

'Mary, I'm so pleased I found Fentiman Road.' He laughed. 'I have such a poor memory and thought that I'd forgotten and could only think, Dentiman, Rentiman...oh dear, what a hopeless clot. Got there in the end.'

Mary breathed heavily. A thousand words ran through her brain in different excited directions, but all she could do was blurt, 'So you have,' and was aware that her face hurt because she was smiling so much. She added, awkwardly, 'it's such a surprise, I'm so glad to see you.'

Giles recognised her nervousness and said softly, 'And for what it's worth, I'm glad to see you too. How about a walk and a cup of tea?'

'Sounds good to me,' she replied, almost breathless with joy. She tried to sound casual but wasn't certain she'd succeeded.

They strolled along the main road and came to Vauxhall Park. Giles took her arm and they headed for a small, orange-coloured tea shack. The man behind the counter wore a flat hat and had a weather-beaten face. When he smiled, gaps in his remaining nicotine-stained teeth made him look rather comic.

'What can I do for you sir? Tea and perhaps a wad, only got margarine I'm afraid. No jam, bloody sugar rationing,' he turned to Mary, 'but you, my dear, look sweet enough.'

'Just two teas, please,' said Giles, as he counted out the pennies.

The man smiled his shed-door smile again, but as he did so, a short, large-breasted lady came up the steps and whacked him lightly on the head with a dishcloth. A kitchen apron fought valiantly with her curves, and she wore a headscarf with the ends tied in a bow above her head at the front. 'Off yer go, Albert, I'll get these. Stop ogling at the lady!'

Mary and Giles laughed.

'Sorry about that luv,' she said to Mary, 'it's 'is age. Every time he opens his mouth his mind falls out.'

Mary grinned and put her head into Giles' shoulder, he looked down and smiled at her; her nearness felt good. They gathered their teas and walked across the gravel towards a vacant park bench.

Giles brought out a packet of Woodbine cigarettes and offered one to Mary. She had not smoked since the incident with the salesman on the train, but readily accepted it. It made her feel liberated and adult. She took a drag and tried her best not to cough, then held the cigarette delicately between two fingers with her elbow tucked into her waist to try and look sophisticated.

'Well now, what brings you here?'

'I should have thought it was obvious,' he said, bringing the cup to his lips and sipping the light brown liquid, 'I wanted to see you again. You all right with that?'

Mary smiled at his directness. Her head nodded amiably even though she hadn't told it to do so.

'So, tell me a bit more about yourself, Captain Giles Masterson.'

Giles took a long drag of his cigarette. 'Okay. For starters, I must confess that I'm an ambitious chap. I love the army and want a full military career, even after the war, of course that's presuming we win! The army gives me all I want, excitement and the stability of a structure that I can flourish in.'

Mary drank in his enthusiasm and positivity, he seemed so in control of his life.

'I was a gentle lad, but thankfully the good Lord improved my physique, and I toughened up. But I prefer to think that there's more to leadership than just brawn.'

Mary recalled seeing him in action on the train. He could certainly look after himself.

Giles took another drag of his cigarette and blew the smoke to one side. 'What about you - what do you want to do with your life?'

When someone you like asks a direct question like that, truths just tumble out. Mary pursed her lips.

'I really don't know. Sounds silly, but it's true, nonetheless. Things are not quite turning out the way I wanted, but then, oh heck, I'm not sure what I wanted.'

He tilted his head to one side, she later noticed he did that when taking an interest in what she was saying. It was a supportive gesture and she liked it. She wanted a friend, someone to talk to and laugh with; someone who wouldn't be judgemental.

Giles obliged. 'Look, I noticed your uncertainty when we talked the other day. But there's nothing strange about that at all. Let's be frank. You've been educated and brought up in the rarefied atmosphere of Devon and, frankly, you haven't seen enough of the world - how would you know which work direction to take? Relax, look around, take your time, and try jobs when they come around. The right one will come along.'

Mary was relieved. He didn't think her silly. He showed her respect. He showed her consideration.

'Tell me about your family,' he said.

'Oh, dear. Well, things are not what I thought they would be.'

'Why?'

'I'm beginning to think I wanted to get away from Devon so much I formed a picture that just doesn't seem to represent the true situation. I thought coming here would be the answer to my prayers, but it isn't.

How naïve of me. I'm here, and yet belonging to no one, aimless, going nowhere. I'd look for the light at the end of the tunnel, but I can't even find the tunnel! It's painful for me to say that.'

This time Giles was silent and leaned over and hugged her gently. 'That's quite sad,' he said supportively.

Mary warmed to his patience and consideration and enjoyed his gentle touch. She looked up idly and caught sight of Mrs Knight walking nearby carrying food shopping. Their eyes met and Mrs Knight smiled from ear to ear. She felt deliciously decadent – caught out, with a man!

Suddenly, Giles straightened and looked at his watch. 'Damnation, I'm so sorry, it's been truly wonderful, Mary, but I must go. Duty calls. This is all too brief. Can I see you again?'

Mary's pulse raced. *He wants to see me again!*

'Why, yes, that would be so good. When and where?'

'How about next Thursday? I'll call at your house at about eleven o'clock.'

Mary hesitated. 'No, let's meet outside the Fentiman Arms public house. I'd rather do that.'

'Hmmm. Are you ashamed of me already?'

'Oh, no,' she said urgently, and then corrected herself. 'Look, my mother can be a bit of a tyke, I would simply rather meet you somewhere else. She would interrogate you and frankly, I just don't want that.'

'I think I understand, the pub it is then.' He winked at her, and she tingled. They walked slowly back to

Fentiman Road and at the steps to the front door to the house he turned and faced her. Such moments are made for amusement. He didn't know whether to kiss her cheek, and for her part she didn't know whether to shake his hand. In the end, they just stared at each other, burst out laughing and after a moment, he kissed her forehead.

Even that was enough for her, she glowed, and her heart raced.

'Goodbye, Mary, see you on Thursday,' he said softly.

'Yes, see you Thursday. I'm looking forward to it already,' she replied through a thickening throat.

Mrs Knight had seen them arrive and opened the door. As Mary came into the hallway, they exchanged glances. 'Nice feller,' she said, with a knowing smile.

Mary didn't answer. *Nice feller indeed, Mrs Knight, he's my captain!*

3

Mary still felt buoyant despite the low-key reception. When all said and done, it was good to be away from the rectory. No more Aunt Agatha, no more rows. She was content to be home and drank in the sight of her beloved papa. How different he was from his sister and the other relatives. Despite the fact he was looking paler and more tired than when she last saw him, he radiated intellect and poise: he was a true member of the Henslow family line – someone to be so proud of.

On top of that, a handsome army captain had courted her.

Yesterday's family mealtimes were just minor irritants, at least they were relatively lively, compared to the morgue-like occasions at the rectory. She'd never seen eye-to-eye with her mother anyway, so there was no loss; her mother talked at her, rather than with her. At least she had more of papa. As for her sisters, she would work hard to get to know them. Things would change.

Mary spent the day walking around the local streets. The bomb damage was indiscriminate and direct hits had chewed large chunks out of buildings. Amazingly some interiors remained intact, pictures on walls remained and curtains flapped in the breeze. Personal belongings, stained and broken, toys, material, boxes, and ornaments, remnants of lives now shattered by war, were placed in heaps by the road.

She stopped and stared at barrage balloons in the local park, hovering barely twenty feet from the ground. They resembled large slugs tethered to stop them escaping. One of the Home Guard tucked his khaki shirt into his trousers and regarded her with amusement.

'You must be new to all this?'

'My goodness, do I look that innocent?'

'Yeah, you do. I must admit, they do look a bit ugly.'

He pointed skyward. 'The balloons are hauled down every day and we give then the once over to ensure they're serviceable. When we hear the air raid sirens, up they go again. They're supposed to keep the bombers away, but sadly the buggers just fly higher.' He added ruefully, 'never mind, every little helps.'

Mary wished him well and walked on. As she passed the walls of houses and gardens, she was surprised to see so many posters advising citizens to beware of strangers and to remember what to do if the air raid sounded. There was even exhortation to the women of Britain to wear makeup and look good for their menfolk, and encouragement to purchase War Bonds. The war imposed a whole new structure on so many aspects of everyday life, with rules and regulations and the hated rationing. The tranquillity of London's cheerful tree-lined mews and open parks had been punctured and she wondered whether things would ever get back to normal.

Mary felt refreshed after her long walk and returned to the house just after mid-day. She stretched lazily on a sofa in the lounge, read newspapers and leafed through papa's plentiful collection of gardening books. There was no sign of her sisters and she mused that they might have shot each other. Chattering along the stairs at around five o'clock proved that this was not the case.

After supper, her Hazel and Mavis drifted off to their rooms, this time without staying to make conversation. Mary helped Mrs Knight clear the dishes, earning a smirk from her mother. It was time to chat to Papa again and she went upstairs to the second floor and walked quietly into his study. She was disappointed that he hadn't made time to talk to her – so she was determined to take the conversation to him.

He was sitting at his large mahogany desk facing the window, the net curtains glowing in the early evening light, turning the pages of one of his large notebooks. On the desk to the right was a circular wooden cannister with shapes of animals etched on it, crammed with pens and pencils. An old-fashioned pen and inkstand with the shape of a carved dog sitting on its wooden base was the centrepiece. A frame holding the Henslow family crest, featuring five cockatrices, hung on the right of the window, alongside was a small collage of portrait photographs and black and white silhouettes of long dead relatives.

Her wide eyes roamed over the bookshelves that covered walls, containing not just books but pictures and photographs. A memory crept into her mind of her, Hazel, and Mavis sneaking into the study when they were very young. Her sisters climbed the shelves, whilst Mary eagerly grabbed and read various books, relishing in the knowledge they held and the new words she encountered. Her father came into the room and went berserk at their trespass on his hallowed space.

Mary felt irked that he had given them all the same telling off – she remembered thinking, *say something about me reading the books and how I love to learn* – but he didn't.

Hearing a sound, papa turned his captain's chair on its swivel and leaned back, regarding her with a slight smile.

Before he could speak, she stuttered, 'Uncle Raymond helped me, Papa!'

'That sounds like my brother,' he said in an almost disinterested way.

'But he was good to me. We always spent time walking and talking. I got to know and like him.' She paused, adding. 'He gave me money for the train fare and helped me plan my escape.'

'Escape? You make it sound as though you were incarcerated. How do you think your aunt feels about all this?'

Mary sat on a nearby chair hugging her knees tightly together and thought about her answer carefully. 'Papa, you don't really understand what she's like. I hate to tell you this but when I went to Devon in the early days, she would beat me with a stick if I did anything wrong.'

Papa's eyes opened wide, and he frowned.

'When I grew older, her control was more over my mind than anything else. She was a bully to me, and to her sister Veronica for that matter. Raymond kept me sane. I never really wanted to tell you. I'm sorry, but I feel nothing for her sensibilities and I'm never going back.'

He frowned.

'Oh dear, that disappoints me. Well, she has called us and vented her fury. I won't tell her about Raymond, he's not a strong-willed chap and she'll make his life hell.'

His face clouded and he fumbled with his Montblanc fountain pen, drew a deep breath, and said, 'You're old enough for me to explain things, Mary. Your mother and I have been through tough times during the last decade. The Wall Street crash crippled our finances and we moved from one cheap house to another. We were desperately short of money and had to make sure you were all looked after. You, and your brothers and sisters were shared out to relatives. In your case it was a bit longer because of your persistent ill-health – the Devon air is so good for recuperation.'

He reached out and touched her hand. 'Believe me darling, we didn't want to do it, really, we didn't. But there are times in life when you must make tough decisions and hope for the best.'

Mary said urgently. 'I do understand, Papa. There's no need to torture yourself.'

He looked relieved.

'Look, Agatha hasn't always been severe. She fell in love with a country gentleman who treated her very badly. She then turned her back on the gaiety of life, preferring her now husband, Reverend Leonard Dreyfuss. Though honest and upright, I must tell you I thought him to be just about the most boring man I ever met. Nevertheless, Mary, what you say upsets me and I feel very responsible.'

Mary waved her hand supportively. 'Let's leave it alone. As far as I'm concerned, it's all in the past. I'm home and that's all that counts. It was thanks to Uncle Raymond that I'm here. He did say something strange, about making mistakes.'

'That's healthy I suppose,' her father momentarily looked at the ceiling as if examining his own mind, adding, 'we all make bags of those, that's for sure.'

'Oh, dear, poor Raymond.'

'Yes, oh dear indeed - but poor all of us. Now, listen to me, Mary. Times have been changing for over a decade now – nothing is the same, there is so much turbulence in social and political life.' His voice seemed to falter. 'Mary, I need to be sure that you understand things I alluded to earlier. After you left for your last recuperation, we were made aware of the improvement to your health and that you had settled well, making a new life for yourself. Then there was the hint of a possible engagement to a young priest, which I now know was not correct. But naturally, based on that, we were satisfied that you had fallen on your feet.'

Mary couldn't help flirting with the notion that she was a 'job done' as far as her bringing up was concerned, but at least she understood a bit more.

'That was, as you now understand, Papa, not the case. As for the young priest, he was never a marriage contender. You thought Leonard Dreyfuss was dull, well this chap is a remarkably close second!'

Papa just nodded with the hint of a smile.

It was a new experience – her father was being frank, and he was listening. She regarded him carefully; she was never able to make him out. As if sensing her thoughts, he forced a smile and talked easily about his latest 'Easy Gardening' book that was now selling very well. Gardening was not on her list of interests, despite it being his passion, and she felt a little guilty. He had once tried to convert her by giving her an envelope full of his articles published by *The Wiltshire Gazette* and *The People* newspaper, to which he was a contributing journalist, but didn't succeed.

Back in her room, she listened to the radio, feeling pleased with her chat with Papa, she had never been able to do that before. However, she remained uncertain how to deal with her mother, or, for that matter what to do about discussing work opportunities. It was so frustrating, she just wanted to get going, but the time never seemed right.

The next day, as arranged, Mary met Giles outside the Fentiman Arms public house at around eleven o'clock. His face beamed when he saw her. When she reached him, she said, 'Eleven o'clock on the dot.'

'Crikey, I've been here since five a.m.!'

Mary laughed and thumped his arm. She noticed he carried a wicker basket.

'So, what's this?'

'I thought we'd go for a picnic.'

'A picnic, how wonderful. What a great idea.'

She playfully tugged at the basket, and he resisted, feigning defence of precious cargo.

They walked, arm-in-arm, along the dusty streets, past The Oval cricket ground and the nearby underground station, closed from the start the war when plans for extra tunnels for air raid defence were briefly abandoned due to the proximity of the river and watercourse. The wind made the leaves in the trees rustle and the warm sunlight flickered on their faces as they passed. Mary felt relaxed and happy.

They reached Parry Street, stopped at the river Thames, and looked across at Vauxhall Bridge. A couple of seagulls swooped down to the water level in the hope of grabbing a morsel to eat.

'I love London,' said Mary, wistfully, 'I hate the idea of the Germans bombing the guts out of it. It upsets me.'

'Me too. Wait, is that a bomber coming?'

'Where?' Mary looked up, alarmed.

He quickly gathered her in his arms and held her tightly. 'Don't worry, I've got you, stick close...'

She put her head in his chest. 'You rotter, there's nothing coming at all.'

'Ah, well, there might have been. I think it was a bus, or train, or...'

Mary looked up at him. 'Or anything, you opportunist!'

Giles hugged her and they headed back down the road. In a short while, Mary stopped in her tracks. 'Giles Masterson, this is Vauxhall Park, where we were last week.'

'Ah, I can explain. I have the picnic but, er, nothing to drink. Besides, there's that lovely tea shack we used last time and to be honest I'd rather spend more time with you than wandering aimlessly around London looking for somewhere to park our bottoms. I hope that's okay with you?'

'How could I object to such a kind thought?' she said indulgently, and they headed to a bench nestled near a large chestnut tree, catching the midday sunshine. Giles placed a blanket along its base and opened the basket. Inside there were two apples, rounds of sandwiches wrapped in napkins and what looked like two scones.

'The officers' mess chef did me a favour,' he said with a broad grin.

'Oh, goody,' said Mary as she peeked at the sandwiches, 'cheese and ham, oh, look, egg too!'

The sun warmed their faces and there was no need to talk - they were content in each other's company. Their hands touched lightly. Ten yards away by the side of a large rose tree, a man in a baggy suit who looked like Alfred Hitchcock, was playing an accordion. A worn tartan cap placed on the ground immediately in front of him was ready to collect whatever passing people could afford to give. The music infused the air with happiness - then it stopped.

Without a word, Giles stood up and strode towards the man. He returned with a satisfied look on his face and the music began again.

'He was about to go, sixpence did the trick.'

'Oh, Giles, you hero. The music is so jolly, I don't want it to stop.'

They sat together swaying to cheerful French music hall tunes. After a while, Giles tapped his stomach, 'My tummy rumbles, shall we dig into the picnic?'

Mary had decided to miss the verbal flak at the breakfast table and was now ravenous. As she enthusiastically unwrapped the sandwiches the lady from the tea shack approached.

''ello darlings,' she said, clutching two mugs of steaming tea that spilled a little as she reached out to them. 'I remember you two from a couple of days ago. A gent just ordered these then had to rush away, so I thought I'd give them to you. I like to treat a soldier and his lovely lady.'

She left without waiting for thanks. Today was full of wonderful things.

Giles stared at her tenderly, "my lovely lady', I quite like that.'

'Yes,' Mary mused, 'I quite like being your lovely lady too.'

They gazed at each other without saying another word – there was no more to be said.

Mary's emotions heightened. The feelings of attraction and the closeness of a man and woman enjoying the same space were new to her. She felt so content being with him and noticed that her body warmed to his touch. Would she kiss? Should she kiss? What would it be like? When, how? The uncertainty made her nervous.

'Giles, this is so delicious. Thank you.'

'My pleasure, lovely lady,' he replied tilting his head to one side.

'You're going to wear that expression out.'

'Why not, why not indeed? I must tell you, *lovely lady,* I am really very happy.'

After the picnic, they settled back on the bench, Mary's head on his chest, quite unselfconscious at the closeness.

Giles reluctantly looked at his watch and said urgently, 'Cripes. Time has marched on. Sorry, Mary but I have a meeting to attend to back at the barracks early this evening.'

Mary playfully pinioned his arms and sat across his lap. 'I'm not letting you go!'

He pretended to struggle, 'Argh, calling the Chief of Staff, come and rescue me, help!'

They laughed, then stopped and stared at each other, before slowly coming together in a soft lingering kiss. It was Mary's first ever kiss and it made her fizz with joy. Now, she certainly did not want him to go. They parted slowly, their eyes locked on each other; the magnetism of their being was trying to hold them tightly together.

They slowly walked back to Fentiman Road, occasionally gazing at each other. Mary supressed the urge to simply grab him and kiss again - once was definitely not enough.

Giles stopped a short distance from her home and said urgently. 'Look, I need to talk to you. I'm really sorry I must dash off like this. We must meet again, but it won't be until next week, pressure of work and all that. What about Wednesday, at noon, same park, and same awful tea, what say?'

'Why, yes of course.' Mary was about to get inquisitive but noticed the shape of her mother at the far end of the road talking to a woman. She looked up and saw them both.

It was time to make a run for it.

'I'd like that too.' She leaned towards him, and he instinctively put his arms on her shoulders and gently kissed her cheek. He walked away slowly, and she just wanted to stand and gaze after him but was aware of the fast-approaching form of her mother.

The steps up to the front door of the house seemed steep and her mother joined her at the top, breathless from a fruitless attempt to get closer to Giles.

'And who may I ask was that?'

'Giles Masterson, captain, Royal Engineers.'

'Army,' her mother sniffed. 'And where did you meet him?'

'On the train from Devon. He intervened when an oaf tried to get personal.'

'Well, perhaps you can introduce me.' Her mother fixed her with a stare.

'I'd like to do that. You'll like him.'

'Thank you,' said her mother. Ever the mistress of the last word, she added, 'I'll be the judge of that.' She pushed past Mary, unlocked the door, and disappeared up the stairs without further conversation.

Mary grimaced, *but not until I've warned him!*

The next week was empty after the excitement of Giles' company. Mrs Knight sensed that Mary was feeling wan.

'Mary, fancy helping me with the shopping?'

Mary readily agreed and they left the house just as the sun started to shine on the streets, wet from a short but heavy shower.

'Look at that,' said Mrs Knight dejectedly. Before them lay the resentful landscape of bombed houses on one side of the street, like skeletons looking down at the rubble that was once their flesh. The other side of the street was completely untouched. 'Life's such a lottery, isn't it?' she said with a sigh.

'Yes, it is. How's your home?'

'Oh, it's fine. Our street is all right. I think Hitler likes me!'

Mary laughed. 'In that case, lucky you. It was bad in London for a while, wasn't it?'

'I shouldn't joke. Yes, my dear, 1940 was truly awful. The bombing went on for fifty-seven nights. The bravery of them fire fighters and casualty workers, and the way people stuck together was amazing. A lady I know who lives nearby was washing up in her kitchen when a bomb hit her house and she found herself half-covered in plasterboard, which probably saved her life. She remembers a young fire-fighter coming in and throwing himself over her, covering them both with the front door that had come off its hinges. She could feel bricks and mortar hitting the wood. When the raid was over, he moved the door and said, 'Sorry dear, I usually knock before I come in.' She chuckled. 'How About that?'

'I heard some folks weren't so pleasant though?'

Mrs Knight stiffened. 'True, there were bad 'uns, but thankfully they were in the minority. Anyway, Adolf must have lost interest. Stone a crow, we were so glad it stopped. Mark you, they still come over from time to time, so you mind yourself, and do exactly what you're told when the time comes.'

They walked past closed shops, before coming to several market stalls selling fruit and veg' and old clothes. Mrs Knight stopped and craned her head around slowly as if looking for somebody.

'Ah, there he is. Stay here, dear.'

Mary watched Mrs Knight walk up to a man dressed in a dirty grey raincoat and wearing a flat hat that was too large for him. A battered cigarette hung from his lips. After a brief conversation, she handed him an envelope and he gave her a rolled-up newspaper, which she pretended to look at before tucking it into her shopping bag.

Back with Mary, she explained. 'Beef. It cost a bob or two, but your mother's paying.' They walked on and Mrs Knight looked around her adding, 'It's just as important not to get caught buying illegal market goods as it is selling them. So, I must be careful.'

As they walked on, avoiding the puddles that filled the many small holes in the streets, a stocky, bald stallholder dressed in a leather apron stood by his second-hand goods and gave Mrs Knight a playful salute. 'If it isn't Annie Knight, well I never did!'

Mrs Knight laughed and waved him away, 'And you never bloody will, Albert!'

This earned guffaws from the other stallholders. Mary enjoyed listening to the exchanges between Mrs Knight and those about her. There were inducements to buy and plenty of banter - these people were survivors.

Mary pointed down the road, 'Oh, look over there, it's a tea cabin, let's have a cuppa?'

Mrs Knight readily agreed.

They sat on a low wall with their feet propped up on a couple of sandbags. Mary nursed her hot mug of tea and gazed into the brown liquid. Without looking up she said, 'Mrs Knight, I often think that I'm destined to conflict with imperious women like my aunt and my mother. Why do they always try to bend me to their will? It's just so exhausting.'

Mrs Knight leaned back with a serious expression. 'Look, I don't talk freely with members of the family, but I like you. You're honest and don't have any side to you, don't ever lose that. But you need to stop kidding yourself. By that I mean that you were always such a spirited little devil, simple as that. You never took no for an answer and when you wanted something you went all out to get it. You weren't a bad child, as I say, just spirited. Your sisters play your mother by not responding to her curious ways, they may be younger than you, but they are a bit savvier.'

A double decker bus drove past, and they shielded their mugs from the rising dust.

Mrs Knight sipped the tea and continued. 'I've been with your mother and father for over ten years now. I won't tell tales, it would be wrong of me.' She looked thoughtful and added, 'there is one thing that should be kept out of sight. So don't even ask or pry.'

'No, of course not,' Mary, reluctantly accepted the need for discretion.

'Now then, that apart, I can at least give you some background, as I see it of course, but keep it to yourself or I'll be in big trouble. The fact is, your father has always been a genuinely nice man, strong in his own way, and yet,' she paused, 'he just doesn't seem to be of this world, almost as though he's marooned between social levels.'

Mary recognised the description.

'He's written gardening books and beautiful poetry and he never gives up, writing every day, sometimes until late. I'm not sure if it brings much money in – it's not my place to know. There are pressures, though.

Your mother has slowly taken the reins over the years. She's always been very organised and he, well, he's an arty kind of a man and how shall we say, not that good at office stuff. Anyway, she rules the roost now and they just don't inhabit the same space.'

Mary touched Mrs Knight's shoulder. It couldn't have been easy for this disciplined older lady to address these matters with her.

'While we're together, can I give you some personal advice, luv?'

'Why, yes of course.'

'Stop rising to the bait, by that I mean not everything needs to be responded to. Be confident in yourself. My gran, bless her, once told my mum not to take so much to heart and to accept that people say silly things because they feel under threat, something might be on their mind, or it's just their nature – nothing horrid, just their flippin' nature. After that, mum never argued with her sister again, she let soppy comments just float over her head. It did the trick. Good old gran. So, take a tip, there will be battles to fight, if so, then fight 'em. Otherwise, ignore everything else. Have the good sense to know what you can't change, including your mother.'

Mary gave her a big hug.

'Thanks. I appreciate that. But I suspect that there's something you're not telling me?'

Mrs Knight recognised the deft inquisitive segue into dark corners but remained steadfast.

'Yes, my girl, and it would do you no good to know. So, no more prodding!'

Mary grinned resignedly. 'Yes, I promise.'

They walked back to the house, talking about the war and the damage to lives and hopes for the future. Not once did they discuss the family circus of Fentiman Road.

As they came in through the front door, Mary saw her mother look up surprised. She had assorted items of mail in her hands and appeared to hurriedly put them straight into her jacket pocket.

'You're late,' she said abruptly, in a tone that defied anyone to take issue with.

Unsurprisingly, as is the way of those who suffer repeated controlling challenges, neither answered, rather, they just both went their ways, Mrs Knight to the kitchen and Mary to her room.

It had been so refreshing talking to Mrs Knight. Her honest down-to-earth nature together with good-mannered confidentiality was what Mary liked about her. It amused her to be thought of as feisty and although that was no bad thing given the array of quirky family members, she knew she had to take note. She thought more about what Mrs Knight was not saying rather than what she had said.

The house was quiet for the rest of the day and her mother went out again presumably to do more charity work or play bridge with her friends - Mary thought that she spent more time away from the home than in it. She fiddled around with the contents of her room, trying to make it look feminine and stopped when she heard the door open and close downstairs and Mrs Knight give a small yell. A young man's voice called out, and the thump of footsteps came up the stairs.

She gave a yelp of her own. It was her younger brother, Tony, lanky as ever, his fair curly hair dishevelled. He stood at the door, smiling broadly.

'Mary, how are you? I saw Hazel yesterday and she said you were here. It's so lovely to see you.' He sounded the same cheerful Tony, high spirits and always laughing.

Mary hugged him tightly, closing her eyes. 'I'm okay-ish. Great to be back, but...'

'Say no more, I understand!'

In this respect they were *comrades in arms.*

Mary remembered how her mother used her ring hand to whack Tony's head when he misbehaved – at one time she thought that he would be knocked out. He was always the butt of her anger. They sat on the bed and chatted merrily, reminiscing, and joking. It felt so good to be laughing and not having to guard what they were saying.

'So, what have you been up to?'

Tony's face darkened and he shuffled as he looked down at his shoes. 'Well, I'm sorry to say that I made a few enormous blunders. You know me, hot-headed and frankly, a bit of a chump.'

Mary put on a playful frown, 'Go on.'

'Promise you won't hate me?'

'Dope, how could I? Now get on with it.'

'Well, oh dear, here goes. I unwisely attended a political rally or two. Rallies by the, er, British Union of Fascists...'

Mary exploded. 'Tony! The fascists. Bloody Moseley's bunch? Even in Devon we read the newspapers.'

'Well, yes, but you must understand, famous people support Oswald Moseley, he's a very clever man. He still has wide support from all levels of society. Everyone thought him to be just the right man to deal with the emerging political chaos. He swept everyone off their feet, including me. I met so many interesting people. There was a man called Henry Williamson who returned from the Great War determined that never again would brother Europeans fight among themselves for the sake of greed and selfishness. He also expressed a deep hatred of communism which he saw as a threat to world order, and so do I. These were the key BUF messages. There were others too, ex-soldiers, writers, and politicians.'

He twisted his hands and paused as if seeking justification. 'It was so vibrant and seemed to provide all the answers to the problems of our time. I met disciplined, articulate, and logical people. I care about what goes on in the world, I really do. I just wanted to be part of changing the country for the better.'

Mary looked at her brother in the way she used to when he was making excuses for his boyish misdemeanours and said without regard to his explanation. 'And now he's safely away in the clink!'

'Yeah,' he said sheepishly. 'I know now that it was all a bit unwise, but he was so magnetic, so seductive. You should know that he held a rally at Earls Court in the July shortly before the war started and implored the government of the day to avoid getting into a spat with Hitler. He preached peace and didn't want war and actually claimed his views were shared by many in government.'

'That's possibly his only redeeming feature, except of course that he said that we should make friends with Hitler, which is not quite the same as peace, Tony.'

'Well, even Papa was taken in.'

'What – you involved Papa? What a thing to do.'

'Calm down. Yes. I thought he would be interested because of some things he was beginning to talk about, you know, the state of the government, socialism, and suchlike. I brought one of Mosley's acolytes here, a brilliant chap called Marendaz who was an ex-RFC pilot in the Great War and fiercely patriotic. Papa liked him and was swayed by his views on English nationalism. He had seen so much in the last war when he was in the Argyll and Sutherland Regiment, and this left an indelible image on his mind. He was convinced that the war would stop soon with some sort of compromise, because he thought that the country was in no shape to fight. On top of that, the emergence of communism made him so angry. We argued about all sorts of silly politics. I'm not sure where his head is now – we don't talk much anymore.'

Tony recognised Mary's anxiety. 'You probably read in the newspaper that the NAZIs whom Moseley held in such high esteem turned out to be a dubious bunch that harboured vile views about Jews, and for me the shine began to fade fast. Anyway, after a lot of political upheaval and local protests in the East End, the BUF were considered pariahs and their popularity waned. Then the war started, and fascists were rounded up, and that meant me too, because my name appeared on the membership list.'

'Oh, dear, Tony. Poor you, what happened then?'

'Thanks to Papa and one of his high-placed contacts I was spared the incarceration under legislation termed, Defence Order 18b, and released, but banned from military service. I'll be forever grateful for that. I was placed in work with London's emergency medical centres. I really like it. We've been terribly busy of late. It can be dangerous at times, but I feel that I'm doing good work.' He looked down, 'It certainly makes me feel a bit better about myself.'

Mary hugged him. 'Oh, my dear Tony, you're not a fascist and never would be. But it was a very narrow escape, little brother.'

The uncomfortable hurdle was soon cleared, and Tony began telling tales about helping people who were gravely injured in the bombing raids or through other accidents. He made light of his escapes from precarious situations involving falling masonry and incendiaries, and Mary was impressed with his bravery. But in her heart, she was upset with her father for even giving fascism houseroom, even if it had entered in disguise and through the back door.

Mary hugged him. 'Oh, Tony, I'm so sorry. It'll blow over, you'll see.'

Tony hugged her back. 'I've got to go. It's been great seeing you. To be honest, I'm taking advantage of mother's absence, it's her 'tea' day with her posse of up-market friends. If you think your irritation with my blunder was strident, hers was positively volcanic!'

Mary kissed him goodbye and watched him leave the house, smiling as he looked back at her.

Some things stuck in her mind.

The headboard to the bed was hard on Mary's scalp and she pulled up a pillow. There was yelling from her sisters' rooms, and she heard a door slam. It was time for her to try and make conversation again – she would keep trying her best. She passed Mavis's closed door, a sign there had been an argument, so she walked on to Hazel's room.

'Hi there, how are you today?' she said invitingly.

'Oh, pretty good really. I'm seeing Roger tonight so forgive me if I carry on doing my nails.' She foraged in a linen bag and brought out two bottles of coloured nail varnish and selected a bright red one to match her lipstick.

'Ah, this will entice him, he likes red. He thinks it's decadent. What do you think?'

'Don't ask me, I've never actually used the stuff.'

Hazel looked at the ceiling disdainfully and reached for a nail file.

'Can we talk?' Mary went on.

'I've been expecting you to ask. Yes, why not. Our little sprat of a sister is ensconced in her room sulking – I said she had spots, and she took umbrage.'

'How very diplomatic of you. The fact is that everyone seems rather, well, fractured. The family dynamics are just not the same. It worries me. I left that terrible woman, Aunt Agatha, to be back with Papa and you all, and well frankly it's just so disappointing.'

Hazel stopped filing her nails. 'It certainly sounds as though you had a tough time.' She paused and uncharacteristically touched Mary's arm. 'You always were the serious one, tough as leather, but principled and sensitive. Do you know our brothers would never argue or tease you as they did to Mavis and me?'

'Why?'

'Because your style was, and still is, to wrap up your arguments in such a way that to disagree with you would be to take a position that is so illogical or against all common sense – you seem to pluck facts supporting your views from the clouds. Look, Mary, you have this air of persistence that sucks the oxygen out of a subject leaving little for anyone else.'

Mary responded. 'Yes, but surely that's just the way I...'

'See what I mean? I've just told you something you don't like, and you question its validity, rather than considering the nuances of the statement.'

Mary blanched, her younger sister was smarter than she thought.

Hazel noisily placed a bottle of varnish on the bedside table and clasped her hands. 'Anyway, enough of us. We're older, Mary, we've all moved on and we're not children anymore.'

'That's true, sadly. I just wish mother and Papa talked more or showed a spark of life.'

Hazel huffed loudly. 'I agree that their relationship is a bit neutral and strained. Over the years I've noticed that mother has taken the reins regarding the running of the house and many other things.'

'Everything?' said Mary, wanting to put more flesh on what Mrs Knight had said.

'Oh, yes, I'll say. The accounts, tradesmen doing work and all household arrangements. She even vets Papa's choice of agents and publishers. It's like watching an intellectual siege, absolutely nothing passes her by, and she's always right!'

Mary reflected on Mrs Knight's words. Hazel continued. 'What really gets me is to see their relationship dwindling, especially when she lays into him over minor matters. The next day she's all sweetness and light. She's the ultimate controller.'

Hazel grinned and added mischievously, 'She may be a tartar, my dear sister, but she gets her way. I'm taking notes!'

Mary sighed. 'Once upon a time when we were small it was all so different.'

'Yeah, but that's life.' Hazel paused for a second. 'Come to think of it, mother did say something strange the other day and I'm not sure what it meant. I was in the kitchen searching for Mrs Knight's stash of biscuits when I heard them arguing in the study. Mother was laying into Papa about his smoking, adding sarcastically that he always excused his flaws as if they were badges of honour, but added cryptically that there would always be one secret too many.'

Mary's mind raced. Was this to do with his flirtation with fascism after Tony's silly introductions? Was he in trouble somewhere else?

Hazel interrupted her thoughts. 'Mary, let's leave this conversation, it's all speculation and is going nowhere. The boys have left home and are in the military, now making lives for themselves. I won't be long behind them, I can tell you. The sprat next door has years to catch up yet, so she will remain at home. But what of you?'

She returned to the task of polishing her fingernails.

Mary realised that there was an ominous thread of sense in that statement. She had swapped being controlled in Devon for indifference in London – would she really end up here forever?

The thought worried her.

Mary needed fresh air so went outside the front door and sat on the step. Her mother caught her doing that years ago when she was a child and scolded her for making the place look untidy and working class. Today she didn't give a fig. Her mind whirled around what Hazel had said and now she understood why her Papa looked so worn down. The issue of a secret stuck in her mind, and she couldn't get rid of it.

Mrs Knight called her in. 'Come on, cheer up. I'll bring you a cuppa in your room if you like, and perhaps an oat biscuit or two?'

Mary readily agreed and later sat on her bed drinking tea; the home baked biscuits crumbled and left bits on her sheets, and she had to brush them away. She declined an offer to go to the park with her sisters who had made up – she quite admired how they both rode the high waves of disagreement, eventually settling in the low swell of calmness. They had the ability to let go and not bear grudges, something Mary realised she had to cultivate. Her father was out visiting his agent and her mother was long gone to yet another afternoon tea. The silence felt heavy and fed her growing curiosity – it was an itch she couldn't resist scratching.

Except for Mrs Knight banging around in the kitchen, she was quite alone.

It was difficult to explain why, but she was propelled to papa's study. The room smelled of tobacco smoke and his cologne, it was as if he were with her. She sucked him into her lungs.

She imagined she was his secretary and sat swivelling in his captain's chair. This tempted her to rummage in his in-tray on the left of the desk. Leaning back casually she put an imaginary telephone to her ear and said in a haughty, prim voice, 'Ah, yes, this is Miss Mary Henslow, speaking. So, you want to give Mr Henslow an offer of one million copies of his latest book? That's wonderful, we'll give it consideration and call you later.'

Carelessly, her elbow slipped off the desk and she nearly fell off the chair, and this brought her back to reality. She rubbed her arm, sat back, and continued to flick through the papers in his tray. Surprisingly, all were dated over six months ago. Many of them were from agents and publishers who praised his poetry but declined to publish because of the uncertainty regarding potential sales during the war. Emboldened, she looked in each of the drawers only to find paper, pencils and pens, and a stash of cigarettes and whisky, there was nothing that gave a clue to a possible secret.

Disappointed, she turned and faced the centre of the study. Her eyes fell on a medium size walnut cabinet. Its drawers were quite thin, about three inches high and twelve inches wide. A quick search of each drawer produced nothing of interest, except that one of them was locked.

There is nothing more seductive to the curious than a locked drawer.

She searched in vain for a key but found nothing. Irritated, she sat back in the chair and swivelled aimlessly. On a shelf above Papa's collection of published works, she noticed Brer Rabbit - dressed in a blue waistcoat, holding a pocket watch - looking down on her mockingly. His large ears cast a shadow on the wall. Mary remembered breaking the plaster head when she was young. Papa had been so understanding and dried her tears, then carefully glued the head back on. He exclaimed loudly, 'The rabbit is new again!' and they laughed together. She noticed the line around the neck where the glue had aged over the years.

Something else caught her eye.

It was the faintest of lines of what looked like a very thin brass chain. She jumped out of the chair and grabbed a stool and was soon reaching for Brer Rabbit's neck. Slowly, she pulled the chain and at the end of it was a small key. She was so excited she slipped but managed to regain her balance and the stool stayed upright.

The lock was stubborn at first but with a hard twist it opened, and she slowly slid out the drawer. Inside were assorted brown envelopes and she removed them carefully, putting each one onto the floor, noting the order in which they had been in the drawer.

Curiosity fought with guilt.

With shaking hands, she opened the first envelope and found it contained letters from traders for household and personal items. The top one read:

Dear Mr Henslow,

I regret to have to pursue your outstanding debt to my company in respect of items of clothing you purchased, but the bill has remained unpaid for several months now. Our previous correspondence to you has gone unanswered.

I have no other option but to advise that should you not clear the bill within ten working days I will have no alternative but to take legal action to recover the sum involved.

My solicitor advises me that he is aware of similar claims on you, and I am therefore acting without delay.

I very much look forward to a successful outcome.

Yours sincerely,

Isaac Cohen
Director
Cohens Tailors
St James Street
London

The letter, dated March 1930, had a note boldly written across the top: *Izzy, if you were my brother, then I would change my mother.*

Papa was obviously very angry – it was only a bill after all. The tradesman was surely being quite unreasonable.

There were other letters written in a similar vein. Mary didn't want to know more about this or any other such matter and replaced them in the brown envelope. Three other envelopes contained private letters from army comrades, freemasons and one, dated 1910 from the Bishop of London, expressed his sadness that Papa had decided to leave the church and he hoped that he would return.

At the bottom of the drawer was an envelope, that was torn in places from frequent use and very smudged. It contained photographs. The top one was of an attractive young woman, who sat at a large desk in front of a typewriter. She had a pleasant face and was dressed in a white high-necked blouse and a grey full-length skirt. Her dark hair was folded high on her head, and she wore a chain that held a large medallion which bore a bright silver crescent moon. It looked as if she had been disturbed, there being paper in the typewriter half-typed on, but she was looking not so much at the camera, rather, at the person taking the picture. Her smile was captivating and so attractive it made Mary want to give one in return. Turning the picture over revealed a scribbled date of 1923. Pinned to the back was another photograph, this one of a small boy of about two years old that had a date of 1926. If she was a relative, then Mary couldn't place her. Who was she?

She picked through other photographs, mostly groups of soldiers marching in highland uniform, or in front of wooden-clad trenches, obviously from the First War. She noticed one of the family taken when she was just a toddler. Her mother stood close to her father, gazing up at him and holding his arm. He stood proudly, looking happy, with his family at his feet. Her heart fell – what a contrast with the family latest picture that was hanging in the hallway, where Papa was upright and serious, her mother tight-lipped at least a foot away to his left.

She heard a sound and her stomach churned. Papa's voice followed the slamming of the front door as he acknowledged Mrs Knight and called for a cup of tea. He slowly trod up the stairs. She scrambled to ease the envelopes back into the drawer and didn't want to leave any clues.

The footsteps clumped louder.

The drawer stubbornly resisted being put back into its place and Mary had to give it an enormous shove. She cursed when she looked down at the floor and saw a piece of paper with scribbled verse on it and scooped it up and put it in her blouse pocket. She quickly locked the drawer.

Papa was now at the end of the landing, and she heard his rasping, as if out of breath.

She sprang up and stepped onto the stool, but in her rush unwisely leaned too far on the edge and it tilted, and she dropped awkwardly to the floor, painfully twisting her ankle.

In pain, Mary held her ankle tight, but had the sense to pull the stool closer to her as she hobbled behind the door. She put her hand over her mouth as the pain seared through her leg. Her mind raced to put together a reasonable excuse for her trespass.

To her enormous relief, papa stopped momentarily outside the study, then he made his way to his bedroom, shouting, 'Second thoughts, just off for a nap, Mrs Knight. I'll have some tea in about an hour.'

'Right you are, sir.'

Mary leaned back against the wall, relieved, and her heartbeat slowed. Certain that her father was now in his bedroom and settled, she put the stool back in place and limped to her room. Once on her bed she noticed she still had the drawer key in her hand, so wrapped it in the notepaper she had picked up and put it into her handbag. She would replace it later, when Papa went out again, but for now she needed to nurse her throbbing ankle.

That had been a very close call.

Mary didn't sleep very well, her ankle hurt all night and her mind roamed over images of the photographs and contents of the envelopes in the secret drawer. She got up and was glad to find her ankle was better. Breakfast was taken in its usual awkward silence - nothing was wrong, it was just that no one bothered to talk.

Her mother came in and sat at the bottom of the table, a waft of 4711 Eau De Cologne filled the air. Mrs Knight was behind her, rudely and amusingly waving her hands in front of her face.

'Mary,' said her mother, prodding the porridge for lumps, 'have you given any thought to what you are going to do now you are here?'

Mrs Knight glared in the background and noisily banged a dish of devilled kidneys on the warming tray on the sideboard.

Mary felt awkward, expecting the subject to lead to a row. 'Actually, I haven't...'

Her mother did not wait for her to finish. 'Well, now you're here please don't just run off like you did in Devon. I should rather like to be kept in the picture.'

Mary felt awkward and flushed red.

Hazel and Mavis stared into their teacups not raising their eyes for an instant, listening in anticipation to the next salvo. Only Hazel had the flicker of a smile on her face. Papa looked exasperated and frowned into his copy of the daily newspaper, taking out a sharp pencil to begin the crossword.

Her mother's expression telegraphed that she was about to say something that was beyond question. 'As you clearly have no plans of our own, my dear, I'm sure you will be glad to know that a good friend of mine has offered to take you on. She has a clothing shop on Oxford Street. It's only part-time, but beggars can't be choosers. No salary as such, just pocket money and a bit of lunch each day.' She pursed her lips and added casually, 'you start on Monday.'

Mary was about to object when her father put his newspaper down abruptly and touched her with his foot under the table, and she recalled Mrs Knight's advice.

Papa said quickly and softly. 'That's jolly good. Mary, you'll have time to settle into London life and perhaps find a more suitable position as time goes on.'

Her mother dabbed her lips with a napkin and said with a hint of sarcasm, 'Perhaps!'

Out of respect to her father, Mary held her tongue and counted to ten before answering. '

'Thank you, mother, you are so thoughtful.'

The words stuck in her throat like stodgy dumplings.

Mary was perplexed. It was Wednesday and no Giles at the park. He was nowhere to be seen. Her chest felt heavy, and she was confused - had she done or said something? Was she too ordinary and boring for him? Walking around the trees and flower beds did little to settle her. Perhaps the important thing he had to talk about was the fact that they should not see each other again. Yes, that must be it - he was going to tell her but must have felt that he couldn't face it. She tried to be strong but couldn't help feeling deserted, unwanted; it was such a counterpoint to her previous feeling of happiness. It had been too good to be true, and now it was no more. Nevertheless, Mary waited and waited, but gave in and, returned home disappointed and miserable.

Her heart ached as the days passed. Each morning she woke to a new day of hoping the Giles would arrive, flowers in hand with a sweet apology on his lips - but nothing. She kept to her own company over the weekend, preferring walks along the Thames embankment, looking at the barges as they pushed through the deep brown water. The city was almost unrecognisable, with many of the older buildings sand-bagged and windows crisscrossed with white tape to reduce the shatter effect of bombs. Some walls had been covered in graffiti urging the government to end the war, and had been overpainted with insults such as, 'Commie bastards.'

What cheered her was the friendliness of everyone she met, despite the destruction and ugliness of it all. So many people were in uniform: air force, navy, and army. They all bustled rather than walked, each as though they had an important appointment to attend to.

Sunday arrived and she still felt gloomy, on top of that she contemplated her first day in the London clothing shop belonging to her mother's friend. Perhaps it wouldn't be that bad – but then again, perhaps it would!

As she idled her way along Embankment an old lady wrapped in a large colourful woollen shawl, despite the warmth of the day, reached out a scrawny hand to her. She was sitting on a low wall surrounded by small bunches of lavender. Her eyes were bloodshot and her hair grey and matted.

'Lucky lavender, dear? I can tell your fortune too.'

Mary opened her purse and took out pennies and handed them over. The old lady grimaced as if wanting more.

'That's all I'm afraid. I'm broke.'

The old lady shrugged and gave a half-smile but had heard the jingle of more coins in Mary's purse. 'Come on luv, just two pence more and I'll let you know what the future holds.' Her hand shook slightly, and she looked up pleadingly.

'Oh, all right. Two more pence it is. But if Jerry comes over, we scatter.' Mary placed the coins in the lady's palm and sat beside her on the embankment wall.

The lady put the money and lavender to one side and pulled her shawl tightly around her shoulders. She took Mary's left hand and after staring at it for a long time, looked straight into her eyes.

'You're not happy,' she said soberly. 'But you will be soon, I can't say when. You are becoming a woman, an adult with determination and pride, and I predict that events will call on you to use these qualities. You will meet a tall dark, handsome man and fall in love.'

The old woman frowned and seemed ill at ease, fidgeted, and said hesitantly, 'there's something mysterious, but I can't quite make it out. Your life is a bit of a puzzle I'm afraid, my dear.' She abruptly let Mary's hand drop. 'I can see no further than that. No, that's it, no further.'

Mary stood up and thanked her. Tall, dark, and handsome, eh? She wondered how many young women had been given that script. Had the lady ever said that they would meet a man, short, bald, and pot-bellied - she thought not! Besides, if the dear lady could tell her why Giles had mysteriously failed to turn up that might be a start. Perhaps that was the puzzle she referred to?

As she walked away, she looked back and saw the woman looking after her.

4

Mary regarded her reflection in the hallway mirror and was not at all pleased. It dawned on her that she looked frumpy. A beige gaberdine raincoat covered her simple blue gingham dress, over which she wore a white cardigan. At least she wore stockings, even if the suspenders dug into her flesh; it was her one concession to growing up. Otherwise, she just wanted to wear corduroy slacks and boots and walk in the countryside.

She pulled her collar up, wrapped a scarf around her neck and set off for Oxford Street. On the way, air raid alarms sounded. They made a low mournful moan, increasing as if agitated to a higher pitch. The steps down into Piccadilly underground station were crowded and she had to be careful as she joined hundreds of others into the station. There was no panic, no moaning, everyone just took it all for granted. A member of the Women's Voluntary Services, with a cheerful face encouraged people to be careful and asked after anyone with children. Another WVS lady was unlocking a large canteen unit that was placed near the ticket barriers, a sign declared it to be a 'Gift from the American Red Cross.'

It was musty and uncomfortably warm, and Mary was glad when the 'all-clear' sounded – it had been a false alarm. As she climbed the stone steps back to the pavement, she overheard two women talking. 'Silly sausage-eating sods. My Fred's waiting on his ack-ack gun, just ready to say hello and what do they do, they turn around and go 'ome. Waste of aircraft fuel if you ask me.'

'Your Fred's probably down the pub anyway.'

The lady responded. 'Yeah, when he's there at least he's not pestering me!'

That earned laughs from all the ladies. It was ironic that the stoic Londoners were more upset that Jerry hadn't turned up than if he had. Mrs Knight explained to Mary that as soon as the long overdue ack-ack guns had been installed, Londoners' spirits rose, and they felt exhilarated – they were fighting back.

When she reached street level, she looked about her. There was no danger immediately above them, all the action was going on in the distance over the Thames estuary. She could just about make out fighter aircraft darting about the sky leaving white trails of smoke in their wake, some creating circles and others straight lines. They were in their own deadly dance-world.

Good luck boys!

Mary finally arrived at Oxford Street and followed directions to the clothing shop and eventually found a sign proclaiming 'Allana's' in black and gold lettering. The window display was full of everyday items of clothing and against each one was a small card with the price and a short description of the number of ration points needed. She went in.

The bell above the door clinked and a severe looking lady came out of a room. She wore a tight-fitting black dress that exhausted itself trying to cover her fleshy figure, a short white neckerchief in the middle of which there was a crystal brooch, and black court shoes. Her hair was dark and straight, and her face was ceramic smooth with makeup, punctuated with black eyes and a bright red lipstick smile.

'Can I help you?'

'Oh, hello. I'm Mary Henslow. My mother...' she nearly said, 'sent me' but preferred a more independent response, '...advised me that you had been kind enough to consider interviewing me for a part-time position.'

The woman hesitated for a second then broke into laughter. 'Oh, Nora Henslow. So, you're her daughter.' Mary was aware that she was being surveyed from her shoes to her face. 'Well, my name's Ruth Adams, Mrs Adams to you. I own this place. Now then, if you want to work here then we must put you into clothes that are more in keeping with the atmosphere. Follow me.'

Mary reflected on the shallowness of the introduction.

It didn't take long for her to be dressed in a black skirt and white silk blouse. The blouse felt soft and delicate, it helped to highlight her red hair. She felt good in it. Mrs Adams made a point of saying that if anyone arrived with a package or box and asked for her specifically, Mary was to call her without delay.

Mary's first day at the shop was a success. She managed to find whatever was asked for and use the till, as well as stamping rationing books. Mostly, she enjoyed talking to people and even helped them choose the correct size garments to take to the fitting room. From time-to-time women, very well dressed and exceptionally snooty, arrived with packages or boxes and were taken by Mrs Adams into a back room.

There was always the clink of glasses and the sound of voices not unlike seagulls stuck in a tunnel.

The days were long, but Mary didn't care. She felt happy to be challenged occasionally when items were unavailable, or customers couldn't make their minds up. She was given sandwiches for lunch, albeit with fish or meat paste, and although she received barely five shillings a week it was better than nothing and got her out of the house. There was always a small package or two to bring home to mother.

It was into the third week that Mary began to understand what was going on. Had it not been for the antics of a tall elegant looking woman in a red coat with a fox fur around her neck, she might not have guessed.

'Oh, hello,' said the woman, looking Mary up and down. 'I've never seen you here before?' She gave a tight-lipped smile and put an amber cigarette holder to her mouth. 'Got a light?'

Mary apologised and called for Mrs Adams.

'Darling,' said Mrs Adams in an affected manner. 'Back so soon. Lovely to see you again.' In one dexterous move she produced a crystal studded lighter and held the flame to the woman's cigarette.

The woman sucked in the smoke then blew it out slowly. 'Yes, more parties, despite dear old Adolf's attentions to us all. What a bore. I need more dres....'

Mrs Adams closed the conversation quickly. 'Enough, my dear Sonia, I know exactly what you're after,' she looked casually across at Mary. 'Pop off to the storeroom and tell me how many sets of white vests we have, dear. There's a good girl.'

Mary understood.

The two women whispered to each other, and Mary heard faintly the word 'sorry.' When she returned, she heard the familiar sound of clinking glasses and laughter.

Thirty minutes later, as Mary was serving an elderly lady, the snooty woman exited the back room and walked past her without a word. She was carrying a bigger bag now. The bell on the door clinked and she disappeared into the bustling London streets.

As Mary was getting her coat to go home, Mrs Adams approached her, smiling broadly.

'Mary, give this parcel to your mother, from me. She often pops in, but I haven't seen her for a week or so. Do give her my best.'

Mary held the package tight on the bus home. She was able to add up two and two. Clothes were rationed. Everyday folks had to abide by clothes rationing. Some people got more upmarket items or perhaps twice their entitlement – there was a thriving black market. There had to be a system of exchange. The answer probably lay in the packages that arrived with the customers, who later left with different bags. Mary felt uneasy about this.

She arrived home, bedraggled after a short drizzle, and as she was hanging up her raincoat in the hall, her mother came downstairs. She saw the package and took it from Mary without waiting for it to be offered.

'I presume this is from Ruth, what a sweetie she is.' She felt it and added, 'it's warm. I do hope the contents haven't melted, dear.'

Butter! That would explain the large portions on the table at mealtimes. There were other clues to the

Henslow lifestyle too. Her parents missed a couple of meals at home during the week and she learned that they often went out to eat. She recalled hearing a couple of women complaining that restaurants could only serve two courses including either game or fish. They were not otherwise affected by rationing, unlike most of the country that survived on a few ounces of butter and meat and one egg per person.

Mary's mood worsened. She couldn't face another round of sibling combat and asked Mrs Knight for a simple supper she could take to her room.

'Yes, of course, you look tired, dear. I'll do you some toast. How's that?'

Mary bit her lip. 'Yes, thank you so much. I guess there's plenty of butter!'

Mrs Knight held her hands either side of her and tilted her head and said knowingly, 'Yes, there is, dear. But not for everybody these days, I'm sorry to say.'

It's funny how things change so quickly. Mary's satisfaction at the daily tasks of working in the clothing shop began to pale against the juxtaposition of everyday ration-constrained customers and those with money who carelessly floated in and out with their paper bags and packages of black-market items. She watched an elderly lady shopping the other day, eagerly counting her ration points, and almost emptying her purse to buy a simple woollen dress for the upcoming winter, it put evcrything into perspective. Mary now went through the motions at work but no longer enjoyed it.

As the London fog choked the streets a young mother and her two daughters, who must have been around eight and nine years old, burst into the shop.

'Can I help?' said Mary cheerily.

'Yes, thanks. I need two coats for my girls. I've got my ration book and money, I think I've done me sums, I 'ope I've got it right,' she said with a nervous smile.

The girls looked excited and fidgeted.

Mary readily agreed to help them select coats. After looking at the few that were available, one style – navy blue with six big buttons – was selected, a far cry from the threadbare garments the girls were wearing. Their mother fitted one then the other, then got them to turn around in front of the mirror. The girls giggled gleefully.

'These are just the job. We'll take them. Thanks so much for your help.'

As Mary prepared the items, Mrs Adams came to the desk and picked up the ration book and inspected it carefully.

She frowned.

'Oh dear, you seem to have added up your points incorrectly. Look here, you are short by two points for two coats. I'm sorry dear but you can only have one – it's the rules you see.'

The young mother looked crestfallen.

There was an awkward silence.

'Use mine,' Mary blurted. 'I've no need for them now. We can do that, can't we?'

Mrs Adams stiffened. 'Mary, that's not allowed.'

Mary persisted. 'If that's the case then put them on my card and the lady can pay. Simple.'

Mrs Adams shooed the mother to the other side of the shop and returned. She gave Mary a stern look, which reminded her of Aunt Agatha.

'Mary, times are tough I know, but we are not a charity. For goodness' sake, she'll tell her friends that there's a naïve assistant here and then we'll have every Tom, Dick, and Harry in here wanting special treatment.'

The young mother heard the conversation and looked embarrassed, she called over. 'Look, I'm sorry. We must go. We should wait for the next allocation. I'm really so sorry.'

Before Mary could stop her, the mother, and girls, who were by now crying, left the shop. She was fuming and glared at Mrs Adams. 'Surely you could've made an exception just this once?'

'It's not your place to question me, young lady.'

By now Mary's safety valve had been bypassed. She angrily regarded Mrs Adams. 'Oh dear, perhaps if she'd turned up with a pound of steak or packs of butter, two little girls would've got a warm coat for the winter!'

'That's enough,' said Mrs Adams, by now red with rage of her own.

It was all too much for Mary. 'You're so right, enough is definitely enough. I resign, or as they say in American films, I quit!' She turned and grabbed her coat. 'I'll return the blouse and skirt tomorrow. I don't want to leave your profit margin short. Goodbye.'

She marched noisily out of the shop.

Mary's father looked sheepish and ill at ease, and the red blotches on her mother's neck were an indication that she was in high dudgeon – she was, in fact, visibly boiling. Mary stood in front of them, hands clasped in front of her.

'I cannot believe it. My friend makes a place for you in her shop, and you treat her rudely, disobey rules and...,' her mother stopped and looked at the ceiling, 'you walk out on her. You seem to have a habit of biting the hand that feeds you.'

Her father intervened. 'Let's hear your side, Mary.'

Mary was not about to give in.

'Papa,' she said addressing him and not her mother. 'I'm not naïve. I know how those with money can survive this awful war rationing, in fact I accept that this is the way of an imperfect world. But when I see someone being treated badly, in this case a young mother with her two daughters who needed coats and were just a couple of points short, I get angry. A little bit of grace and creativity in these situations goes a long way. Mrs Adams showed not a jot of sympathy.'

Her mother got up. 'I've heard enough. You see life through rose-tinted glasses my girl, nothing and no one...' she glared pointedly at Mary's father as if to strengthen her point, '...is perfect. Life is not perfect, and we all try and survive as best we can. Doubtless this young mother went to a second-hand shop and got the girls properly kitted out. What are you, some kind of bloody communist?'

'Nora,' said her father, patiently trying to defuse the situation, 'no more. I see the problem and think that we had better let the dust settle. What is done, is done.'

Her mother stormed out and her father leaned back in the chair.

'Mary, let me explain something to you. I've always been fair to people below my station. I learned that in the army during the last war. Everyone deserves to be treated well. Rules are rules, and sometimes sticking to them is difficult. Nevertheless, it's very important, in our society that everyone knows their place, to work hard, succeed or fail, but within their own milieu. Once you start to blur the edges you create problems.' He added ruefully, 'Heaven knows we daily see the result of over liberalism in society.'

Mary sighed – she didn't agree.

Her father rubbed his temple. 'Mary, I can't say that I disagree with your motives, but losing self-control and throwing rocks is no way to win an argument. You're kind-hearted, but you are also in danger of being put upon.'

Kind though his words were, it was too much for Mary. It was not in her nature to see people abused – to hell with expediency! This was absolutely the last straw.

'Papa, I know a bit more about life now and I'm so sorry, I don't want to upset you, but it's not really working out, me staying here, is it?'

Her voice shook with emotion. 'I'm fed up with being controlled and the odd one out. I have tried, I really have. For now, can we just say no more. You can lie to mother if you like, say I'm distraught, apologetic. I really don't care. I just don't want you to be the whipping boy for my actions. I need to move out of the house, it's the only solution.

Her father let out a sigh and touched her hand. 'Oh dear. All right, darling. If you say so. No more to be said.'

Mary leaned forward, looked into his eyes, and kissed his forehead. Then she went to her room She didn't cry, she was just angry, particularly about not being understood. Nothing would change her views of fairness. Why could her parents not see her point of view?

She reached for a large dictionary and hurled it at the wall.

Mary's anger cleaved to her all night. The last thing she wanted was to have to sit in an ice-cold atmosphere at breakfast time, watching her siblings' schadenfreude at her situation. On a positive note, at least it kept the attention away from them, especially Mavis, who had been getting a lot of unkind verbal remarks. Their mother was bad-tempered, yet another tutor had been called up for military service, and she had to carry out home-schooling herself.

Mary left the house unnoticed and walked calmly along the embankment. The pigeons were busy scavenging for food and the occasional barge pushed its way upstream through the churning brown water. She stopped and looked at sandbagged areas; barrage balloons were tethered low to the ground for maintenance and people scurrying about, almost all of them in uniform.

So why wasn't she?

That was the answer. She should join up; a uniform, regular meals, training, comrades, and the feeling that she was doing her bit for her country, just like many others. *Why not?*

Papa can't be right, it can't be that bad.

Without a second thought, she enthusiastically sought out and quizzed several soldiers and airmen passing by, who regarded her urgency with amusement. Nevertheless, Mary got the directions she wanted and made her way to a recruiting office. She picked the WAAF as her objective; she liked the uniform.

The recruiting sergeant regarded Mary with mild interest as he leaned back in his chair and listened to her. 'So, you want to join the WAAF?'

'That's why I'm here,' she replied, straightening herself, 'is there a problem?'

'No, not at all. It's just that, well, with your background there's usually a formal education and a sponsor.'

'Ah. You mean someone to ease me into a cushy number?'

The sergeant was embarrassed. 'No, it's just that–'

Mary interjected, 'Can we just fill the forms in and get me into uniform, please?'

'All right. Let's take down your details first. Then I send them to the Air Ministry for approval. If you are accepted for consideration, you'll soon get a letter telling you to turn up to an RAF unit, together with your overnight bags. You will be interviewed and if successful, allocated to trade training as the recruiters see fit. We're desperate for WAAF recruits so there'll be no delay. If you pass, I can assure you that you'll be straight in.'

Mary nodded and enthusiastically filled in the necessary forms, and the sergeant seemed satisfied. He stood up and held out his hand. 'Thank you for applying. You are a determined young lady, put it to good use in your service. Let's all give the Nazis a kick in the pants.'

Mary left the recruiting office in high spirits – as high as if she had just ridden her beloved Enfield.

Each day was agonising as Mary waited for a letter from the Air Ministry. The household mail was usually placed on a silver salver in the hallway under the mirror; her parents' mail to the left and everyone else's to the right. She chided herself for being impatient, but it had after all been eight days since her visit to the recruiting office. What was going on?

It was a dismal rainy day, and she heard the letterbox clatter, and dashed downstairs to check the mail herself. She rifled through the envelopes; all were for her parents, nothing for her. After flopping the envelopes onto the tray, she looked up and saw Mrs Knight in the kitchen doorway.

'My goodness, Mary, you do look forlorn. What's up dear?'

Mary looked left and right; she trusted Mrs Knight. 'I'm waiting for a brown envelope, Air Ministry.' Looking around furtively again, she added, 'I want to join the WAAF.'

Mrs Knight's eyes gleamed, and she put her hands to her mouth. 'Golly, you'll be so good, I just know it. Why, Hitler will surrender just at the thought of it!'

They both giggled like schoolgirls.

'Be that as it may, I still haven't got my letter calling me to be attested. I'm worried they don't want me.'

'Silly girl,' said Mrs Knight. Her eyes narrowed, and something seemed to cross her mind. 'A brown envelope you say?'

'Yes, unless they can afford Basildon Bond stationery for all their candidates!'

'I think not, my dear. Look, your father is away to a meeting with his agent and your mother has also left early to meet her bridge partners, who are several bus rides away. Join your sisters in the dining room – I've only just put a pot of tea on the table. I just need to go upstairs.'

A cup of tea was just what Mary needed. She watched Mrs Knight hurry upstairs.

In the dining room, Mavis and Hazel were unusually friendly to one another and talked about make-up and clothes. Hazel was instructing her younger sister on the art of applying rouge properly.

Father had eaten kippers and the girls complained of the smell.

Hazel poked her spoon idly into her porridge. 'We are all alone today. Ma and Pa are off in town.' She smiled wickedly, 'Perhaps Mother has a secret job, a stripper maybe?'

Mavis put her hand to her mouth her eyes wide open, 'Hazel!'

As Mary poured her tea, she noticed Mrs Knight come close to the door and, unseen by Mary's sisters, beckoned her into the hall. Mary pretended to spill her tea and made an excuse to get a cloth. The girls were too absorbed in conversation to notice.

Mrs Knight handed her two envelopes. One was beige and the other cream-coloured. 'I was dusting near your mother's writing desk, and these had fallen on the floor. I thought I might bring them to you straight away,' she said, 'if you know what I mean.' She tilted her head back, raising her nose in the air.

'Wha–'

'Oh, for goodness' sake. I know where to look. Now open it up, dear.'

Mary impatiently ripped open the envelope and stared at the title:

Notice to Attend RAF Innsworth No 2 WAAF Depot, Gloucester, for Interview and Attestation Into the WAAF.

The date to attend was 1 October 1941 at 1400 hours – today! She was distraught and her hands fell to her sides.

'I'm doomed, it's today and I must pack, say goodbye and...and...!'

'And nothing, Mary, get into your smart day clothes. I'll pack as much as I can for you, while you do the rest, including writing a farewell note to your parents. I'll get you to this Innsworth place if I have to carry you myself.'

She shooed Mary upstairs.

It was all such a whirl. True to her word, Mrs Knight arranged a taxi to Paddington railway station and presented her with a packed suitcase. It was easy to locate a train to Gloucester and to Mary's enormous relief she sat hemmed in by a large number of young women; their chatter revealed that they were all on their way to Innsworth. It was like being late for school then finding that you've been joined by others in the same situation.

She settled back and felt the stress of the moment lessen. One thing bothered her. She reached into her handbag and pulled out the cream envelope addressed to her; it was handwritten and not postmarked, so had been delivered personally. Moments later her face flushed, and her hands shook. The letter read:

Dear Mary,

I called at the house the day before yesterday and your mother said you were away, you'd left London – I thought that was strange because we agreed to meet for tea and tiffin later in the week, but no matter, we all make mistakes. The reason for my visit was to take you out and give you the bad news that I have been posted to North Africa and so I cannot make Wednesday. Montgomery needs a bit of help and picked me – well, someone in Army Postings did!

It wasn't entirely unexpected, but I'm disappointed to have missed you. I hope that I have done nothing to offend you. I've written a telephone number for you to call so we can catch up before I set sail, but it needs to be within the next few days - I am packing my kitbag as I write.

You know what - now that I've got my posting date, I realise that I am going to miss you, a lot.

When we meet, and I do so hope we do, bring a photograph and I promise to keep it by my bedside whilst I am away.

Looking forward to seeing you.

Very best wishes,

Giles

XX

The letter was dated three weeks ago and explained why Giles had not turned up for their date. Her stomach tightened and she felt angry at her mother's vindictiveness. Why, oh why did she do that? Giles must have thought her uninterested and she guessed that he would eventually make other female acquaintances - who would blame him? Her eyes brimmed with tears, and she scrunched up the envelope, and thrust it into her handbag. Now she was convinced more than ever that it was important to get away from her chaotic family, particularly her meddling mother.

That really was the last straw.

Mary was jolted out of her mood when mournful air raid warnings sounded just as the train left the station - the compartment fell ominously silent with the passengers now in a crowded small space without an easy exit. There was a palpable sense of fear.

'Come on driver, shift this bloody thing!' stuttered an irate soldier. No one else spoke.

The train slowly moved forward at first, then to everyone's relief got up to a good speed as it steamed through the outskirts of London. No aircraft, no bombs, and no explosions. It was probably a false alarm for the area - it meant that some other poor souls were being pounded elsewhere.

The relief was evident, and everyone suddenly started talking excitedly at the same time. It had a strange bonding effect and cigarettes were handed around to complete strangers and the chatter lasted for an hour afterwards. After that, tiredness followed relief and heads lolled for the rest of the journey.

Mary couldn't rest, and she looked out of the window and saw the terrible damage done to the railway infrastructure and town buildings of Swindon. There were craters, piles of rubble and buildings with no roofs and gaping holes in the sides. She gulped. This underscored that the danger was everywhere, not just London.

It was all so easy. At Gloucester railway station a WAAF officer and several airmen guided them along the platform.

'Okay, ladies,' said a burly sergeant, 'follow the signs to the buses outside.'

That would be the last time the WAAF recruits would be called 'ladies' by any staff. They embarked and it took no more than twenty minutes to get to Innsworth.

'Oh, my goodness,' said one of the recruits, as she surveyed the dreary desert of long huts.

A girl with a sense of humour retorted, 'Don't worry, gel, it's one hut per person.'

That got a lot of laughs and lightened the mood.

They debussed outside a building with a sign that said, Administration – New Recruits. Inside the building she joined several other young women in a queue to a desk where a harassed woman, in round-rimmed glasses wearing an RAF uniform, sat furiously filling in forms.

'Take this.' A label was hastily handed to her. 'Put this label on your case and leave it by the door.'

Mary felt uncertain about this. 'Ah, yes, well you see I'd rather...'

'By the door, do it now. Then sit over there.' The woman pointed. 'Next!'

She obeyed.

The chairs were tubular metal with green canvas seats and backs and were not at all comfortable, but she saw others wriggling on them and resolved that it would not take long before she would move on. She was wrong. An hour later she was still there, and the room had filled with young women. She listened to the vibrant chatter around her and took in the various conversations. It was as if the forming process which led to every girl staking a claim as to why they were there. Each shared experience being more graphic than the last one.

One girl demonstrably tried to put on lipstick and talk at the same time – it was so comic. ''Ere, Shirley, whatever 'appened to them Yids who lived next door to you? I never could make 'em out. Our dad said it's a Jew's war and nothing to do with us. He got a bit silly and said they shouldn't come into our local air raid shelter. Mum wacked 'im and told 'im to shut up.'

Her friend huffed and replied, 'Dunno. They're a strange bunch, but never did me any 'arm.'

Another girl with wiry hair and sullen cheeks mused. 'I'm just glad to be 'ere. I'm free of my feller. It'll be so good not to get home and receive a smack in the chops for nothing.' There was a murmur of shared recognition and sisterly support as though this was an everyday occurrence.

Mary was amused by frequent references to people with airs and graces, and a dislike of being looked down on, despite no tangible evidence offered of it ever happening. There were occasional comments that the war only hit the working class and the rich never suffered. Mary's experience in the clothing shop lingered.

She watched as the girls moved around and formed cliques, drawn by accents, or familiar backgrounds. It was all a kind of normalising of emerging social confidence brought on by the war. The one thing they all shared was that this was a portal to a new life – liberating and exciting.

The door to the canteen swung open noisily and a robust smartly uniformed older woman strode into the room and addressed them sternly.

'Right, now listen in. My name is Roberts, Warrant Officer Roberts, and you will address me as 'ma'am'. Understand?'

There was a low murmur of agreement.

'First off, no smoking. Second, listen for your name and when called go to the office indicated by the airwoman who calls you. When you've finished, proceed down the corridor to the medical centre for examination. Any questions?'

Silence.

'Good.' Without further conversation the warrant officer left the room and the throng burst into chatter and raucous laughter.

Mary had lived a solitary life in Devon and never developed the art of conversation with a large number of people of her own age. She resigned herself to the situation, saw it as a challenge and put it to the back of her mind. Looking around her, she saw a slim young woman two seats away, who returned a nervous smile. Her hair was in tight bun. She wore no lipstick or rouge and was dressed in a woollen dress and wore brogue shoes. Her fingers fidgeted as she held her hands together on her heavy woollen skirt.

'Hello,' she said nervously, her left eye twitching slightly.

'Hello,' said Mary supportively, 'how nice to talk to someone. I'm not really used to all this. My name's Mary.'

The young woman's face broke into a smile, and she looked relieved, and gushed, 'Oh, my name's Jane. I must confess, I'm very nervous about all this. But determined, yes, very determined to join the WAAF and do my bit for my country.'

Mary felt strange, almost superior in the face of this quivering young person. True, she felt awkward in the throng of strangers, but it didn't worry her at all, in fact she quite liked the challenge.

'You seem so at ease with all this. I wish I was.'

Mary softened, 'Well, let's look at it this way, you are at least here today ready to do your bit for your country and many aren't. So, you're one step ahead and that's to be applauded. That makes you more confident and courageous than you think.'

'Oh, yeah. When you put it like that...'

There was a shout, 'Jane Collins.'

'That's me, crikey, which way...?'

Mary touched her shoulder and pointed at an aircraftswoman standing by one of three doors that was open. 'Over there, Jane. I'm sure it will all be just fine. Good luck.'

Jane smiled self-consciously and scurried towards the open door.

Mary regretted not having a surname closer to the beginning of the alphabet and settled down to wait. After what seemed like ages her turn came, and she strode towards the door. Inside the office there was a desk behind which sat a man in a smart uniform, with two rings on his sleeve. A desk light shone onto papers in front of him and the room smelled of furniture polish.

'Sit down, Henslow. I'm Flight Lieutenant Baker and I am one of several administrators here at RAF Innsworth. I need to get more details from you to add to those you gave at the recruiting office. Are you happy with that?'

'Yes, but I'm not sure that there is much more to tell.'

'I'll be the judge of that. So just relax. Now then, let's see, you've left the question about schools open. Which school did you go to?'

'When I was small, up to about nine or perhaps ten-year-old, I went to a church school, in London. I think it was called Holy Cross primary. Anyway, after that, I kept getting ill with all sorts of lurgy and was tutored at home until I was fourteen then my parents sent me to live in Devon with my aunt. Country air and all that. Must have worked – look at me now!'

The officer tapped his teeth with his pen, 'And your education in Devon?'

'I was tutored by my aunt and my uncle Leonard – he's a vicar.'

'I see, so no formal schooling then. From what you record here, your father is an author?'

'Yes, he wrote many books on gardening as well as poetry. He started his career writing small articles for the Surrey Herald, as well as many poems. I have some here if you want to see them...'

'No, really, thank you. Not now.' He paused. 'You see, Henslow, we need to ascertain your level of education so we can decide where to best employ you. Frankly, there's not a lot to go on.'

He furrowed his brow and fiddled with his pen. 'Tell you what, I'll make a note for your superiors to keep an eye on your aptitude. Meanwhile, we'll pop you into photographic duties, I'm sure you'll find that interesting. That's all I can do. Sign here, please.'

He pushed the form towards Mary who signed without reading it.

'Before you go, I researched your family name, it goes back a long way, and you have a crest too.'

'Yes, that's right. I'm very proud of that. The name and crest indeed, goes back to the fourteenth century. Of course, for my family, the depression and stock market crash pushed everyone to the edge, but you are what you are, and I hang on to my heritage. It's so important, isn't it, family, and all that?'

'It is for sure. Look, I'll be blunt. If you'd had a better education, then we could've considered you for a commission. Perhaps if you attend night school we could move you along, but it won't be easy from the ranks. Never mind. I'm sure you'll be an asset to the RAF. Thank you for volunteering.'

Mary left the office excited at the prospect of working with cameras - she had a box model but was sure that her new job would entail something more interesting. She reflected on the comment about a commission and wondered what the difference was between serving in the ranks and officers.

As Mary approached the entrance to the medical centre, she saw Jane coming towards her. She was blushing and held her left hand to the top of her blouse and looked in a bit of a state.

'Jane, hello there, how did it go?'

Jane looked upset and stuttered. 'Another time. I really must go.' Then she scuttled away.

Mary watched her, bemused and wanting to comfort her - what about she did not know.

The outer office to the medical centre had six chairs but all were empty. A stern-looking nurse with dark hair and a rather large nose looked directly at her and barked.

'Henslow?'

'Yes,' she said, edgy at the haughty tone - such bad manners. In the outer office she could see a doctor through the half-open door, sitting at his desk writing.

'Right, go behind the screen and take off all your clothes.'

Mary's jaw dropped.

'And I mean everything. Here's a blanket. When you've finished, wrap yourself up and then sit over there. The doctor will see you when he's ready.'

Just like that. Strip. Wrap in a blanket. Wait. No conversation or appreciation that this might just be a little embarrassing. She wanted to leave, but of course she couldn't. The reason Jane was so upset dawned on her. She had a choice, get jittery or get on with it.

It felt so odd. She had never undressed anywhere but her bedroom and as for wearing nothing but a blanket, that just never happened. Taking a deep breath, she removed her clothes, folding them on the chair. When she finished, she wrapped the blanket around her, it was thin and very itchy, and then came out from behind the screen and sat on a chair by the office door. The nurse looked up from her desk and smirked.

Mary stared back resolutely, and the nurse looked away.

'Come on in,' announced the doctor.

The nurse ushered Mary into the doctor's office and joined them.

'Henslow, I just need to ascertain some medical facts, listen to your heart and chest, check your tummy, and give you a good look over before His Majesty can let you join the WAAF. Now it says here you had rheumatic and scarlet fever when you were in your teens. Is that all over now?'

'Yes, you should have a letter from my doctor explaining how much I have improved.'

'Yes, *sir,'* urged the nurse.

'Oh, sorry. Yes, sir.'

'It's all right, I'm a doctor first and an officer second,' he glared at the nurse. 'Your local doctor has indeed cleared you. You've ticked all the right boxes I see, no allergies, no current medical problems and, I'm sorry to ask, you're not pregnant?'

'No,' Mary spluttered.

'Then let's get on with things.'

The doctor turned and retrieved his stethoscope from a cabinet. The nurse approached Mary and with a smirk said, 'The blanket, Henslow.'

Mary felt a flush of embarrassment flow through her tummy. But the sight of the nurse holding out her hand was enough to galvanise her feisty nature.

She raised her head high, whipped off the blanket and threw it at the nurse so that it partly covered her head. The nurse flapped her arms about like a penguin, trying to get the blanket off.

It felt so silly. The cool of the room against her warm body and the involuntary blushing as he moved the stethoscope across her chest, then her back. After a while she noticed that he was totally absorbed in his task and not her nudity. After poking her tummy, checking her eyes and throat he declared the examination over.

'All right then, Henslow, that's it, you're quite fit for service. You can go now.' He paused, adding, 'Do you want to get the blanket, or shall I get the nurse to throw it back to you?' He craned his head and gave her a supportive, knowing look.

Back outside, Mary dressed and left without a second glance at the nurse; if she had hoped for a jittery, stuttering recruit she must be disappointed. Stupid woman.

In the main waiting room, several girls were preparing to leave, and others queued to receive a final set of papers that cleared them for service in the RAF.

One girl looked at Mary and nodded in the direction of those women heading for the door. 'That lot either failed the interview or the medical. We all made it. We're special.'

Mary nodded and felt pleased she had crossed a starting line – yes, she felt special.

Reunited with their suitcases the young recruits were led to a wooden hut called a billet and allocated bed spaces. How strange, sleeping with twenty other women – a far cry from a small bedroom, on one's own in a rectory. But she got on with it.

To her delight, she saw that Jane was two bed spaces away and negotiated with her neighbour to swap places. Jane was pleased and Mary was now aware of how the poor girl must be feeling after the medical examination.

'Come on, Jane. Buck up. Let's follow the other girls to the canteen.'

'I'm not sure I can eat, I'm...'

'No, Jane, you must eat. Come on, follow me.'

Jane did as she was told.

The canteen was plainly decorated with beige walls covered with posters urging everyone to not 'talk to strangers' and to be aware of things out of the ordinary. Large round white lights hung from the ceiling. Mary and Jane joined a queue at the counter and were soon sitting at a table with a tray of food. To her surprise, it was good wholesome grub and well cooked.

'It's been a long day and I'm ready for this,' she said and tucked into sausage and mash; the rich gravy made her tongue tingle.

Jane fiddled with her food, which irritated Mary; then, as if realising that it was quite tasty, she hurriedly finished her plate.

'There you go, you were hungry after all.'

Jane nodded and was visibly more cheerful.

Mary looked around and saw girls laughing and gesticulating, mimicking the movement of a stethoscope across their bosoms. They had no inhibitions, and it was all a joke to them. She turned to Jane.

'You looked so upset earlier, Jane. I know why. We all went through it, you know. Did you want to know something? Seeing you gave me courage to remain positive. I've never removed my clothes in front of anyone before, it was a challenge for me too you know.'

Jane nodded. 'You're so confident.'

'Yes, but it's all bravado. Besides, your confidence deserts you when you have no knickers on!'

Jane put her hands to her mouth and burst out laughing, it was a release of repressed angst.

Mary pretended to look left and right then said, 'And guess what?'

'What?'

'When the nurse smirked and asked for the blanket, I stood straight then threw it at her and it nearly knocked her hat off!'

That did it for Jane and she laughed until the tears rolled from her eyes. 'Oh, Mary you are so funny.'

She was still laughing until after the apple crumble and custard.

They walked back to the billet and on the way talked about their lives.

'Jane, you say you're an orphan, and your French mum and English dad were killed in a car accident in Paris when you were in your teens, that's so tough. Where did you go after the orphanage?'

'Oh, I went to work for a middle-class family in Guildford, Surrey. He is a banker. I didn't like him. He was always brushing close to me when his wife wasn't around and tried to get into my room one night, but I put a chair against the door. I knew I had to get away but had nowhere to go. The next day I decided to join the WAAF. He thinks I am visiting a friend.'

'Ah, how brilliant. So, you can sign up tomorrow, and after we are attested and sworn in, then send him a post card?'

Jane's eyes lit up and she giggled, 'Why, that's an idea.'

Once back in the billet they prepared for bed and after the day's events there was no embarrassment about being in dormitory with a large group – in fact, it was amusing to hear the chattering and laughter, quite liberating.

Lounging on the bed opposite Mary was a dark-haired girl who confidently bantered with the other girls. She had an easy-going nature that encouraged conversation and commanded attention.

'Ere, girls, did you see that handsome sergeant on the main desk? He's a regular feller if ever I saw one.'

''Ands off, he's, my dad!'

There were catcalls and howls and the dark-haired girl stood up and put her hands on her hips and looked at the ceiling. 'Just my bleedin' luck!'

As the noise died down, she looked across at Mary and Jane who both seemed a bit out of place and walked over to them.

'Hi, my name's Betty Wilson, what's yours?'

'Oh, hello, I'm Mary...'

One of the girls at the far end of the room mimicked Mary's accent. 'Ooooh, helloooo. Don't mind if I dooooo!' Some of the others laughed.

Mary blushed.

Betty turned and faced the girls, one hand on her hip and the other pointing at one of them. 'Leave it out, Sandra.' She was playfully stern. 'We're all in this together, right. So, we're mates and look out for each other, got it? Mary is 'er name.' Turning to Mary, she put a friendly hand on her shoulder. 'Mary you've got a great accent, you should be on the radio, you just keep it that way.'

Mary saw an opportunity and took her cue. To Betty's surprise, she stood up, went to the end of the room, raised her chin, held her hands in front of her and addressed the billet.

'Ladies, good evening. I'm Mary Henslow of the BBC Home Service. News time. The economic situation is dire with stocks and shares very wobbly - sadly, for haberdashery, shirts and pullovers are stable but undergarments are down.'

The girls hooted with laughter.

She raised her chin and continued. 'The local situation at RAF Innsworth is decidedly awkward, as five elderly men in white coats were arrested when caught peeping through the windows in the medical centre. They were gas fitters who happened to be passing and said they only popped in for a cup of tea and got carried away. They were undone when one of their number recognised his neighbour as she removed her blanket.'

By now the room was convulsed in laughter.

'Finally,' Mary said loudly above the laughter, and with a flourish of her arms, 'Prime Minister Winston Churchill welcomed twenty-five new WAAF recruits. He paid tribute to aircraftswoman Betty 'What's-her-name', saying she was an inspirational leader of her billet and praised her offer to buy drinks for every one of her new comrades.'

A loud cheer filled the room and Betty wagged her finger at her new friend. They hugged and there was more laughter. Mary's outgoing nature and years of helping to direct and act in the local village pantomime paid off.

Betty stayed with her and Jane, and they chatted for a while, but it had been a long day and returned to her bed space. The chatter in the billet died down, the lights were put out and soon there was a gentle sound of snoring.

Mary pulled the crisp white sheet up to her neck, turned on one side - so far so good.

5

The canteen was a cacophony of noises, pint mugs clunked as they were taken from the trays to be filled with steaming tea, and the chatter and laughter of airmen and airwomen rose and fell. Mary stood holding her mug and a plate on which there was a large slice of bread and margarine, and looked around for a place to sit. She paused momentarily, taking it all in. Most of the girls looked up and regarded her with mild interest, a couple smiled before continuing their conversation or flirting with the men opposite.

'Come on, darlin',' said a familiar cockney voice just behind her. 'If you stand around too long your tea'll, get cold. Get a bleedin' move on gel.'

She laughed. 'Thank you, Betty, lead on then, I'll follow you.'

Betty barged through a small group of airmen in front of her, her elbows moving left and right, and her language better suited to Billingsgate fish market. The men laughed and acknowledged her, some backing off theatrically as if she were a modern-day Boudica. They found a table and both sat down.

'I wish I was like you, Betty. You're so vibrant and able to banter with everyone you meet. I thought I could. Well, I could, but only in my own small world, that's to say, my local pub.'

Betty regarded her with interest. 'Mary, after your performance last night how can you say that? You made my night. Take your time, you're just not worldly wise that's all. I grew up in the Elephant and Castle and if you didn't speak up for yourself then you got picked on. Human nature, I s'pose. You're new to all this, so just be yourself, and for gawd's sake don't let Sandra Grant get to you.'

'Betty, thanks. I feel good already. I'm okay, actually.'

'Actually,' Betty laughed and teasingly repeated, 'actually, actually...!'

Mary gave her a playful shove.

'Oh.... why, you little devil. You can...er...sod off!'

Betty shrieked, 'Wahey, that's it girl. Fuck off is better but sod off will do.'

Mary and Betty bonded through humour and shared values. For the next ten minutes their conversation was open and lively as they laughed and gossiped about one or two of the other girls, and even some of the men. Mary's shell had been cracked wide open and although there was more to do, she was on her way.

The billet smelled of mothballs as the new blue uniforms were laid out on beds. Mary's fitted snugly, and she turned this way and that, looking at herself in a long mirror in her locker. Raising her hat with both hands, almost ceremoniously, she put it on. She felt wonderful. – liberated, almost a new person. From the back of the billet, it seemed that others did not feel the same way.

'My gawd, look at this will yer?' said Agnes her cockney drawl full of contempt. 'No colour, fits like a sack and I reckon I look like an escapee from Holloway.'

One girl put her jacket on back to front and jumped up and down like a penguin, to the delight of the others.

Interestingly, Mary saw Jane standing at the long mirror for quite a time admiring herself, she had a smile on her face, not so much like the cat that got the cream, rather one that had just been given a big dollop of it. Jane looked just like all the other girls in uniform - one of the crowd, a new person.

Betty was busy tucking her shirt in and then adjusting her tie. She looked across at Mary. 'You look great, darlin'. Uniform suits you - I reckon you were made for it. Anyhow, it's better than the boring rags you turned up in!'

Mary pretended to look shocked and threw a towel at her. The frivolity was cut short when the stern looking WAAF warrant officer burst in.

'All right, calm down now and get yourselves outside - now!'

They obeyed without demur.

Mary spent the previous evening talking to some old hands about what to expect during initial training and they regaled her with anecdotes about 'square-bashing', the nickname given to marching around the parade square learning drill procedures. They explained that getting men or women to form what is known as a squad, and to subscribe to the ancient art of drill, can be both hilarious and perhaps a bit frightening, depending on the players of the game.

Today's perambulations called up both experiences.

A smart WAAF corporal with strong, aggressive features addressed them. It was a slightly comical sight because, as was the fashion of anyone who was part of the drill machine, the rim of her peaked cap had been cut and fashioned so that it almost covered her eyes. It looked as though she had walked into a brick wall, but nevertheless, had an intimidating effect. She held a wooden pace stick to one side – almost as though she was about to use it to beat someone, rather than measure the steps taken by the squad.

'Right now. I want you to line up and we'll complete what is known as a "right dress".'

'Undress?' shouted Agnes. 'Naughty, corporal.'

The corporal went red, and the girls laughed. The WAAF warrant officer walked over to Agnes and said loudly, inches from her face. 'Just think, when you are up to your delicate little elbows in dirty dishes tonight in the mess hall kitchen, with no end until at least nine o'clock, you will regret saying stupid things.'

That did the trick. Good behaviour was thereafter assured.

The girls were 'sized', shortest on the left and tallest on the right, and through the deep art of drill manoeuvres they learned to form a squad. Then came the technique of shouting, 'one, pause, two' to give timing in between the raising of one foot, putting it down and raising the other. Finally, they were told to step off with the left foot, each step obeying the command, 'left, right, left...'

Early attempts to come to a coordinated halt were comical, but the threat of dishwashing in the mess hall concentrated minds and after several attempts, slowly succeeded.

They went up and down the parade square, many taking it all very seriously and others simply wishing that it was time for tea.

As they marched along the corporal strode alongside timid Jane whose nervous gaze had been all over the place instead of straight ahead. She shouted at her, 'You girl, do you fancy me?'

Flummoxed and embarrassed, Jane responded, 'No, corporal.'

'Well stop bloody well staring at me then!'

Jane got the message and so did the others, they were intimidated and yet each of them tried to suppress amusement.

There followed rudimentary first aid training and lectures on security, and military procedures and processes. It amused them when they were told what would happen if they misbehaved: they would be 'on a charge', nicknamed 'a fizzer'. This resulted in a kind of mini court hearing but only in front of a flight commander, who would most probably give them a number of days punishment, known as 'jankers', as the instructor playfully explained: guilty or not!

After the medical examination experience, the free from infectious diseases inspection, known as an FFI, was completed as hair, underarms and other parts were checked for lice and rashes, and caused little embarrassment.

But worst of all were the series of Inoculations required. It proved to be frightening for those who had not experienced being pierced with a needle and was made worse by those who stood in line telling everyone how painful it was going to be. The low lighting in the medical centre with masked nurses dressed in green gowns, standing stiffly at linen covered tables holding syringes was a severe setting.

One of the girls said alarmingly, 'O'er, mate 'o mine said her arm nearly fell off because of an infected needle.'

Another squealed, 'Oh, goodness, don't say that. How far does it go in?'

As the line edged forward with arms angled to one side, a hardier recruit teased, 'Don't worry, it only hurts if it goes out the other side.'

At that, two girls fainted.

Mary felt Jane's hand tighten, 'Don't worry,' she said, 'the girl was being silly, it's not that bad.'

Later, as they queued for mugs of tea in the NAAFI canteen, Betty said irritably, 'Jankers, wankers, I can't wait for the end of today, I'm whacked!'

Mary looked around at her companions. It was such an inclusive experience, not always pleasant, but they were all in it together – it was a great leveller. How strange that she felt more at home with these strangers than with her family. There again, like her relationship with her family, she was the outsider.

Jane joined them. Her uniform was spotless, and she kept adjusting her tie which didn't need it. She was poised, confident and held her head high.

Betty caught Mary's eye and winked.

'I've got good news,' Jane said, looking left and right.

'Goody,' said Mary, 'have you been posted or what?'

'Sort of. The flight commander called me in and quizzed me about my knowledge of French. I can speak it quite well actually. Anyway, he's arranged for me to go to a place in the country to be interviewed for a special role, one where my French language can be used for the war effort. I feel quite excited.'

They drank their tea and chatted about the latest big band music then Jane left, almost skipping as she went.

Betty grimaced. 'I hope she's gonna be okay.'

'Yes, I heard the other day about people being chosen for special ops in France.'

Mary was jealous at Jane's special selection. She craved validation of her worth, to be able to hold her hands up and say, *this is me, I have a trade and I'm good at it.* Had she done the right thing? How she wished her education was better.

She finished her tea and returned to the billet. It had been a busy but boring day. Mary realised that there was so much to learn and wrestled with her impatience that it was taking so long to get into proper work training.

After only two weeks, they paraded and were given certificates that indicated they had successfully completed basic training and received posting notices. Although it was a huge relief, Mary was disappointed because she was posted to RAF Kenley, near Caterham, to work on general duties, pending a place at the RAF School of Photography.

Despite that, Mary felt so much happier now that she was at last on her way. She knew Papa liked photography and couldn't wait to complete the training and surprise him with her new knowledge.

The first week at RAF Kenley was full of settling in and being allocated tasks. She was delighted to be in the same billet as most of the girls she had got to know during initial training, including Betty, whom she had bonded with, unlike some girls who were less accepting of one of their number who spoke 'proper'.

Friday arrived and they were all grateful for the upcoming weekend - except those who earned the inevitable 'jankers' for minor offences.

It was now after five o'clock and Mary said goodbye to Betty who was off to the bus station to make the most of her twenty-four-hour pass to see her sick mother.

Her shoulder bag and gas mask rattled against her side as she walked around the road to the billet - no walking on the grass allowed. The sun was almost out of sight on the orange horizon and the evening air was beginning to cool. As she passed two WAAF billets, she heard the sound of Glen Miller's jazz orchestra coming from a nearby window. The tune was lively, and she was taken by the low bass-notes; but the notes lingered - too long. It was not the music that now produced the bass sounds, but the noise from an aircraft that was getting louder.

She looked behind her and gasped. Approaching, was a German Dornier bomber, with a large glass canopy at the front. Suddenly, small flames darted from a position in the turret just below the pilot and bullets sprayed the ground around her. One WAAF was hit and thrown into the air like a rag doll, it was so sudden the poor girl had no time to avoid danger.

Mary threw herself to the ground. *Oh, my God, I'm in the WAAF for five bloody minutes and I'm about to die!*

Terrified airmen and airwomen ran in all directions and Mary looked up and saw the black bar-cross on the underside of the Dornier's wing. It pulled up and wheeled around to the left, circling fast and it was clear that it planned a second run. Sure enough, the aircraft banked and then took a straight-line approach towards the operations building. Despite her fear, Mary was angry. She got to her feet and raised two fingers defiantly.

'Sod off, Adolf,' she shouted, then in amendment said, 'No, fuck off, Adolf!'

The aircraft was almost overhead when she saw an object fall from its belly. Mesmerised, she followed its path as it fell – straight towards the operations building. The sound of the explosion rent the air and bits of wood and glass flew in all directions. Although the bomb missed the centre of the building, it landed alongside and blew a hole in the wall. Without support, the roof sagged, windows began to collapse, and parts of the building caught fire.

Mary ran towards the debris as everyone else ran against her. Brown smoke billowed from the hole. She gingerly moved a little way inside and peered through the gloom into what had been a large operations room and saw that blackboards, tables and chairs had been thrown all over the place. The smoke almost blinded her. To her horror she saw a uniformed woman, her head blood-soaked and her leg trapped under a wooden structure.

Without hesitation, she put on her gas mask and clambered over the debris. Smoke had entered the mask as she put it on, and it made her cough and her eyes water. It was almost impossible to see anything in the room.

Mary heard the sound of a woman's loud wailing and was able to feel her way towards her.

'It's okay, it's okay,' she yelled, her voice blunted by the mask.

She held the woman's hand to comfort her and looked at the structure holding her leg. Thankfully, it was part of a plasterboard partition and not brick - but it was heavy. A piece of bone sticking out of the woman's shin shocked her, but she remained composed.

'I'm going to try and lift this bloody thing off you, when I lift then you must do your best to quickly get clear, understand?'

The woman's face was covered in tears and her voice quivered. 'Yes, thank you so much...'

'No time for thanks, just get ready.' Mary stood up, grasped the edge of the structure, and bent her knees, remembering the advice of farmhands to do that to get better purchase and protect her back when she moved bales of hay. Her fingers dug into the wood and plaster structure.

'One, two, three...argh!' she shouted and lifted the structure. At first it only moved inches, but she took a deep breath and with another mighty shove created more space and the trapped woman slid out quickly and screamed in pain. It was just in time, as Mary could hold on no longer and let go – the structure fell to the ground with a thud. As she did so, the unmistakable sound of an aircraft could be heard.

'Come on, it's not far, you can do it,' shouted Mary encouragingly.

The bastard's coming back.

She grabbed the woman, and dragged her towards the hole in the wall, following the dim daylight almost obscured by acrid smoke, hoping for the best. Exhausted, they both stumbled outside, the woman was crying, holding her head, and limping. Mary encouraged her to move to open ground as fast as she could. After about fifty yards, the Dornier passed over them and another bomb was jettisoned, hitting the building in the centre with a mighty thump, blowing it to smithereens. Mary flung herself over the woman and they fell to the ground just as bricks and sharp debris flew through the air. She received several sharp smacks on her head and body and tasted blood. Her head buzzed and her ears rang.

The aircraft moved away slowly and there was the sound of an air raid siren, then the recognisable ringing of a fire engine bell.

She blacked out.

Mary awoke in a ward in the station medical centre. The sheets felt crisp and cool, and there was a slight trace of ether in the air. She felt the stinging to the cuts on her hands and face, and there was a bump on her head the size of a duck egg. She looked at the window and saw that it was dark outside.

'Aircraftswoman Henslow,' said a stern but soft voice, 'glad to see you stir. You've been out for the count for over three hours.'

Standing in front of her was a tall and elegant-looking woman wearing a nursing sister's uniform with officer's insignia on the blue cape-like jacket.

'You did bloody well. There's a young woman who owes her life to you, Henslow. You will be up for a commendation, for bravery. Well done. Where do you work?'

Still dazed, she managed to mumble, 'I'm waiting for a training course at the RAF School of Photography, ma'am.'

'Not anymore. We need people with your kind of courage and compassion. I'm getting you transferred to the medical centre. We'll soon get you trained up.'

Mary didn't know what to say; besides, she got the impression that one didn't argue with superiors in a military environment. The sister left, and she was given some tea – it was welcome and washed down the remnants of dust that remained in her mouth.

Three days later, Mary was pronounced fit for duty. The walk back to her billet seemed longer than usual as she passed areas damaged by the air raid. When she came to the rubble that had been the operations centre, she gulped at the sight. A passing airmen stopped.

'What a mess,' he said. 'This isn't the first time. It happened last year, and they had to move the ops people down to a local newspaper shop, because it had the only working telephone in the area. It was all a bit comical.'

Mary remembered the explosions and shuddered at how close it had been to disaster as she and the hapless WAAF had struggled to get away. Nevertheless, it was her initiation into the war, and she felt quite proud of it.

She gently rebuffed the airman's offer of a date and limped away.

As she walked through the door of the billet, she became aware of a strange silence – the quarters were never as quiet as that. The air seemed heavy and warm. Suddenly, the room filled with excited airwomen who gave a loud cheer and crowded around her, and she was hauled into the throng.

'Here she is, our very own heroine!'

There were yells of, 'Good on yer, Mary,' and 'You were brave, gel!'

It made her laugh and she said modestly, 'I feel sore, not brave!'

'Maybe so, but sore or not, you get into your civvies and we're all taking you out for a drink in the NAAFI.'

Mary just wanted to rest, but there was no chance of that. She reluctantly gave in and got ready for a night out.

She went through the motions of sorting out suitable civilian clothes and Betty shouted, 'Hey, Mary, wanna borrow my lipstick?'

Mary had seen Betty's blood-red lipstick before, 'No, that's kind of you.'

Another girl yelled from the back of the billet, 'Yeah, 'n if you want to borrow my nail varnish just ask.'

Mary felt a mixture of emotions: relief from being out of danger and the joy of appreciation. She was also divided between being cheated out of a good sleep and receiving such friendliness. The room was buzzing – it was almost as if they had been brought to life by her actions. Her part in the excitement was now almost incidental.

The NAAFI was noisy and smoky. She spent the evening in a daze but was aware that this had been her 'rite of passage', she had earned the respect and now friendship of her fellow comrades in the billet. Fate had worked well – the WAAF she saved had been none other than her nemesis, Sandra Grant, who was now languishing in a hospital bed, singing Mary's praises.

The evening took a more jovial turn when someone mentioned songs and jokes. Mary felt anxious; she couldn't sing or recall any jokes, other than 'why did the chicken cross the road'. Each girl took it in turn to perform. Those that sang were really very good, but the jokes were, in the main, quite feeble, or quite disgusting. Nevertheless, comrades being what they are made a lot of noise cheering even the most hapless provider.

Mary was aware that it was approaching her turn. Sure enough, one of the girls shouted, 'Come on then, Mary, your go.'

A couple of the girls nudged each other.

Mary gathered her wits, her mind raced, thankfully one of her father's short poems sprang to mind and she slowly got to her feet.

The girls looked awkward - she was one of them now, and yet not really, had they put her in a vulnerable position?

'A poem,' she said.

Mary noticed the girls' expressions tighten.

'It's called: The Mighty Hunter.'

The girls politely, ooohed and aaahed.

Mary took a deep breath and began.

The Mighty Hunter

'*The mighty hunter fit and tall; his fat bankroll he holds above all.*

His sport is to kill creatures, but not from near.

A natural coward, he harbours fear.

At home he treads on the working man; in Africa he shoots whatever he can.

He towers over his now dead prey; bidding all to listen to what he will say.

A foot upon the lion, and full of misplaced pride; a mosquito bit him - and he died!'

The girls were awed. They cheered and clapped, and Mary blushed at the sudden outburst.

'That was brilliant, upper-class twit done in by a mossie. I love it.'

'Knew she was a good 'un.'

'Well done, Mary!'

The comments flooded in.

It felt so good, Mary even laughed at herself. The drinks flowed and the night out lasted well beyond closing time.

Three days later Mary was invited to the Station Commander's office and given a commendation. He was pleased and said that her action had underscored that to win this war, bravery and discipline were what was needed. Looking at the typed paper, Mary wondered what her parents would think. She had earned special recognition and wanted to show them but was uncertain. Would they take it for granted or feel proud of her? Not knowing the answer made her feel awful.

Two months passed and Mary spent a lot of time learning her new job in the medical centre. Although only an assistant, she worked hard on every task given her and earned praise from the sister and trained nurses. Because her duties involved looking after injured people it drew the best out of her. She was able to be decisive and yet kind, and always put the patient first. It made her feel better about herself and helped draw a veil over her disappointment with her family. What she did now had real meaning.

When it came to Christmas duties Mary volunteered to work as many shifts as she could, insisting that those with families far away from RAF Kenley should be first in the queue for home leave. She sent cards and small gifts home, and a note regretting that 'duty calls'.

Betty stood by her bed and regarded her carefully, 'Mary, you're doing a lot of shifts over Christmas and that means no parties. You must enjoy yourself too, y'know.'

'I promise you, Betty, I'm happy with my choice. Some young girls are from the north or Scotland, and this is their only chance to get home after months away. I feel good about that. I'll make up for it.'

Betty put her hands on her hips. 'You're an angel, just don't wear yourself out.'

Gradually, the billet emptied. The silence was a blessing and Mary felt content in her own company. The next day she joined with another auxiliary nurse in putting up simple lines of loop decorations around two of the medical centre wards and when Christmas Day came, every patient got a small piece of chicken for lunch. In the afternoon she led Christmas carols and there was much laughter when a soldier with a broken leg sang, 'We three kings from Orient are, one in a bicycle one in a car...' The feeling of team spirit and genuine warmth made her happy. It contrasted with the pious celebrations in Devon and indifference of Fentiman Road. She felt part of all this – she owned it and wanted more.

New Year's Eve was a bit flat because the war overshadowed everything, leaving everyone wondering what it would bring. Would it bring an end to misery, or would the misery remain?

Soon the shifts were back to normal and the returning nurses brough Mary gifts in gratitude for her selflessness.

It was Friday and there was much excitement in the billet at their promotion and one of the girls shouted, 'We're no longer erks, we're leading aircraftswomen now - how about that! Let's enjoy spending the extra cash down the pub?'

Betty yelled back, 'Wattenden Arms it is then!'

Until now, Mary's socialising with her comrades had been limited to the NAAFI or the dining hall. The girls shouted with glee at being 'let out' - but she felt strangely uneasy about this new sense of freedom.

'Come on, Mary. We're gonna let our hair down tonight, you'll see. What's more you're gonna join us and that's all there is to it,' Betty said, as she layered on bright red lipstick. 'One of the pilots from 15 Squadron is a pianist and has promised to bang the ivories for us tonight, wahey!'

Mary gave in gracefully and knew it would be fun. 'Yes, sorry. Time of the month. Let's have some fun.'

'That's my girl,' said Betty, who knowingly popped her lipstick back in her make-up bag and walked over to her bed. 'Don't think I don't know how nervous you'll be tonight.'

Mary went to speak, but Betty held up her hand. 'Stop! It's okay, y'know. Once we get into the throng, you'll feel better and when I see that, I'll let you fly solo - until then, I'll be by your side.'

Mary smiled in submission. Tightening the towel around her wet hair she opened her make-up bag, the contents were significantly less than those of the other girls. She usually preferred nothing more than a shadow of powder - but tonight would blend in and raised the red lipstick towards her lips with slight trepidation.

For all that, she felt relaxed and completely at home with her new comrades. They were a million miles away from people she had mixed with. She watched them laugh and joke. They looked out for each other, but above all it was their basic honesty she liked so much; no airs and graces. If dropping the aitches meant being a good person, then she might just set about dropping hers!

Any thoughts of visiting Fentiman Road in the coming weeks were miles away.

The girls swaggered down the road, happy to be in civilian clothes and at least momentarily away from the discipline of their daily routine. Four of them linked arms and they swayed back and forth singing, '*Roll out the barrel, we'll have a barrel of fun...*' Out of uniform they looked radiant, with make-up, hair fluffed out, wearing tight-waisted dresses with bodices that showed a cleavage, very much in the style of the latest leading-lady film stars. Mary hung back with Betty who held her upper arm supportively.

The Wattenden Arms had been repainted a dull green, replacing its bright white exterior. It was clear that the public bar was almost full, judging by the number of people lounging outside against the wall. The sound of a piano being played and the noise of intoxicated revelry, drifted out of the door every time it was opened. Immediately outside the main door a young corporal stood, his uniform battledress open and tie loosened; he dragged on a cigarette, cupping it in his hands.

'Ullo, ladies. Who wants a date, then?'

Betty retorted, 'Only if you ask your mum first, darlin'.'

The other girls screeched with laughter, but Gwen sidled up to him and they were soon chatting like old friends.

'Good old Gwen, she'll get a pint or two out of that one,' said Betty, nodding her head in their direction.

They pushed their way inside and Betty effortlessly elbowed her way to the bar with Mary in tow. Within minutes she was holding a pint of shandy and Betty was sipping port and lemon.

It wasn't so bad after all. The young soldiers and airmen were jovial and polite, and she enjoyed their company. Then the singing started – Mary thought how amazing it was that when people started to sing lively songs, they seemed to forget the tough times and bond together.

The fourth shandy meant that she had to leave Betty and make her way to the ladies' room. She followed Betty's example and elbowed her way through the crowded bar to the rear of the pub. She was almost there when she bumped into an airman who stood alone at the edge of the bar, and he spilled his drink. He looked up angrily, but his face softened when he saw her.

'Oh, goodness me, I'm so sorry. I must get you another one. I do apologise.'

The man held his hand up. 'Oh, not at all. If I had a pint given me for every inch of beer spilled on me in this crowded pub, I'd be drinking free of charge all week.'

Mary felt relieved.

He gave a wry smile and stroked his chin. 'Hmmm, on the other hand...!' Standing up abruptly, he began brushing away non-existent beer pretending to be soaked and shaking non-wet hands.

Mary laughed. 'You don't look very wet to me. If you are I suggest you take your trousers off and hang them over the bar to dry,' adding, 'but I suspect you're just teasing me.'

'Frankly, yes, but I think I'll maintain my modesty. Besides, I'm very tired today and at a loss for chat up lines.'

'Chat up lines? What does that get you I wonder?'

He stared at her. 'Well for starters, it gives me a chance to talk a pretty lady to raise my spirits. In this situation, a lady christens me with brown ale, and she is not only pretty but extremely good at banter.'

She returned his smile. 'What's that on your arm? Ah, I see sergeant stripes. What do you do at Kenley if I may ask?'

'You may. I'm a pilot. A sergeant pilot. Having no upper-class family background, nor a university education, I am awarded sergeant stripes. It means that if I am captured and sent to a POW camp, I must be given some privilege over the average soldier in the field.'

'Oh, that's interesting. Do you intend to get captured?'

He smiled mischievously. 'Well now I've made your acquaintance, that's the very last thing on my mind. My name's John King, I came to the UK from

South Africa to fight Nazis, but instead, I'm talking to a beautiful woman.'

Mary smiled and shook her head. 'My goodness, you have an answer for everything. I must get you a pint to make up for the one that got spilled. My name's Mary Henslow by the way.' She beckoned the barman and paid, then turned to him. 'Well, I must go back to my friends now.'

'Must you? Why not stay a while and we can chat, you're the liveliest person I've talked to all week?'

Mary waivered. He was very handsome and oozed charm. However, the memory of Giles lingered, enough to make her careful. She wanted no more disappointments.

'Sorry, perhaps another time.'

The ladies' room was signed directly ahead, and she made her way towards it; when she got there, she looked over her shoulder - he was still gazing at her.

Someone pulled back the curtains in the billet and the morning sunlight burst in, earning a dozen rebukes.

'Oh, my sainted aunt,' Betty sighed as she tried to move here head off the pillow.

Gwen groaned. 'That corporal was bloody generous, but my 'ead don't 'arf' 'urt.'

'Generous?' shouted one of the girls two beds away, 'and what did he get for such largesse?'

'Dirty cow,' said Gwen, 'He got great company and a snog or two...or, perhaps three of four!'

The billet filled with ribald laughter. Then it quietened.

A voice from the back of the billet teased, 'And what about Mary last night, eh?'

Mary flushed and wanted to sink beneath the sheets.

There was a loud cry of, 'Oooooh!' from the girls.

'Okay, Mary,' said Betty. 'I set out to look after you, but you didn't bleedin' need it. You hooked up with a sergeant pilot, no less. Is that a New Year treat, or what?'

There were more shouts and Mary had to sit up and face the music.

'Look, okay, we chatted, very briefly. His name is John King, and he is indeed a sergeant pilot. He came over here from South Africa and ended up in the RAF at the outbreak of the war. If you must know, I spilled beer all over him!'

'Before or after the introductions?' yelled Gwen.

'Did you lick it off?' said a young Scots lass, and there was more laughter.

Mary tutted and tried to keep to the high ground. 'Anyway, I said I had to get back to my friends and that was that.'

'Mary, gawd luv yer, you silly dolly, what did you do that for? You should've stayed with him.'

The other girls hooted, and Mary blushed. It occurred to her that she may have made the wrong decision.

'She ain't never snogged!' yelled Gwen.

Betty came to the rescue. 'Okay, enough of that you lot.' She turned to Mary and said gently, 'Are you shy of blokes?'

Mary spluttered, 'Not exactly, I just...'

'Mary, you're such a pretty lady, I predict that it will not be long before you enjoy the delights of puckered lips!'

The girls yelled supportively and what could've been an embarrassing admission had been turned to expressions of support - and fun.

Mary could relax. For the moment, Sunday would be a day of recovery.

If dull, rainy mornings had to pick a favourite day then it would have to be a Monday. The wind moved the wetness around as though it was cleaning the airfield. The mess hall was quiet today, many airmen and airwomen preferring the warmth of their bed until the very last minute before going to work. Mary was aware that Betty was watching her eat her porridge.

'Betty, is it my table manners?'

'Oh, heck, no. Sorry. I was just thinking. I'd love you to meet my mum and dad. We've got time on Saturday to go my place, Turnpike Lane. It'll be a good laugh. It'll be a brief visit. D'you fancy that?'

Mary realised that this was Betty's way of cementing their friendship and felt privileged. 'That would be very special indeed. If they are as nice as you then it would be a special day for me.'

Saturday came and Betty was up and about, fussing with her make-up and shooing Mary to do the same. She was clearly excited. The underground was in operation and the tube trains ran regularly. They chatted and laughed throughout the journey. Mary thought Betty was one of the liveliest people she had ever met.

They got out at the Tube Station at the end of Turnpike Lane and Mary was grateful to swap the stale air for the cool breeze. They walked arm in arm past the local park and down the lane. Two dark-uniformed ARP wardens with their battledress open and helmets hanging on their belts were smoking and drinking mugs of tea at a tea shack. Mary had been encouraged to wear her hair long at the sides and curled up at the front – she didn't feel comfortable, but it was how the other girls dressed so she gave in gracefully.

The shops held few new goods and were mostly full of second-hand items. Emptying lofts and wardrobes of unwanted clutter helped to bring in a little extra cash. The area was so far untouched by the bombing. Betty explained with a grin, 'I know this will seem a bit nutty, but they say that this is due to Mr Elliot Follett,' and gave a wry laugh. 'Apparently, he communes with the spirits, and they told him that the Turnpike Lane would be spared the horrors of the aerial bombing. My mum has always been into that stuff, you know, tea leaves, spiritualists, tarot cards, you name it. I Daren's debunk it because she holds onto it like crazy. Trouble is, I know Follett came here from Croydon and his street got obliterated!'

Mary chuckled and considered the facts. 'Well, Betty, when you think about it, the good Mr Follett avoid getting flattened after all didn't, he?'

'Oh, yeah. I suppose he did.'

At number 71, Betty fiddled for her keys and the door opened easily.

'That you Bett'?' said a woman's voice.

'Yeah, mum, and we've got a guest so get Dad to put his shirt on.'

There was ribald laugh, 'Some bloody 'ope!'

The walked down the dark tiled corridor, passed the stairs and into a living–dining room that had an enormous coal fireplace, with red glazed tile edging, on the left. The beige painted walls were covered with pictures and family photographs, magazines and papers lay everywhere. A battered sofa was at the back of the room, which made sitting at the large table a bit difficult. Next to it was a cabinet with countless glass objects such as models of animals, glasses, and paperweights. A man lay curled up on the sofa, gently snoring.

Betty looked annoyed. 'Don't mind dad, it's his constitutional!'

Mary raised her hand to silence her and whispered, 'please don't worry, I'm the one intruding.'

Betty's mum came towards her, drying her hands on a cloth.

'Hello, and who've we got here?'

Mary didn't have a chance to answer. 'She's my best mate, Mary. And she's a heroine, she saved one our lasses from getting fried after a bombing raid!'

Mary blushed and laughed, not knowing what to say.

'What's more, she comes from an ancient family and her father writes books, poetry and the like.'

'Ooh, there's clever,' cooed her mum.

Just then, the shape on the sofa stirred. A man slowly sat up, yawned, and scratched his ample belly through his vest. 'Posh, eh?'

Betty spun around, but before she could deliver an admonishment, Mary brushed past her. She held out her hand. 'Mr Wilson, lovely to meet you. I envy you having a nap, I think I could do with one too.'

He flashed her a suspicious smile. 'Be my guest,' and he pointed to the sofa as he got up. 'Gotta go to the khazi.'

Betty put her hand to her temple.

Her mum stepped in quickly. 'Well, Mary, any friend of Betty's is very welcome here, now sit yourself down at the table and we'll get the tea on.'

She scurried to the kitchen.

Mary noticed that the tablecloth was very thick to the touch, almost like a thin carpet. It had deer and trees embroidered into its green colour. As Betty fumbled inside her handbag, she grabbed the opportunity to go into the kitchen.

'Come on then, Mrs Wilson, let's both do the tea.'

'You are a dear, yes, let's do it together. Name's Audrey, by the way.'

They fussed and apologies were offered for a cracked cup, but it was decided that this was a sign of acceptance. Like many homes in London, a secret stash of biscuits was kept in the kitchen cupboard and Audrey tapped her nose, 'Fell off the back of a lorry!'

By now Betty was more relaxed and grinned as Mary and Audrey chatted. Her father came in from the outside lavatory that was now shaking from the water pressure that gushed into the cistern, and noiselessly went upstairs.

A sallow-looking young girl came in with a baby on her hip. ''Ello, someone new?'

'This is Mary—'

Mary stood up quickly, keen to prevent Betty from giving a long description of her exploits and father's writing.

"Hello, I'm Mary. I heard you could get a decent cuppa and biscuits here at the Wilson's, so I popped in.'

'You're not wrong there. I'm Betty's sister, Marjorie, Marje for short, and this little tyke is Albert.'

On cue, the baby gurgled. 'Sorry, must go, I need to see the local district nurse about his bum, it's a bit red and sore. That reminds me, where's dad?'

They laughed and Marje left as quickly as she had arrived.

Audrey leaned towards Mary. 'Just a heads up. She lost her man some time back. HMS Ark Royal, off Singapore. She doesn't talk about it at all. Baby Albert is her joy, and ours too. We're family and will do all we can to help her.'

Mary pursed her lips and gave Audrey a gentle hug.

For the next hour she enjoyed flicking through the magazines and talking about everyday things, like hairstyles, clothing, and the latest film stars, laughing at the antics of politicians and other newspaper headlines. It was all so ordinary and yet so relaxing, no arguments or pointed remarks - just good honest fun. She had only been in the house for a short while and yet felt as though she had known everyone for years; she was already sharing a bit of sadness.

It was soon time to eat and though fish and chips was suggested, money was short and so was the fish. Audrey did her nose tapping again, went to the kitchen and came back with a dozen eggs saved over the last weeks.

'I've got spuds, so how about egg and chips?'

There were gleeful shouts as they busied themselves laying the table.

After the meal Audrey leaned back and patted her stomach. 'Love a duck, that was yummy if I say so myself!'

Betty beamed at her, 'Yeah, mum, runny yolks and crispy chips, you're the best.'

'Lesson for you, my girl. Rationing maybe a pain in the proverbial but keeping the fat for longer than necessary helps to brown and crispen the chips. I've got lots of tricks like that to teach you.'

Mary watched the mother and daughter exchange and was envious. She raised her glass of ale and said, 'Here's a toast to chef Audrey.'

Audrey stood up and gave a half-bow.

Betty beamed and gave her kiss.

Full and warm in front of the roaring fire, they listened to a comedy programme on the wireless, featuring Tommy Handley; it made them all laugh.

'I do love that Handley bloke, don't you?' said Audrey.

'Yeah, I like the title, ITMA, it stands for It's That Man Again.'

Mary broke in, 'Oh, yes, and that dreary character, Mona Lott, what's her line? I remember, *it's being so cheerful that keeps me going!*

Betty laughed and got animated, 'No, no, what about Colonel Chinstrap, *I don't mind if I do.* He reminds me of our squadron leader, you know the one with the wobbly left eye?'

The next half an hour was full of calling up all the other characters in the series in detail, such was the popularity of the show. The gossipy chat and laughter made Mary feel a mile away from the dangers of wartime London.

Betty's father had been silent and now, after lighting a cigarette, he joined in, mimicking one of the characters, the German agent, Funf. He coughed violently and Betty looked worried.

Mary could've sworn that he was about to spit into the fire as he leaned forward in its general direction and pursed his lips when Audrey glared at him. He swallowed, frowned, and went upstairs.

Minutes later Harry returned, he sat down and looked challengingly at Mary. 'So, your dad's a writer, what about?'

'Gardening, poetry, and he's written articles for the Daily Telegraph.'

'Rich then, is he?'

Audrey bristled, 'Harry, that's rude.'

Mary sat straight. 'No, let me explain. He does what he likes to do - write. Nothing wrong with that. We all have to make a living. For the record, despite all the trappings of a family crest and so on, there really isn't that much cash in our family. In fact,' she leaned forward, looked at him and winked, 'I rather wondered if you could lend us a couple of quid?'

There was a moment's silence, then they all burst out laughing. Harry's shell had been punctured, and he smiled broadly. Betty looked relieved.

'Dad, play your records,' she said excitedly. 'Go on, please.'

Harry looked thoughtful and Audrey threw him a gaze that made his mind up for him. Soon the record player was on the table and wound up, then they were dancing around to big band music from the twenties and thirties. They sat back and listened to the bands of Harry Roy, Henry Hall, Joe Loss, and Hugo Rignold,

It was music that reflected the improving economic situation after the last war and the arrival of a new social independence. Mary found her spirits rising. She thought how funny it was that music could do that. It was almost revolutionary as people were encouraged to enjoy 'hot rhythm', swing and jazz.

Harry went to the kitchen to get more bottles of beer and Audrey whispered to Mary, 'He was in the Royal Artillery in the last lot. He saw a lot of young men die and it was this type of music that stopped him from going doolally. All that cheerful stuff about places we've never been to, Mexico, Paris and songs about love and heartbreak. Keeps our heads up, doesn't it?'

Mary readily agreed.

They went to bed late and she was happy that Betty's dad had softened and joined in with the fun. He was certainly more relaxed, and she was careful not to use the word 'actually'.

Mary and Betty left the house after a modest breakfast of toast and margarine and countless cups of tea. Audrey was sad to see them go – they had spent a lot of time laughing and joking. It was so uplifting. The journey back to Kenley took a long time on the Sunday service. During the ride, Mary saw Betty gaze at her several times.

'Mary, I really enjoyed your company. I know we come from different places, but you're kind and fun, and I know my mum really likes you. You're always welcome at Turnpike Lane, you must remember that.'

Mary felt good, the inclusion and friendship from Betty's family was very special to her now. She gave Betty a hug and noticed her expression - it said, *she's my mate!*

6

Mary enjoyed working in the medical centre. Most of all, there was a sense of camaraderie that came from helping people. She was a quick learner and although giving injections and other technical stuff was beyond her training, she was able to change dressings and watched carefully as many other treatments were administered. Her good nature and intelligent approach meant that she was often trusted to help, but importantly, her kind personality calmed those in most pain. She kept herself busy and volunteered for many hours of overtime. Another week passed and she was beginning to forget what life had been like before she joined the WAAF. The daily routine of learning new things and meeting and talking to fellow recruits was totally absorbing.

She wearily returned to the billet and flopped onto the bed. The evening meal of Woolton pie, consisting of a cheese-based pastry and vegetables, but no meat, had been disgusting. Decent vegetables were in short supply, except for those in the countryside, and how she wished for a large plateful of them, cooked lightly, and not boiled to glutinous submission by RAF cooks. Her waistband was tight and when she undid the clip, it eagerly sprang open. *I must cut down the grub or I'll end up a 'tubby'.*

Later, she went to the domestic area to make a brew of tea. Two of the girls came in, laughing as usual. It was Gwen and a rather gawky looking Scottish lass. Gwen waved an envelope.

'Something for you, Mary. It didn't come through the post. Internal I think.'

Mary studied the neat copperplate handwriting. She could see that the girls wanted her to open it and was amused by their cheek. She put it on top of her locker and set about making tea for three.

When she was finally on her own, Mary opened the letter.

Dear Mary,

I do hope you don't mind me writing this note to you – it was the briefest of encounters the other night and I must confess that it left me wanting to know more about you. I felt we had a lot in common. But off you went to your friends – lucky them! I would really like to meet you again. I have therefore taken the liberty of booking us both into a small restaurant in the village for tomorrow, Tuesday – if this is not convenient or you feel that I am being a bit forward just tell me. Otherwise, I will meet you at the Wattenden Arms at 4 p.m. My mate here on the squadron will lend me his MG sports car and I thought we could go for a spin, then a walk in the hills, before we dine at 6 p.m. so I'll see you about 4 p.m. Sorry it's a bit early all round but I'm flying early the next day.

Respond by note to: Sergeant Pilot John King, c/o Sergeants Mess, RAF Kenley.

I look forward to your quick reply.

Yours,

John.

PS. I will save you a few bob and bring a small bottle of brown ale for you to spill over me before we set off - to make you feel at home!

Mary's hands shook, as she read the note. A second chance to meet this amusing man. Her heart thumped and her mind worked furiously. What should she wear? How should she behave, easy-going or reserved? She stopped herself - what a fool. Perhaps he just liked her as she was.

She wasted no time in looking for her writing pad.

'No bloody way, Mary, that's flippin' great.' Betty was beaming and began to fuss. 'How are you off for clothes, make-up, and stockings? You must wear stockings.'

'Betty, you are the sweetest person I have ever known. I have everything I need. Because you're a friend, I'll admit that I am a bit nervous, but I'm determined just to be myself.'

'That's my girl. Now then,' Betty paused, tilted her head to one side and looked playfully serious, 'I must ask. Do you know much about, er, men, and sort of...'?

'Oh, you mean, snogging?' Mary made it sound functional, learned in a 'how to' book on pruning plants or tennis.

Betty sat down and burst out laughing. 'Well, my girl, that'll do for a start!'

They talked frankly for the next hour - nothing was left out - Mary took it all in. Betty had to meet a friend in the NAAFI and left her alone with her thoughts.

Mary wrote a note to John King and sat back against her pillow, sipping the remains of her cool tea. She was surprised that she was feeling warm at the thought of seeing him again, and his face came to mind. His company, albeit brief, had been light-hearted – he had the allure of a slightly open door.

Days in the medical centre could be lively or boring, depending on events. Due to an overspill in local hospitals patients had suddenly been brought in following a bombing raid on Kenley town and needed special attention until space could be found for them locally. There were six in all, one older lady, four middle-aged and a young woman who could not have been more than twenty years old.

Mary was given a list of the patients' names and addresses and assigned to general duties. She was happy to make tea, attend to dressings and chat to the patients to help keep their spirits up. She was just pouring tea for the oldest in the group, when the lady began to grumble about her stomach.

'So sorry, dear. No tea for me today, I'm not feeling particularly good in the tummy region. To tell you the truth I'm a bit shocked. It was the sight of my kitchen wall falling towards me – I'm so glad I was under the table. Even that gave way and pinned me down, but it saved my life. The army boys were marvellous and got me free in less than an hour.' She winced. 'Oooh, I feel rotten.'

Mary touched her hand, 'Listen, you must put all that out of your mind. Lie still, sip the tea if you can, but try and get some sleep. Let your body heal itself.'

'You are so kind, dear.'

The old lady lay back as instructed and closed her eyes. Mary felt sorry for her. The woman was a widow and vulnerable, a bomb hit her house and the debris nearly crushed her. The rescuers joked with the medical staff and said that although covered in dust and injured, she said, *sorry to be such trouble.*

The other middle-aged women were only slightly injured, mostly bruised limbs and grazes, but the younger woman worried Mary. She had a doll-like face, with corn yellow hair, blue eyes and a frame that was a product of food rationing. She looked totally lost and stood by her bed staring at the wall.

'Hello, it's Louise, isn't it? How are you today?'

The girl slowly turned her head and wrapped the blue medical dressing gown tightly around her. 'I, er...I...' Her eyes were brimming with tears, and she appeared anxious and confused, and kept wringing her hands.

'Slow down, dear. You're safe now. Relax, sit down, and have a cup of tea.'

'Safe, yes, me, but...er, ... I want...'

Mary was worried about her distress. Something wasn't quite right. A whole line of terraced houses had been badly damaged by the air raid and Louise's house was on the end. No one knew much about her because she had only moved in four days previously.

'But you don't understand, I...er...Oh God. What can I do?'

'Louise, I'm going to get help. Just settle down and I'll be back.'

Mary turned and hurried past the other ladies towards the door.

'Is she okay?' said a large lady with a handful of oat biscuits at the ready, 'She's my new neighbour. Poor luvvie, what a shock. You move in and then whoosh, your house is demolished around you, it must have been frightening for her, especially with the babies and all.' She slurped her tea. 'If there's anything I can do, just let me know...'

Mary was half out of the door when she heard the words, '...especially with the babies.'

She stopped abruptly, and then rushed back the lady.

'What was that? Babies? But she's listed as the only occupant.'

'Bloody hell!' said the lady. 'The rescuers probably just noted who they found, her place was next door to me, number 57 the end of the terrace. Oh, yes, I can tell you for sure, she has babies. I heard the little bleeders crying like crazy the other night.'

Mary looked at Louise, the door and back to Louise again. The girl was in shock and had been unable to express herself to those around her. Her pulse raced and she knew that she had to get to the rescuers as soon as she could – time was of the essence.

'Where have you all come from, please tell me quickly?'

'Grosvenor Terrace, near the gas works. But there's not much left.'

She ran down the long corridor almost skidding on the newly polished brown lino. As she reached the entrance, she saw a couple of soldiers having a smoke beside a dusty truck.

'Lads, I need your help. I've been talking to a lady from Grosvenor Terrace–'

A young soldier with fair hair matted with brick dust sighed, 'Yeah, well we've just been there, what a mess!'

'Okay, but I have reason to believe that two babies are trapped in the end terrace. The mother arrived here but she was so shocked and said nothing, everyone assumed she was the sole occupant. Lads, we've got to search for them.'

The men stood up quickly. The older soldier grabbed his haversack. 'My goodness, we'd better get going. Fred, tidy the truck and make some room, come on now, no time to waste.'

Mary turned and ran to the accident department, shouting over her shoulder, 'I'll be back in a jiffy.'

A young doctor looked up as she ran to his desk.

'Please, no questions. I believe two babies are trapped under the rubble at Grosvenor Terrace. We must get there before nightfall and the temperature drops. We cannot take chances. Can you come with us?'

'Damned right I can,' said the doctor. 'I'll grab my medical bag.'

He hurried to get a bag of medical equipment and Mary returned to the truck; the engine was running and ready to go. Minutes later the doctor arrived, and they both climbed into the back, and the truck roared away. Luckily, because of their earlier involvement, the soldiers knew the best route and picked their way past obstacles and bypassed closed roads. They headed straight for the end terrace.

It was an awful sight. Two thirds of the building had been completely blown away, the roof hung down at a thirty-degree angle and the remaining walls were cracked and under stress from the irregular weight from the damaged interior. Debris and broken garden walls obstructed an easy entry. They looked on silently.

'Shit!' said the one of the soldiers.

'Succinctly put,' said Mary.

'Doesn't look safe to me,' said the doctor fearfully.

Mary considered the situation and felt their understandable anxiety, but would not hold back, and gently coaxed them. 'Let's just go to the edge and just have a peep, shall we?'

Babies are babies, they can't walk out of danger. She would get them inside that shell if it was the last thing she did.

Making their way across the bricks, mortar, and twisted timber, they carefully approached the largest gap at the side of the house, over which hung the remains of the roof joists and tiles. A lonely hall lamp, still attached to half a ceiling, swung slowly in the breeze. It felt surreal as they stared at the devastation. Around them there were noises of vehicles driving away and shouts from soldiers on guard duty to stop possible looting.

Mary instinctively looked towards the remains of the stairway, strangely intact.

'I don't think you should do that,' said the doctor urgently. 'It could all fall at any moment.'

The air was electric with tension.

Mary said nothing – there was nothing to say. If there were babies in this rubble, she would find them and that's all there was to it.

The doctor nervously continued. 'Look, I said–'

'Stop,' Mary shouted. 'Stop and listen.'

No one spoke further. Then came the faint but unmistakable sound of a baby crying. It stopped. They all looked worried, and Mary prayed for the little thing to make some more noise. The minutes ticked by. With the building in such a dangerous state, it would be difficult to carry out a random search. She put her hands to her face. *Come on little one, cry, cry, cry...!*

They were resigned to going into the building via the hallway when baby cried again. One of the soldiers shouted excitedly, 'From that window up there!' He pointed to a bedroom that had been spared most of the damage but was nevertheless without a set of stairs to access it.

Mary darted forward. The men following her, uncertain of what to do, but her bravery motivated them. They nervously entered the house, the sound of the baby's cries rallied their courage. Picking their way through the rubble was difficult and once inside they found themselves looking at a large irregular hole in the ceiling.

They stopped and listened.

There it was again, up in the blackness. 'Leg up, please,' said Mary, hitching up her skirt, 'and eyes down or I'll belt you!'

The soldiers smiled and one held out his palms, whilst the other pushed her upwards. She was halfway into the ceiling and the plaster around the edges of the hole began to crumble – a large chunk fell away, and her heart jumped with fright. The rest felt firm, so she carried on, eventually pulling herself over the edge and into the gap. The doctor was a slightly built young man and followed, more easily than Mary had.

'I thought I'd join you. Besides, we'll need this.' He held up a torch and switched it on.

They stood in silence, moving the torch beam around what remained of a bedroom, now resembling a rubbish tip, with bits of brickwork, timber, and plaster dust all over the place. They waited.

Mary watched the torch beam as it was waved this way and that.

'Wait,' she shouted, 'over there!'

The doctor held the beam into the corner and Mary scrambled towards a pile of crumpled pink blankets. She fell to her knees, struck by the horrific sight before her. A baby lay in a pool of blood with a large piece of the chimneybreast across the top half of its body.

'Oh, my God.'

She put her hands to her face.

'Poor little soul.'

Her eyes moistened and she felt the doctor's hand on her shoulders. As she sniffed back tears, she touched the baby's hand. It was stone cold.

'Hang about. This poor dear has been dead a long time.' She stood up abruptly and looked about her.

'There must be another one here.' Urgently looking around she got the doctor to continue to sweep the room with torchlight. They moved between the now broken bed and a wardrobe, when suddenly a baby's cry broke the silence. It was from the corner of the room. Mary rushed there, moved pieces of plasterboard to one side and saw in an oblong box that had once been a cot the unmistakable form of a baby, erratically moving its limbs left and right. Its face was dusty but otherwise it had been protected from debris by the canopy of the cot.

As Mary lifted the baby out it cried softly. She hugged it tightly and the soldiers downstairs cheered enthusiastically. Wasting no time, the doctor got Mary to leave via the hole in the ceiling, and then handed down the now wriggling baby to those below. He undertook the grisly task of retrieving the dead baby.

Mary was halfway out of the house, closely followed by the doctor when they heard a loud cracking sound from the infrastructure. They ran for their lives, picking their way across bricks, masonry, and large pieces of wood that littered the ground. Behind them the house emitted a loud groan as its weakened structure shifted. They stopped in their tracks. Tiles slid noisily down the now badly sloping roof and fell noisily to the ground. Mary was startled by the sound of timber snapping. The doctor's grip on the dead baby loosened and he nearly dropped it.

'Go, go, for goodness sake, don't stop!' yelled one of the soldiers.

Mary tripped and only just managed to gather herself and regain her balance, hugging the baby close to her chest. They instantly broke into a run.

Their nerves were at braking point as they quickened their pace, then the doctor shouted, 'It's going, my God, it's going.'

There was a slow, muffled 'whoomph', and the building caved in, almost submissively like a deflated balloon. Clouds of grey dust spewed out and enveloped them, and Mary hurriedly covered the baby's face.

They stumbled over the remaining debris and reached the truck, and stood arms outstretched against the bulkhead, coughing, and gasping for breath. They were covered head to toe in dust. The younger soldier reached inside the driver's cabin and brought out several canteens of water, which they eagerly gulped down and doused their faces.

The doctor looked back. 'That was bloody close!'

It was a bittersweet experience. The dreadful fate of one of the babies hung over them, but the joy of finding one alive was palpable - ten minutes later and it would have been lost. The medical staff were elated and praised Mary's quick action. They had the difficult task of talking to the young mother, Louise, and called in the Padre to help.

Mary accepted a mug of tea, a handshake from the doctor and to her surprise, kisses from the soldiers.

She looked at her watch and gasped. It was three fifty. Her heart sank and she put her hands to her face.

'What's up? You suddenly went quiet,' said the younger soldier.

'Oh, dear. I had a date with, oh hell, with a pilot. He'll think that I stood him up.'

The soldier smiled broadly. 'If he's got a brain luv, that's the last thing he'll think. Righto. Where are you meeting him?'

'But I look a sight.' Now feeling sorry for herself she sniffled, 'I'm covered in dust and dirty.'

'I didn't ask for a description of your lady-like self,' he persisted, 'where are you meeting him?'

'The Wattenden Arms.'

'Blimey, it's only ten minutes away!' The older soldier grabbed her arm. 'Now then, to the truck and away.'

Mary protested but he would have none of it. The others joined in, and despite her uncertainty she found herself laughing through her dusty lips at their cheerful antics, unable to do anything but be carried away. They drove away at speed. It was four-fifteen. As they approached the pub, Mary saw a man getting into an MG sports car.

'That's him!' she said breathlessly.

The truck accelerated and the driver sounded the horn several times. John King looked up, surprised. It skidded to a halt in front of the MG. Mary scrambled out and ran towards John and stopped in front of him. He gazed at her in amazement, her torn uniform, face covered in dust and her hair all over the place.

'Oh, John, I'm so sorry I'm late,' she stuttered, 'I wanted to be on time,' then the tears flowed, and she fell into his arms.

The younger soldier approached John.

'She's in too much of a state to tell you so I will. A mother was brought into the sick bay, shocked and no one knew that her babies were still in their bombed-out house. She quickly found that out and bossed us all about, including a doctor, to go and find them. We found two, one dead and one alive. The one that survived is alive now because of this brave lady.'

The older soldier came over and spoke with unguarded emotion. 'She's pretty special, mate. You take care of her. We'll leave you to it, then.'

They shouted farewell to Mary, who was too distressed to hear them, then drove off, leaving John holding her to his chest.

She looked up at him and sniffed loudly, 'I wanted to look good. Dress, make-up and...'

He touched her lips, and she stopped talking.

'Well, my heroine. You look pretty good to me.'

Then he took her head in his hands and brought his lips to hers and kissed her tenderly.

Mary felt as though a thousand volts surged through her body, it was the most sublime feeling she had ever had in her life.

She didn't want it to stop.

When they parted, John's face was smudged with dust; he stroked her hair and she put her face into his shoulder. It didn't take long for him to drive the MG back to her billet and insisted that he would cancel arrangements for the evening. It made sense, she needed sleep. Letting go of his hand she wearily stepped into the billet and gazed after him as he drove away.

After washing off the dust and dirt from her face and hands Mary undressed and fell into her bed, tired and yet excited at the day's events. She lay, exhausted and on the edge of sleep, and recalled the feeling of her first long kiss – it lingered on her lips, asking not to be forgotten. She tingled with happiness. What could have been a disaster of a first date ended with a man who was patient enough to accept what had happened without criticism, instead showing kindness. She drew her knees up and hugged her pillow against her chest. Sleep began to win the battle, but the kiss defiantly etched itself on her mind and provided substance for her dreams.

The dim morning light crept through the curtains and tickled Mary's face; she stirred after a long deep sleep. Her eyes were sticky, and she rubbed them with her hands. She went to the washroom. It was cool and there was a lingering smell of cheap disinfectant that always made her nose crinkle and didn't spend long there. After dressing in casual trousers and a large jumper, she pulled on sheepskin boots, grabbed her brown corduroy coat, and left the billet, intent on getting a bit of fresh air.

The day was fresh and sunny, and she put all thoughts of the terrible events of the previous evening's air raid carefully to one side – it was a habit that everyone developed in these terrible times. She passed the station football pitch and several of the airmen who knew her yelled out her name – she waved to them. As she reached the road adjacent the guardroom, she noticed the RAF flag, her flag, her life, and her reason for being. She breathed in heavily.

The road outside RAF Kenley was quiet and she was able to amble aimlessly along the hedgerow-lined tarmac taking time to look at the birds as they swooped and swirled catching midges, and memorise where she saw patches of blackberry bramble, promising to come back later into the summer and pick them when they ripened.

After walking for twenty minutes, she heard the distant rumble of a car engine coming along the road behind her. She didn't turn. It could only be him. *Please let it be him, please!*

Tyres skidded on gravel close to her and she heard a shout. She smiled broadly, it was him.

'Well now, you're determined not to look around, do you treat all sports car posers like that?'

Mary looked over her shoulder, her expression resembling that of a child that has just been given a gift they always wanted but doesn't quite know what to say.

He got out and opened the passenger door.

She was about to get in and wondered whether to peck him on the cheek or kiss him. The decision was taken from her, and he gently reached towards her, taking her head in his left hand, bringing her face slowly towards him.

Another kiss, so soft and gentle that the world around her briefly ceased to exist.

'Well, hello,' he said as he released her, 'so nice to see you.'

'And you, er, me, well what I mean is...oh, good grief!'

She stopped burbling and grabbed his head and kissed him again, more urgently; they clung to each other, neither really wanting to let go. A troop lorry passed and there was a loud cheer from the men in the rear. They separated and waved at the now disappearing vehicle.

Mary sat back in the passenger seat as John drove lazily around the countryside; the war was almost on another planet. Her eyes were closed, and she revelled in the warmth of the day and the wind that stroked her face. She felt exhilarated, happy and so very at ease with life.

'I have to confess,' said John mischievously.

Mary looked surprised, 'Oh, something bad or naughty, or what?'

He laughed. 'Not a hanging offence. I bought black market petrol so we could cruise around the countryside without fear of running out of juice. I know a spiv quite well and he likes pilots.'

'Well, Sgt Pilot King, you'd better behave yourself or else I'll shop you!'

John pretended to be distressed and gripped the wheel making the car swerve slight as he shouted, 'Argh, I am undone!'

Mary shrieked with uninhibited laughter.

They drove on and after a few minutes suddenly John slowed down. 'Hey, look, it's a pub. I'll pay a forfeit instead, let's stop for a beer.'

Without waiting for a reply, he pulled into a space close to the front door over which was a sign signifying that it was the Duke of Wellington.

Inside the pub, the walls were mostly wood panelling, festooned with brass bric-a-brac, horseshoes and bridle parts, together with aged landscape paintings that looked as though they could do with a clean. A dartboard was settled invitingly in the corner, its 20-position fuzzy and well-worn and in need of replacement. The owner looked up and gave a cheery smile. 'Nice car young man, nice lady too, you lucky feller.'

John laughed, 'Yes, I am that. I'll have a pint of best, and you?' he turned to Mary.

'Oh, just a small shandy, thanks.'

The owner pulled the pint. 'And cheap to run too!'

Mary cocked her head sideways. 'Just biding my time!'

They made their way to a window alcove and sat side by side on the bench seat leaning inwards, to face each other.

'Thanks for being so understanding about the cancellation last night.'

'Oh, come on now. In the scheme of thing there was no other choice. Anyway, I thought we would catch up soon enough. Besides, I am proud of you – a baby lives because of you, don't forget that. As far as the next date is concerned, I'm afraid I'm flying tomorrow and the next day, but after that is fine, and you?'

Mary looked at him and realised that all she wanted to do was to kiss him, again and again, then corrected herself; new experience or not she had to exert a degree of self-control, but by golly it was difficult.

'I'm not a shift worker so any date will do for me.' She paused adding, 'John, I'd like it if we really got to know each other, you know, background, likes and dislikes.'

John's face was implacable, and it confused her.

'I'm okay with that I suppose' he said guardedly, 'but there's not much to know. As I said in the pub the other day, I grew up in South Africa, my parents were Afrikaans, my surname King is anglicised from Koning.

They came here just before WWI, well after the debacle of the Boer War, and I was born smack in the middle of it all. I was educated at a private school set up by Afrikaans trustees for those who'd emigrated to the UK. I spent my Oxford university days at St Edmunds Hall. I learned a lot about the English class system and emerging socialist ideals. I flunked university; I suppose I was a bit feckless and hot-headed, and got involved with politics and the like.'

He absentmindedly flicked dust off his jacket and went on. 'When the Spanish Civil War began, I joined the International Brigade, it was the most harrowing time in my life. It makes what I do now a picnic by comparison.'

'Gosh, you are brave.'

John's face darkened. 'Mary, it's not about bravery. The Spanish people were let down by all the European governments as they sought to appease Hitler by staying outside the conflict. The ugly truth is they were fearful that communism would take hold in the Republic and then spread elsewhere, threatening the status quo of the privileged. As if wanting fairness and equality were a bad thing!'

'But we are all equal in Britain,' Mary responded uncertainly.

'Oh, dear heart, if you think this sceptred isle is equal, or for that matter fair, you are seriously in need of updating. Do you read a lot?'

'Yes, of course.'

'And?'

'I know what you're getting at. I've read a lot of books, including George Orwell's Road to Wigan Pier.'

'What did you think of it?'

'For starters, the plight of miners who worked for a pittance with terrible working conditions really got to me. It was difficult to reconcile with my life where I never had to worry about the basics such as food and warmth. It was a different world.'

John supped his beer. 'Go on.'

'Well, it seemed that almost every task in their daily lives, like travel and getting their wages or benefits was such a tremendous chore.'

'Ah, yes. Interesting you remember that - the working man being made to feel grateful for everything. Not fair at all.'

'Orwell went to Spain; was he a communist?'

'Oh, my goodness no. A democratic socialist of sorts, yes, but mostly he was an anarchist. If he'd stayed in Spain the communists would have taken him away and shot him, as they did with many others.'

'So, which group did you fight with?'

John stared into his beer and slowly swilled it around. 'You know what? I was just like many others who sought to stave off fascism. I grabbed a rifle and joined any group that shot in the direction of General Franco.'

He paused and looked slightly detached. 'There was so much confusion and division that's why Franco won. But the fight continues,' he added, almost absent-mindedly, 'for a fairer and more equitable life, where all men are equal. So, we must first of all get rid of the

Nazis. He playfully held up an imaginary rifle and made a popping sound.

Mary laughed at his antics, but wondered what he meant when he used the phrase, *we must first of all get rid of...*

Since leaving Devon she was trying to catch up with real life and was lost for words, recalling her father's doleful look as he described the world as 'changing fast'. She had a lot to learn on her journey to independence, perhaps this man could help her?

John noticed her unease and quickly changed the subject by joking about playful antics in the sergeants' mess, playing rugby with the Station Commander's hat, drinking out of yards of ale and so on.

Mary was aware that he was rescuing her from political innocence.

'Perhaps I should tell you about my life but compared to yours it's terribly boring.'

'No one's life is boring, everyone has a tale to tell, go on, I want to know.'

'Don't you believe it. Anyway, for what it's worth, my surname, Henslow, is ancient. It goes back to the 1400s and we have a family crest. But rest assured, no fortune. With families like mine, and there are lots I can assure you, the lines are greatly extended, and descendants come in all shapes and sizes. But although I'm proud of my roots, I'm not at all like my parents and siblings, I don't use it as a crutch for my life.'

She watched John's nose wrinkle and continued. 'My father writes books on horticulture and is a poet; his family were mostly in holy orders, as was he, but he left a few years after ordination. He joined the Argyll and Sutherland Highlander Regiment and fought in WWI.'

John nodded and looked impressed. 'Where did he fight?'

'The Somme.'

'Good grief, that was tough. I knew a couple of Argylls, they were great guys.'

'My dad respected all the men he served with. After I was born the Wall Street Crash decimated savings and investments. After that we lived a chaotic life. Nothing horrid, just plain chaotic. Money was short and that caused frequent changes of residence in London. It took a long time for him to get established to earn good money. During this time, my siblings and I got shared out between relatives. I got the booby prize and ended staying with my aunt in Devon at a rectory.' She paused and added thoughtfully, 'I'm, troubled by the thought that it all became convenient. Perhaps they just forgot about me.'

John looked at her, his eyes soft, and touched her shoulder, all social judgement suspended. 'I'm sure that isn't the case. For the record, I don't want to forget you.'

Mary pursed her lips then faced him. 'That's a lovely thing to say, John. Anyway, there's lots I'm now beginning to understand. Let's park this identity stuff. Suffice it to say, I'm at a kind of railway terminus of life and changing platforms is an eye-opener. And...I met you!'

She leaned forward and kissed him gently on the cheek.

Their faces lingered, inches apart and as John was about to respond, the landlord shouted.

'Another round, I close in ten minutes?'

They both huffed, touched foreheads, and laughed. John looked at his watch.

'Damnation. I've an appointment with a meeting committee for Adolf's boys on the south coast in three hours. We'd better head back.'

They finished their drinks and within minutes were motoring back through the countryside to RAF Kenley. John dropped Mary outside her billet, and she reluctantly got out, closing the door carefully, but leaned over it to give him a lingering kiss. It took a long time and John was flushed when they separated.

She stared at the MG as it drove away.

Mary realised that she was so at ease with her new life but had a difficult decision to make, should she visit her family soon or leave it for a month or so. It was an easy decision and decided to put it off. It was all still too raw. The lack of interest in her needs, the endless childish pecking of her sisters absorbed in fatuous things such as make-up and the possibility of a good match, annoyed her. Whilst indifferent to her imperious mother, she remained deeply disappointed in her father. Where was the *joie de vivre,* and the energy and humour he used to have? Or had it all been in her imagination, a kind of balm for her pointless, painful existence at the rectory? The RAF station commander's letter of commendation for bravery was crumpled in her handbag, but she was sure that even that would not elevate her to any place of respect with them.

John's face came to mind, and she smiled instantly. She thought, *of course, don't waste bloody time - spend more of it with him.*

Mary worked hard in the medical centre, but outside those hours and when John was not flying missions, they met at the pub for a drink, or simply walked in the countryside and talked about anything and everything. She looked forward to those moments of sheer joy. Their gentle kisses had long since turned into passionate embraces, what Betty termed a great snog. Whatever it was called, she guiltily admitted that lovely though the frequent meetings were, the most anticipated part was the long kisses before that said goodbye.

One night, as they sat on the wall outside the Wattenden Arms, her head on his shoulder, John surprised her. 'Mary, I want to ask you something?'

'Go ahead, but nothing too intellectual - the local ale addles my brain as it is!'

'I've been thinking.'

Mary sensed something important was coming.

'These are such difficult times.'

'Yes, they are.'

'I do so enjoy your company. We've been going out now for long time and I have to say that this has been one of the happiest times of my life.'

'And I feel that way too,' she replied, the weight of his words hung in the air.

'Oh, jeez,' he ran his hands through his hair and appeared ill at ease. 'Look, I've got a dangerous job and frankly, I'm not the best of boyfriends!'

'You are to me, Mr Sergeant Pilot, you are to me.' She grabbed his face and brought it to hers.

They kissed deeply.

When they parted, he looked at her apprehensively and blurted. 'Mary, I would love you to come and stay with me at my flat. We can relax together and not have to kiss goodbye outside the WAAF billet. What do you say?'

Just then several aircraft noisily flew overhead. That seemed to be a sign. John had a perilous job. They both had to take each day as it came, no one knew what would happen next. What was the point of being overly sensible or cautious? In the face of this war, it was sheer folly to turn down anything that provided an escape to pleasure. Staring at his face she thought, *and perhaps, to love?*

'John King, I think that would be absolutely splendid.'

John looked taken aback, 'Wow, you didn't take long to consider the suggestion.'

'No,' she grabbed his neck gently and pulled him towards her again, 'perhaps I had more of this in mind?'

The kiss seemed to last for an eternity and when they finally separated, John was talking wildly about tidying his flat and how wonderful it would be - for Mary it was already wonderful.

7

Mary contemplated John's offer carefully. It would only be for short while - a bit of fun really, or not? But did she know him well enough? Was this the right thing to do, or was it a case of 'to hell with it, there's a war on'?

She stopped - these were just feeble excuses. There was a bloody war on and who knew what the future held. One thing was for sure, there was no doubt at all that she wanted more of John King, and if that meant living in his flat for a while, then so be it.

It seemed to take her an age to pack her things for the night and as she stuffed the last pair of stockings into her bag, Betty came in.

'Mary, now then my friend,' she rushed towards her, 'where are you off to?'

'Well, I...er, that is John, suggested that I go to his flat. It's been a busy time and we've all been working hard. We could go out for a meal tonight and...' she realised that she was talking with the speed of a machine gun, stopped, and looked straight at Betty, adding sheepishly, 'we've been, well, doing a lot of...you know, kissing.'

Betty smiled broadly, put her hands on her hips and tilted her head, 'Oh, have you now. You dark horse.'

She approached Mary and gave her a hug. 'Enjoy it while you can. Just remember my mum's advice to me when I joined up. She said, 'Take advice from one who knows, keep your nightie tucked round your toes!' Then she giggled.

Mary flushed. She hadn't thought that far ahead.

She said goodbye to Betty and dashed to the door of the billet. John had only just parked the MG and was walking towards her. They hugged, got into the car, and set off to his flat. As they drove away Mary let the wind take her hair, she felt elated, free, and gloriously happy and couldn't stop smiling.

John parked the car, they linked arms, and walked up a set of well-worn steps to a large oak door. Once inside, he put down her case. The flat was simply furnished with a double sofa in a blue weave and a matching armchair. The lounge wallpaper had small roses, now a little faded, spaced a foot apart and they looked a bit out of place. There was a small galley-style kitchen through a door at the far end of the room.

John took her coat and held her in his arms. 'Mary, I'd like it if we didn't go out tonight.'

'But I thought...'

'No, please listen. I really hope you don't mind. I took the opportunity to dash to the restaurant and rebook for tomorrow night. Also, please forgive me, but I spoke to your nursing sister, whom I know, she goes out with my squadron commander. She's aware of the overtime you put in and was surprised that you continued with your duties after the recent incident. Frankly, she's so chuffed that a WAAF in her charge has done something so brave. The upshot is that she agreed to let you have two days off to relax and recuperate; she berated herself for not thinking about it earlier. I have the chit here,' he fumbled inside his coat, but slowed his search, bored with the admin of it all and stared straight at her. 'I am so looking forward to being here with you over the next two days. My flying duties finished today so I too have time to myself.'

All sense of caution flew out the window and she gushed, 'Yes, John. I would really like that, very much.'

He leaned forward and kissed her lightly. 'I'll prepare supper, it won't be the same as the restaurant though.'

'You serve it, I'll eat it. Off you go, I'll have a nose around the flat if you don't mind.'

'Certainly not, go ahead,' he replied and went to the kitchen.

Despite the dowdy interior the flat had a lot of tasteful personal touches. She looked at John's extensive library and saw books by Dickens, Orwell, Virginia Woolf, Aldous Huxley, and on the walls there were several signed pen and ink sketches of animals as well as two of bare-breasted women. Various artefacts like a brass telescope, and a lot of African wooden objects with carved animal and African faces, fly swatters made of animal tails, walking sticks and even a couple of shields and spears, littered the room. This small space was a whole new world of interest to her. It had character, his character, and she felt exhilarated to be part of it. She sat in a large threadbare armchair on top of which were coloured cushions and flicked through the books. Thirty minutes later John entered the room with a tray on which lay a serving dish, knives, forks, and plates.

'Nosh up!'

'Smells good, chef.'

'Corned beef cottage pie,' he said, turning his head to one side, 'courtesy of a box of army K-rations from stores.'

They ate in silence, and the meal was soon over.

'That was delicious. The flat's great by the way.'

'Yes, I'm lucky to have found it. I must stay in the Sergeant's Mess when I'm on operations, but this is my main home. My space. Now you're here, it's my haven.'

Mary touched his hand. 'Thank you for sharing it with me.'

'No, thank you for being here.'

Mary smiled at his boyish charm. She knew he was pleased – his face said it all.

John got up and switched the radio on and the sound of Joe Loss orchestra broadcast from the Savoy Hotel in London – the lively music filled the room.

'Dance, ma'am?'

Mary stood up and took his hands. At first, they touched lightly. Their gaze was electric. As the music quickened, so did their embrace and it became more of an excited tangle. They parted slowly, red-faced, grinning at each other.

'If you want, I'll run a bath for you,' he said, through a tight throat.

Mary's pulse quickened at the thought of a hot bath, and him.

'Yes,' she replied and started to clear the table, her hands shaking in anticipation. She heard John running the bath and the plopping sound of liquid being emptied into the water.

'Bergamot and lavender oil good enough for the lady?' he shouted.

'Good enough.'

She quietly deposited the dishes in the kitchen then went into the bathroom. John was busy checking the water temperature and fussing around; he looked very nervous. Strangely, this gave her confidence. She was surprised at how aroused she felt.

He looked up.

'Can you help?' she said softly, 'you see, it's these damned buttons, I can't seem to get them undone easily.'

He looked like a boy given a bag of sweets, got up and kissed her lightly. 'Of course, anything to oblige.'

John's hands fumbled with the buttons - minutes later Mary's outer clothes lay on the floor. He backed away, then turned and dipped his hand into the water, announcing, 'Nice and warm.'

Mary breathed deeply. She felt deliciously sensual and held her arms apart. 'The only problem now is this bra' – it's also a bugger to get undone.'

John was kneeling on the floor and nearly fell over. He got up and Mary submitted to the completion of the mission. The cool air on her skin made her body tingle.

John kissed her, turned to stop the hot water tap and put on a little-boy-lost expression. 'Well, fair's fair. My buttons are a challenge too!'

Mary wasted no time.

Moments later, she had seen her first fully naked man, and her man had for the first time seen her naked. They lay in the hot water, and she watched the steam rise, and drank cool lemonade, spluttering at the large seductive quantity of gin.

After what seemed like an age, John got out of the bath, and as Mary stepped out, he wrapped her in a towel, and they went to bed. He held her tightly for a long time until the feeling of their naked skin against each other was second nature and she was perfectly relaxed. Unrushed, he slowly stroked her back and kissed her neck. Mary's body submitted to his touch, and she was lost in overwhelming physical pleasure.

Later that night, as John lay sleeping, Mary nestled her head in his arms, and reflected on something that Betty had once told her. She had said that the first sexual encounter is so wonderful and unlikely to ever be fully replicated. That explosive moment, that innocent feeling of joy and that hopeless abandonment of common sense.

It was just like that.

The next morning, John had to take the MG back to his friend and left Mary in the flat. She kissed him goodbye, then sat at the table moving a half-eaten piece of toast around her plate, not feeling at all hungry. Dreamily basking in the rays of the sun that reached out to her from the kitchen window she contemplated her situation. When she had been in the rectory in Devon, she felt isolated and had to create her own niche. It was such a dead atmosphere, devoid of laughter – a joyless place where to laugh was a sin. In the WAAF, she had earned a place for herself with her comrades but knew that their friendship and respect had come about because of happenstance – it was likely that without rescuing Sandra Grant from the Operations Room after the bombing, she may well have continued to be the outsider. Now, here she was, with a man – her man, and for once in her life she felt whole, complete – all in such a short time.

A thought then struck her: she still had not contacted her family. She put it quickly to the back of her mind as one does with things that hurt and cannot be explained - keep the box closed. Don't think about anything uncomfortable. Don't even try to reason. Deal with it tomorrow.

The door opened. It was John.

'Goodness gracious me, the heroine of Grosvenor Terrace hasn't moved an inch since I left.' He bent to kiss her, and she looked up, submitting to his touch.

'This heroine is exhausted, mentally, and physically, Sergeant Pilot JK! How about a bit more toast?'

'No. That's a silly idea.'

Mary looked surprised.

John put his hand gently under her arm and she stood up.

'I think that you are very, very tired...really tired,' he said, playfully emphasising the word *really*. Mary twigged and laughed as he continued. 'And you so need a bit more rest. Let me take you to the bedroom...'

By now Mary was laughing loudly and put her fingers to his lips. 'Very cute, but I have a better idea. Let *me* take *you* there, eh?'

John looked surprised then took her hand and she led him to the bedroom.

The old Mary had re-established herself.

Mary was back at work in the medical centre and did her best to concentrate on her work but couldn't get John out of her mind. Three weeks later, he had a series of intense briefings to attend, so she decided to take a few days leave and visit Turnpike Lane and take time out for herself.

Mary stared at the tea that Betty's mum put in front of her, it was her usual dark brew that she termed, 'builder's tea', achieved by leaving the mash brewing for a little while longer than usual.

She looked across at Betty who was applying thick red lipstick, turning her head this way and that to get a better view in the mirror.

Betty saw her and said, 'Just a tip, Mary. You remember Gwen, she had the bed at the back of the billet? Well, her mum was killed by a doodlebug.'

'My goodness, what happened?'

'What happened? It went boom, that's what bleedin' 'appened! Her mum and other folk went to do liaison work and welcome American servicemen just off Sloane Square, when out of nowhere the flippin' thing fell out of the sky and whoomph! The grim reaper did a good job that day, over ninety people got killed, mostly Yanks.' She said wearily, 'I'm really fed up with this bloody war, it just seems to go on and on. No bombing raids, just them bleedin' buzzbombs!'

Mary looked at her supportively. 'But there is hope, John was saying...' She realised she was straying in her language and was careful. 'Well, he was saying that all is going well, and we have reason to be hopeful.'

Betty shrugged. 'Anyway, tonight I'm on the pull,' she straightened and tilted her head upwards. 'Besides, I'm quite a catch.'

They burst out laughing, sipped their tea and fell silent.

'And as for you Mary H, how's that pilot of yours?'

Mary blushed, 'He's fine and he...'

'So very matter of fact. Flippin' 'eck, gel, I mean...how's, *it* ?' She winked expressively.

Mary blushed, 'Since you put it like that, it's, well, it's simply beautiful - I'm in seventh heaven.'

Betty sat down heavily in a chair. 'At bloody last!'

They laughed, uninhibited as true friends can be in the circumstances.

Audrey sat quietly in the corner knitting, a broad grin across her lined face. She looked up. 'I cannot think of a nicer person to be in love, Mary. Sharing your life with someone special is the best thing in the world. Even Harry!' She nodded towards the image of her husband out in the back yard, relentlessly banging metal with a hammer, filling the air with expletives. 'We've 'ad our hard times but pushed through 'em. I still love him to bits.'

Betty got up and kissed her mum on the forehead, then turned.

'Come on Mary, we'd better get the last bus, or I'll be on jankers.'

Mary reluctantly got up and grabbed her overnight bag. Being reminded of how lucky she was made her feel warm and content.

H*ow the heck am I supposed to be in love and concentrate on work at the same time?*

Mary wriggled in the comfort of a warm bed and then stretched her legs as far as they would go. It was nine o'clock and John was long gone, having explained that he had a morning briefing to attend. She sat up then persuaded herself to go to the kitchen. Padding over the linoleum she cursed as she picked up a couple of pieces of grit in her bare feet. A teapot, a mug, milk, and porridge ready to be cooked had been laid neatly on the table. This simple, humble piece of preparation for a partner was a gesture of love.

Gazing out of the window, she saw a woman throwing a stick for a collie dog and noticed how quiet it was – it was unusual for a flying day, normally the sound of circling Hurricanes could be heard as they took off then gathered in tight formation. She made a mug of tea and held it to warm her hands.

There was a knock at the door. She tied her dressing gown and went to answer it.

A small woman with pallid skin and a hairstyle that resembled the contents of an exploding armchair looked at her sheepishly.

'Good morning, oh my gosh, I'm sorry did I get you out of bed?'

'It's okay, I work long days at the medical centre on the base and I'm taking advantage of my free time. Can I help?'

The woman nervously brushed away non-existent crumbs from her green apron day-dress, clasped her hands before speaking. 'I'm your neighbour and I sort of thought that I would pop in and say hello, but if it's inconvenient...'

'No, no. You come on in. The kettle has just boiled.'

Mary told the woman to take a seat, poured her a mug of tea and went to get changed.

She returned in corduroy dungarees and a scarf around her head but felt awkward because the woman was quite scruffily dressed.

'So, how long have you lived here?'

'Four or five years, or thereabouts. I remember when John moved in a year or so back. He's no trouble and keeps to himself. You're the first person I've ever seen him bring home. There's a bloke who calls in. He's a bit of a scruffy bugger and looks a bit dodgy, but no one else. The name's Daisy Mullins by the way. Are you Mrs King?'

Mary thought for a moment. *What the hell am I?* Then decided that being straightforward was best. 'No, I'm a friend, that's all. Mary Henslow.'

The woman gave a knowing smile.

'Actually, I'm his landlady,' adding supportively. 'But don't you mind, it's the war and we're all broad-minded these days. He never misses his rent and I'm grateful for that. I brought you this.'

Daisy handed Mary a brown paper package and she opened it carefully.

'Black pudding! I kind of know a bloke what makes it, and it was going spare, so I thought I'd give it to you as a moving-in present.'

Mary repressed a grimace. 'Gosh, Daisy, thank you, how kind.'

'Well, I'll go and let you get on with your day. Thanks for the tea.'

'And thank you, I'll give this to John when he gets home.'

Daisy left the flat, taking short fast steps, resembling a sparrow looking for somewhere to peck. Mary peered into the package. The contents looked dark brown and felt quite solid and she reflected that her culinary tastes hadn't quite moved to pigs' blood and fat.

It was after midday when John returned – he looked tired. As he came through the door Mary smothered him with a big hug, kissing him firmly on the lips. 'The pilot returns. Shot any of the enemy down?'

John picked her up and she wrapped her legs around his body. He looked directly into her eyes. 'Since you ask, four Heinkel bombers, two fighters and a milk-float I mistook for an enemy tank.'

'Oh dear. Such a hero. But bad news, your landlady, Daisy Mullins popped around and she's kicking you out for living with a loose woman.'

'What...?'

'Only joking. She popped in to say hello and gave us this. I'm going to be mighty generous – you can have it all.'

John grimaced, 'No, we'll both give it a miss. She is rather sweet but the last time she gave me this stuff I spent days on the throne.'

They lunched on black market eggs and toast – how John got such a regular supply she did not know. He lay on the bed resting after his early start and Mary got changed for an unexpected late shift. She was in her underwear, and he lay gazing at the ceiling deep in thought. Impulsively, she went to the bed and sat across his stomach.

John looked up, surprised. 'Oomph! You beast.'

Mary dug her knees in. 'Give in or else.'

John got his breath back and he stared at her. 'Or else what, my little red head?'

Mary's breathing quickened. John ran his hands up her thighs and he hooked his fingers over the satin-covered elastic around her waistband.

Mary tingled, not just from his touch, but from the way he looked at her.

She held her head high – a gift from the pompous Henslow genes – and gasped as he began to slowly pull his hands downwards. Mary felt herself flush. Unbuttoning her bra slowly, she threw it over her shoulder and concluded that she would be late for tonight's shift.

The night shift was quiet, and the off-going team accepted her apology for lateness. They had nowhere to go anyway. She didn't mention that she had to make her way in from the town rather than the nearby billets where she still maintained a bed space. Almost all the girls had a relationship, and they were no longer trainees who had to be chaperoned. There was work to be done and that was the priority. The ward sister knew, but Mary's currency was good after the incident where she saved the baby.

''Ello deary',' said a voice from the end of the ward. It was an elderly lady who had been taken in due to worsening gangrene in a damaged leg, not helped by bad hygiene and a poor diet.

Mary approached and tucked in her sheets. 'And what are you doing still awake? You need all the strength you can get.'

'I was looking at you, nurse Mary.' She smiled broadly. 'That's all I can do these days – look! You look happy and wistful. I suspect that there's a bloke responsible for that!'

Mary smiled, 'well now, you might just be right.' She playfully looked left and right. 'But that's just between you and me, eh?'

Gratified at her correct assessment the lady quietened, accepted a glass of water and was soon asleep.

By the middle of the night, with only the blue safety light on, Mary sat turning the pages of the *London Illustrated News*, thinking about her situation with John. She had moved from a peck on the cheek to a world of physical pleasure, greater than she had ever imagined. Even her occasional racy adolescent dreams etched on the blank canvas of her mind, had not reckoned with the excitement of it all. Her brain had no experiences to feed off – she had some now!

But there was more to it than that. It was the sharing, the oneness and being inextricably linked to someone else. To give and receive, and to want to be swallowed up in their being – it was sheer joy.

Mary was happy with the quietness of the ward as the hours slipped by and she let her thoughts have free reign. For once in her life, she didn't have to think about anything else.

Shift patterns were generous, and Mary was able to divide her time between work, John, and the occasional visit to Turnpike Lane. It occurred to her that she was beginning to regard Betty's family as more of a priority than her own. It was just that they were so inclusive, so easy to be with and so very thoughtful. Nevertheless, she felt irresponsible and knew that she should try and visit Fentiman Road - things don't get better if you don't try.

It was as though John had been part of her life forever. They never argued and had no big issues, although he had a disturbing habit of disappearing for a couple of hours occasionally, she put this down to him wanting to be alone, away from the crowd so to speak. No matter, when he returned, joy came with him. All was well in her world, apart from the fact that her monthly cycle was late. There was nothing odd in this, it was often the case, and so she gave it no further thought.

It was the month of May and buds were beginning to appear everywhere, on shrubs, trees and even in hedgerows. She resolved to go for more walks, especially along the paths by the RAF station and through Kenley Common where the ground was undisturbed, and wildflowers grow unhindered. That's how she felt - that she was growing without restriction.

Today, she decided to clean the flat from top to bottom. It didn't really need much doing to it because John was immaculately tidy and clean. The kitchen needed only a little work and she turned her attention to the main room. As she moved the bottles of booze around, she noticed a bottle of vodka half-finished – this surprised her since she thought her man a whisky drinker. Her brush and dustpan skills made short work of the floors and she flopped onto the sofa.

The bookcase caught her eye. She hadn't really regarded it too carefully until now. The collection was quite large. One section held a lot of scruffy looking old books, many with bindings that were ripped, titles now indecipherable. Newer books were on a different shelf. Interestingly, there were no books that taught anything, chess, cooking, or gardening. No fun books. But he was certainly not a dullard or lacking in humour – they just weren't in his bookcase.

As she mused there was a loud roar overhead. She froze at first then decided to venture to the window. When she got there, she saw the unmistakable shape of a Hurricane slowly flying away from the flat. It then began to turn in a wide sweep – it was coming back!

Instinctively, she knew it was John and as she dashed to the stairs, she saw from another window that the aircraft was now coming straight towards the building. The stairs were steep, and she had to take care that she didn't fall as she excitedly ran down them. At the bottom she pushed open the door and rushed onto the grass. She was joined by several curious residents.

The Hurricane came lower and lower, then finally flew over the grassed area, pulling up sharply, its engine growling as if in pain. The crowd cheered and Mary found herself jumping up and waving her arms around excitedly – she felt like an exuberant child.

The aircraft made one more sweep, turning slightly so that Mary could see the pilot wave, then it was gone, leaving the small crowd cheering.

One of the neighbours turned to her. 'Oh, isn't it exciting? Those boys are so brave, they're flippin' heroes.'

Mary lowered her hand from her brow. 'Yes, heroes. And that one is my hero, he's my man.'

May surrendered to the warmth of June and Mary's cycle rides to RAF Kenley became much more enjoyable. The birds were in full song and the buds were now in bloom – summer had arrived. Her evening cycle rides were pleasant, and she often wanted them to go on forever.

She arrived back at the flat after her day shift and set about making supper. John had been a bit edgy for the last couple of weeks and she didn't know why – she hoped it was nothing she had said or done and searched her conscience for possible mistakes. Her colleagues assured her that many pilots were susceptible to depression given the dangerous work in which they were engaged.

The leek and potato pie she prepared looked good, and she didn't put it into the oven in case he was late. As she washed her hands she looked out of the window and was pleased to see John but cocked an eyebrow when she noticed that he was talking to a scruffy man in a dirty beige raincoat. They were deep in conversation, more like an argument, and John was waving his hands around animatedly, finally flapping them down to his sides. The man looked around furtively several times then gave him a package and then walked away.

She was curious, but not alarmed.

John came in minutes later with a rather dark expression. 'Hi, darling. What's for supper?'

'Beef pie surprise!'

'What...?'

'The surprise is that beef is still rationed so it's just potato and leek – tasty though, I added a bit of cheese.'

He laughed and threw his flying jacket onto the sofa. 'Chump,' he said and cuddled her.

It felt good. Contact. He gazed straight at her and not out of the window.

'How was your day?' she said, showing an interest.

'Oh, the usual frivolous, mindless briefings, same old stuff. I just want to get up there and shoot the shit out of the enemy.'

Mary held him tighter. 'I can understand that. Listen, I'm not spying on you, so don't think that, but I was looking out of the window and saw you talking to a particularly strange looking bloke in a beige raincoat. He looked rather like a bookie's runner, or at least that's how they are described.'

John frowned and responded a tad over eagerly. 'Yes, he's certainly strange, that's for sure, but he's not a bookie's runner. He sells books and gets the odd one for me. Old books. He tries to charge an arm and leg for them, so I argue with him, it always works.'

He handed Mary a brown paper envelope and she pulled out a thin book entitled *A Story Without a Title* by Anton Chekhov.

'One of his most enigmatic and amusing stories,' said John, half-smiling as if he felt it had relevance. 'An elderly abbot is an outstanding orator. Everyone hangs on his words. After speaking to a visiting vagrant, who tells of debauchery and vice in the local town, he sets off to see it all for himself. After three months he comes back to the monastery, tells the monks all the naughty things he saw and takes himself off to a secluded place to meditate. Unfortunately, his description of the situation to his flock was misunderstood and when he comes out all the monks are gone!'

Mary put her hands to her mouth. 'To town?'

'Yup! They took it as direction to go and see for themselves. I like it. It's all about the power of words that are often taken the wrong way or misused on people ignorant of the real facts of life. In this case the result is amusing. After all, the monks were held in ignorance by stories and misconceptions. Bit like life really.'

'Well, you're in a deep mood tonight...'

His expression changed, almost as if a heavy weight had settled on his mind. He looked irritable and fidgeted.

'We should all be deep. Living in a house made of perfect pictures is unhealthy - we need more realism, more questioning and less moronic acceptance to all we are told.'

Mary tried to calm him.

'I agree. Papa and I ...'

'Oh, yes, the great Papa. Man of letters but not of the people. A talent to write things as he sees them, forgetting perhaps that what he writes can be taken as gospel.'

'That's nasty and not fair.' Mary stood up with her arms crossed.

'Fair - what is fair in life? He gave up the church, *why?* So having sold religious fairy tales to the masses he then decided to write his own in verse, some very antiquated, others just plain nasty.'

'Go on then, what?'

'Since you ask, in his edition *Early Poems* he writes all sorts of romantic and literary drivel about birds and bees, religious virtue and suchlike. Then, bang, he describes a money-lending Jew with vile contempt, as a 'revolting loathsome leper of the East', all fodder for mindless antisemitic idiots in society. To add to that he outlines the personality of someone who is left wing, in his poem, *The Socialist,* as a 'lazy idle drone, no working bee' and 'like it he feeds, and every time asks more.' All this is so wide of the mark and deliberately designed to steer the average man's point of view to a patriotic line underpinning the conformity of the privileged. He's no angel of perfection.'

Mary was stunned by John's quotations from these two pieces of work that she had chosen to overlook years ago when she read the anthology, considering them to be no more than two flaws in an otherwise great collection. Loyalty kicked in.

'And you are? Perfection is difficult to achieve, and we all make comments we wished we had not, but he's a good man. Don't you ever traduce him again!'

She was red faced now and stood in front of John, ready for a fight.

'I don't know about perfection, but I know about real life, the cruelty of men and the way minds can be manipulated by men, particularly those in holy orders. I know he served in the Great War but didn't advance beyond lieutenant in six years military service - where did he serve, in a tent reading the maps?'

Mary swung at him, and he dodged, catching her hand as it lost its force.

He glared at her. 'It's a trial living in his bloody shadow!'

Dropping her hand, he picked up his flying jacket and headed for the door. The whole block of flats must have heard the slam.

Mary's eyes glazed but she was determined not to cry. *Why the hell should she? Beastly man!*

She poured herself a large glass of gin.

The light faded as the evening drew on and there was a strange silence without her man in the room with her, so much so that she could almost hear her own heart beating. It bumped against her ribs as if trying to get out. She put the radio on just as the evening news came on, followed by the inevitable big band music and soulful crooners. The hands on the clock showed that it was nine o'clock, she didn't feel a bit tired and put it down to the adrenaline generated because of the exchange of words.

Almost imperceptibly, she heard the door creak as it opened. He must have come home. She put on her best indignant face and crossed her arms. But for a minute or so there was still no sign of him. Suddenly, she heard – piggy snorts! Honk, honk...silence, then more snorts...honk, honk. *What the heck...?*

As she looked towards the front door, a hand slowly came around the corner wall to the kitchen – it held a large bunch of flowers. The arm lengthened and a body followed. John's face appeared, his mouth deliberately turned down like an upside-down smile, his eyes droopy in a Charlie Chaplin expression of remorse.

'I'm a pig. A big pig...honk! I'm sorry. Forget all I said, beat me, kick me – I deserve whatever you want to do – just don't damage the flowers. They took me bloody ages to find!'

She put her hands to her head and shook it in disbelief at his antics, then smiled broadly – her man was back. All the anger melted, the pre-prepared expressions of, 'now tell me what's up', and 'who do you think you are?' evaporated with her laughter.

John put the flowers on the table.

Soon they were in each other's arms tightly embracing.

'Please, don't ever insult my Papa like that again.'

As they parted, he gazed at her. 'I'm truly sorry. It's been such a terrible week, I'm wrestling with a lot of decisions. But that's no excuse. Neither you nor he deserved my ire.'

'I accept your apologies, so let's put things to rights,' she said, grabbing his collar and bringing his face closer to hers.

The pie stayed uncooked.

Autumn introduced the chill of early winter, and John's mood lightened, he was almost back to his old self. Nevertheless, Mary had a strange feeling that he had to work at it. His words and actions appeared contrived rather than spontaneous.

When he was on his own, he often stared straight out of the window. On one occasion she awoke in the middle of the night to find his side of the bed empty and tiptoed to the door of the main room. She saw him flicking fast through the pages of one of the older books in his collection, stopping making short notes.

Whatever it was that vexed John, Mary decided not to question it straight away. He suffered enough stress, and she was strong enough to put it to one side.

They ate toast for breakfast, and he was cheerful enough - Mary thought that would do for now. Then he was off for a briefing, and she knew that sorties would be flown that day. It was always a torrid time, him flying, her waiting for his return.

When it came to six o'clock in the evening and John was well overdue home, Mary began to get worried. She felt stupid worrying, but on the other hand it was very late. An hour later she lost patience, got dressed in her dungarees and cycled to the base. Outside the squadron office, several officers were talking and looked in her direction, she knew one of them, a cheery Canadian called Justin.

He didn't look cheery today.

'Hi, Justin. I'm looking for John, have you seen him?'

Justin looked at his fellow pilots, then back at Mary.

'Mary, we're not certain, but he hasn't returned. It's all gone a bit quiet. I can't tell you much.'

Mary felt adrenaline surge through her body, and her balance faltered. The pilot rushed to help her off her cycle whilst she retained her balance.

'Is he dead?' she said almost choking the words.

'Mary, we just don't know. He was due to fly a solo mission with special gear on board,' he looked left and right, 'I'm not even supposed to tell you that. Put simply, he hasn't come back. But, of course, he might be traced, it happens all the time.'

Mary knew Betty was in the billet and asked the Canadian pilot to help her get there. He agreed readily and a small jeep was called up.

Betty held Mary in an enormous hug. 'Oh, God, Mary. I'm so sorry. Keep your chin up darlin'. He's such a strong guy, I bet he ditched and he's doing the front crawl all the way through the North Sea to get back to you.'

Mary had no room for platitudes - he was gone, and that was all there was to it. She knew it. He was now just a statistic, just like all the other poor souls.

She was as low as anyone could be and knew she would never see him again.

Days passed and there was still no news. To her anger and surprise, his squadron commander refused to see her. What was that all about? More infuriatingly, the station military police came to the flat and removed all of John's personal possessions, clothes, his collection of statuettes and all his books. She begged to know why but was stonewalled. It was bizarre.

Loneliness and grief are not good bedfellows and Betty was astute enough to see this. She encouraged her to return to the billet to be with her friends. They too were numb with shock and ready to help her in any way they could. It was such a wonderful thing to have friends who care. Her possessions were collected by Gwen and Betty who called in favours from the Mechanical Transport Flight for a vehicle to help move them to the billet.

The next day, Mary went to work and tried to concentrate but it was impossible. News travels fast and the sister in the medical centre showed real concern and called her into her office for a chat.

'Mary, my dear, I'm so very sorry. Truly sorry.'

'Thank you. I feel so empty, I can't even think straight.'

'That's not unusual, so please don't try to fight it. We're all here for you, remember that.' She reached down to her bag and took out a bottle of pills. 'Here, take these. They are very strong indeed so only two a day, when you need them.'

Mary looked at the bottle and shrugged.

'I'd better not.'

'Why?'

'Well, you see,' she patted her tummy, 'I'm late. In fact, very late. We can't jeopardise anything now, can we?'

The sister sat back in her chair.

'Well now young lady, we're going to have to take very special care of you.'

Mary burst into tears.

8

The billet had been silent all day, the girls had thoughtfully come and gone quietly so as not to disturb her. Mary awoke late into the evening, her mouth was dry, and her head felt fuzzy; it was difficult to think. She missed the presence of John's body alongside her - the thought of him brought a shard of pain in her chest. A long walk around the airfield perimeter seemed the only answer.

The dry grass crackled as she walked unsteadily over the clumpy ground. An owl hooted as if trying to gain her attention, but she ignored it. Halfway round she looked up at the fading orange October horizon and prayed to an unseen God to gather up her man and send him safely home. It had all been so perfect, so wonderful. She felt dizzy, but kept asking the question that all partners do in such circumstances; why him, why, why...?

After an hour, it all became too much for her and she fell to her knees and screamed angrily at the sky. Exhausted, she leaned against the fence, tears wet her cheeks and her body shook with her sobs.

Two military policemen found her an hour later, their torch beams falling on her prostrate body.

'Come on, Luv,' said one of them and he gently lifted her to her feet. 'You're in a bad way, so let's get you back to your billet.'

The other policeman located a field telephone used for airfield emergencies. ''Ello, this is MP Corporal

James here, send a vehicle to checkpoint,' he looked up at the marker board, 'Bravo 14, I'll explain later.'

The older man put his arm around her and the vehicle took her back to the guardroom where friendly staff took her back to her billet.

Luckily, Betty was there and was her usual supportive self. 'Mary, I don't know what it must be like for you, but my mum's cried for you, as I have. We all want you to know that you can come and stay at 71, any time and for however long you want to. You and mum get on so well, it'll be no problem. Remember that, please.'

Mary sniffled and looked at her friend.

'Thanks so much, I'm so lucky to have you as a friend. The tears keep coming - I just can't stop them. My man is gone, lost at sea they said, well, a fellow pilot said. I keep asking myself - was it quick or slow?'

Mary clenched her teeth and tried to chase the morbid thoughts out of her mind. Her positive self clung to the slim thread that he may have been picked up by a fishing boat, or the enemy, and it was just a matter of time before she would get the news that all was okay. But her rational mind told her that the RAF was quite accurate when it came to the fate of their airmen.

She reached out for Betty's hand. 'There's more news, to add to my anguish, I'm pregnant. I know the score, it will lead to my discharge from the WAAF.'

Betty gasped and sat back on the bed.

The wooden bench outside the station headquarters was uncomfortable and she was glad when her watch showed five minutes to ten. Time to go. Time to meet the Station Commander, Group Captain Jack Maynard. Time to get answers.

Mary walked unsteadily down the brown linoleum floor that had been recently bumpered and she mused that if Britain lost the war, then at least they could polish the German floors to perfection. She reached the Station Commander's office and stopped, straightened her tie, and then knocked on the door. His personal assistant answered.

Without acknowledging Mary, she sniffed and said, 'The group captain is expecting you.' She pointed to a small wooden chair and resumed typing. Time went on. Mary reasoned that when you are a lowly senior aircraftwoman it is inevitable that a senior officer would not see you as any kind of priority.

After fifteen minutes the door to the office opened and the group captain emerged, he looked past Mary to his assistant. 'Madelaine, I need a cuppa. Henslow, come on in, sorry to keep you waiting.'

Mary followed him into the office, saluted and waited to be asked to sit down. She removed her hat and held it on her lap.

Maynard was given his tea – none for Mary – he sipped it and regarded Mary with interest. A file lay open on the table, and she reasoned that some of the information was about her and John.

'Right then. let's cut to the quick, Henslow,' he reached for a file and opened it, 'I see that you had a relationship with Sergeant Pilot John King. You want to know his whereabouts.'

'Whereabouts? I understood from one of the crew on 15 squadron that he was posted missing presumed dead four days ago?'

He looked decidedly awkward. 'Yes, I'm sorry to put it like that.' Then he paused to think, which surprised Mary. 'All I can say is that he is missing. He failed to return from a mission.'

'I know all that, forgive me for being blunt, sir. I just want to know how and where, a kind of closure really.'

'Henslow, he's missing. That's it, finish! He was on a mission over the North Sea, and I am not at liberty to tell you anything further, simple as that.'

They were both exceptionally tense and breathing hard, and sat in silence, regarding each other defiantly. Mary pressed on. 'Well, can I at least have details about his family and how I can contact them?'

Maynard's eyes widened. 'Well, if he didn't tell you long before he went missing then that surprises me. We cannot disclose that information to you now. Clearly that was his call beforehand. There's nothing to be gained from harassing his relatives at this time.'

'But...'

'No, Henslow! I cannot and that's all there is to it. He's gone. It's sad of course, but it's a scene that is being played out all over the country now. My earnest advice to you is to move on, by the looks of things you have other challenges to face.' He nodded at the bump in her tummy.

Mary looked down at her shoes, beaten.

The station commander softened. 'Look, Henslow, you come from a fine family, and as I understand it, you're certainly very well thought of by your superior officer and fellow airwomen. Walk on. Grieve of course, but don't pore over things.'

The personal assistant came in soundlessly and stood waiting to show her out – she had obviously been listening and needed no prompt. Mary stood, put her hat on, saluted and left the office.

She walked slowly back to her billet. How cruel. Why so abrupt? The RAF had a reputation for being good with grieving relatives and friends, but this was certainly missing now. Several recruits on jankers were using large lawn mowers and the smell of cut grass made her nose tingle. As she approached the billet Gwen caught up with her.

'Hi. How's it going then?'

'Not brilliant. I'm over three months pregnant and my lover is likely to he dead, on top of that I'm not even married. To cap that, I've just been blanked by the Group Captain. I desperately want to talk about John to someone, his friends, or his family, but I'm being shut out. They're either heartless or stupid.'

Gwen thought for a moment. 'Look. I work in accounts so why not let me do a bit of unofficial digging? I'll see what I can find.'

'Oh, would you? You are sweet.'

'No problem. Now you just get your lump and you onto the bed for a nap – you probably need it.'

'Yeah, I just want to lie down and stop thinking. I'll miss lunch. In any case, if I do eat then it'll come straight back up again.'

They parted and Mary headed back to her billet. When she got to her bed space she flopped onto the bed, laid back and tried to quell her thoughts. It didn't work. John's fellow pilot's remark and the recalcitrance of the station commander to show any kind of humanity didn't make any sense at all. After a while, tiredness and stress got the better of her and she drifted off to sleep.

The evening came quicker than Mary expected, and she got up, washed, and dressed in civilian clothes. The billet was silent the other girls had come in from work and left without her hearing a thing.

Mary decided to keep busy and go to the NAAFI for a shandy and company. Before she left, she put on bright red lipstick - looking in the mirror she saw that it brightened her face, but her heart stayed dull. She wondered if it would ever be raised again.

In the NAAFI bar she joined the girls from her billet. They greeted her warmly as one would a sister or aunt; Sandra, who had by now become her friend, was attentive, almost unctuous, bought her a shandy and ordered a large girl off a nearby seat to make way for 'a mum to be' - word travels fast.

Mary thanked her. 'I see that the scars are healing nicely, Sandra, I'm so glad.'

Sandra gave a crooked grin, the skin on her cheekbone failing to keep up with the intention. 'It's all down to you, Mary. Without your brave and quick action, I would be a scorched sausage,' she put her hand on Mary's shoulder. 'But now you're in a bad place and we're all here to cheer you up.'

A record was playing in the background, but lots of scratches spoiled the sound of big band music.

Nevertheless, her foot was tapping, and she was lost in her thoughts.

'Hey, Mary, you look away with the fairies. Do you like big band stuff?' said one of the girls, the others turned towards her.

'Oh, yes, I do,' she replied absentmindedly, 'it's so different. I can relax to it. It gets right inside me.'

Daisy the station photographer let out a shrill laugh. 'Funny old thing that, Mary. For me it's the other way around. My boyfriend Alf gets inside of me, then I hear the music!'

The girls convulsed, and laughed so much, tears ran down their faces. Mary wondered if there was anything they couldn't turn into a ribald joke.

They were still laughing when Gwen joined her. 'Er, Mary, have you got a minute?' Before Mary could respond, she added, 'Over by the bar, there's two seats, let's go.'

Mary followed her and sat down. 'What's up, Gwen?'

'Look, I'm not sure, but there's something up. For goodness' sake, don't repeat what I'm about to tell you?'

'Yes, but...'

'Just listen. I went to my account ledger, which shows the payroll for all station staff and, well, Sgt John King's name had been removed. Not just lined through which is what they do when airmen are lost or killed – it just doesn't exist anymore.'

Mary's jaw dropped.

'That's not all. I casually spoke to a mate of mine in the general office and mentioned your John's name.

She clammed up immediately and said she had no recollection of any Sgt Pilot John King and put her hand up all defensive like and said, 'enough'. That was my cue to take the hint. I said no more. Sorry, but it's all a bit odd.'

Mary felt numb. Grief was bad enough, but this was so confusing.

It was mid-day and the journey to Fentiman Road had been dismal. Mary stood in front of her parents holding her handbag in front of her, nervous, upset and desperately wanting a comforting word or touch. She got neither.

Her father looked worried and stood upright with the rather elegant but odd habit of putting one hand inside his Harris Tweed jacket pocket, which put strain on the middle button. Her mother's face was milk white and her lips so tight they could've been welded together.

'You got my letter?' said Mary.

Her mother spoke first. 'Yes, and frankly, it was a surprise. We expected better of you.'

Her father quickly intervened. 'What your mother means is that the pregnancy is unfortunate, Mary...'

'Don't contradict me...' spluttered her mother.

Mary did her best to remain calm. 'Look. I came here to explain the situation. You completely overlook the fact that I've lost the man I loved. He was posted missing over the North Sea. He was a sergeant pilot, a brave man. He treated me well and we were so happy in each other's company.'

Tears filled her eyes, and her father wrung his hands and looked anxious.

'Your focus is on my pregnancy rather than my loss. I can't believe you could be so cruel.'

Her mother was unmoved. 'It's just like you to shift the blame onto us...'

Mary responded angrily, 'Blame? Falling in love is something to *blame?* Falling for a baby with the man you love is something to *blame?*'

'Not at all,' said her father, trying his best to lower the temperature, 'it's just a shock that's all.'

Her mother pretended to deal with her bracelet and said tightly. 'Well, it needs to be sorted out. Ever since I joined this family all I've done is to run around with a brush and dustpan clearing up the mess. Nothing changes.' She glared at her husband and stormed out.

The silence lingered.

'Don't mind your mother, she's had a trying few days. She'll calm down, I'm sure.'

Mary knew she wouldn't.

'Oh, Papa,' she said, putting her hands to her eyes, 'I just wanted to tell you both what happened. It's no sin is it, to fall in love? I do wish you could've met him, he was quite literary and although you both have, well, had, different political beliefs you would've enjoyed debating them with him. It's such a shame.'

Then she got what she really wanted. Papa came over and put his arms around her and held her tight. She cried and he stroked her head. He kissed her tenderly on the forehead and they sat down on the sofa.

'What are you plans?'

Mary stared at her father. She had rather hoped that he would take the lead and offer her space at Fentiman Road, but after this exchange of views it would prove a disastrous decision.

'For the moment, none, although a good friend called Betty Wilson, has offered for me to stay at her home in north London. I've been to the station Medical Officer, he confirmed my pregnancy and set in motion for my discharge around the end of October, which is about three weeks away. Normally, pregnant WAAFs are discharged almost immediately, but there is sympathy due to my relationship with a lost pilot. The baby is due in March.'

'That sounds very reasonable,' he said, looking down at his shoes. 'I hate to say this, but staying here might be quite stressful, so your friend's kind offer would be just the ticket.'

Mary looked straight at him. 'Yes, it's sad, but you're right.'

Mrs Knight brought in two cups of tea. It was timely and Mary knew from her expression that she had probably been listening to the disturbance in the lounge. She scurried away.

The tea tasted good. Refreshed, Mary summoned up her strength.

'Losing John has been the biggest shock of my life. I have to maintain some kind of stability to get me over the next few months.'

'Have you thought further ahead to, er, the baby that is?'

Mary looked shocked. But it was nevertheless a poignant question; she had not.

'Can we leave that for a bit, Papa. I'm still a bit raw.'

'Yes, of course. I'm sorry. Typical man thing, trying to solve problems too early. You will need money and I'm happy to reinstate your allowance but do please keep it to yourself.'

Mary wondered at a relationship where things like an allowance to a daughter should be kept secret.

It was difficult. There was no other conversation that could possibly be entered into that would remove the hurt of their initial reaction to her situation, or even ride over it. Silence was the only thing on offer. Eventually, her father made an excuse to go and see her mother and she kissed him goodbye.

Mary left the house knowing she had done her duty. She had asked for nothing – unsurprisingly, she got nothing. As she checked her purse for her bus fare, she noticed the crumpled letter of commendation and guessed that pregnancy trumped bravery. That event would now be consigned to history.

All she had to do was to sort out the next move on her own.

Betty's it was then.

Mary folded the RAF discharge papers into her handbag and got annoyed when they caught on the zip and wouldn't quite fit in. The young WAAF clerk who issued them looked nervous as Mary's flushed face glared at her. There had been delays and it was now the middle of November, Mary's bump was now quite pronounced.

'Thank you. What next?'

'Not a lot. You can join the WAAF again after the birth, providing the baby's taken care of. Just contact us via the address on the bottom of the discharge form.' The clerk hesitated. 'Are you alright?'

'Yes,' Mary replied irritably, 'I'm perfectly fine. Thank you.' She squeezed the handbag closed and walked out of the office, pushing past people coming in.

Outside in the fresh air she closed her eyes tightly to stop the tears from streaming down her face. Her head felt cluttered, and she even had difficulty remembering which bus to take to Betty's place. Their concern for her welfare contrasted with that of her parents.

The bus didn't take long to reach Turnpike Lane and Mary got off at a stop close to the park and opposite the underground station and was careful to step over broken paving. She needed the short walk, to breathe the fresh air and settle herself. The streets were surprisingly full of people, women in scarves tied close to their chins and older men in grey raincoats and wearing battered trilby hats - clothes were in short supply. German bombers came infrequently now. Just before her destination, she passed the off-licence owned by the Leonard family. She met them when picking up Betty's father's bottles of 'wallop', as he called them. They were a severe couple, always tidying the shop, which nevertheless looked the same with the badly painted shelves and bare wooden flooring that creaked when walked on. She paused and went in.

'Allo,' said Mr Leonard, as ever lacking charm or manners.

'Hello. Have you any bottles of light ale?'

'Up or over,' he ventured, referring to the business to be contracted either side of the tax man.

'Whatever is good for you – it's for Betty and family. Six bottles, please.'

Mr Leonard half-smiled; that itself was obviously a strain. He liked Betty and family. They had a reputation for being good people. He reached low and brought up a crate, removing six bottles for Mary, which he put into her leather bag. She proffered a half a crown, and he took it and spent ages counting out the change. She remembered the phrase used by one of her Irish comrades: *Every penny a prisoner.*

She left the shop with a wave and cheery goodbye; there's nothing better to fix a feeling of dejection than to see such a miserable creature as Mr Leonard – it was like watching a public hanging – it made one feel lucky to be alive.

At number 71 she was greeted warmly. The family welcome was always the same.

'Mary, darlin', where have you been? You look pale,' said Audrey. 'You just sit yourself down now and I'll make a quick cuppa.'

Mary eased her lumpy body into a chair and rested her hands on her bump. Harry, looked up from his copy of *The Picture Post* and gave her a nod.

'Here's your tea, luv.' Audrey put the mug down and touched Mary's hand. 'How's things?'

'Oh, bloody awful. I'm out of the WAAF as of today. I still don't have any information on my lover's death. The baby is about to enter this world and my parents have made it quite clear, in a civilised way of course, that I am in no position to look after the little mite - no husband, no money and nowhere to live. They reminded me that they're not able to help in any way, and...' with that, Mary's face screwed up and she burst into tears.

Harry looked awkward and Audrey gave him a jerk of the head that directed him in no uncertain terms to leave the room, which he did without demur.

'Mary, don't take on so. Your parents have pressures of their own, I bet. It's never easy. Drink your tea and relax in front of the fire, I'll put more coal on - my stingy old-man has let it die down.'

Mary dried her eyes and sipped the tea - it tasted so good. 'Builder's tea' is what Betty termed it. She felt silly. Controlling her emotions was what she had always been good at, but now she felt helpless.

Mary drifted off to sleep, exhausted and fed up. When she woke up hours later, Betty was standing beside her.

'Listen, I've taken things into my own hands, Mary, and I went to the billet and got all your stuff. I have to say you travel bleedin' light! Anyway, it's all here and ready to be put into this room. Marje is happy to let me bunk up with her when I come home. So, no worries.'

'Oh, God, Betty. You and your family are so wonderful I don't know how I can repay you.'

'I should cocoa! You can forget that. No repayment needed. So, get that out of your mind.'

The next six weeks were long, dismal and grief stricken. The Wilsons worked hard to cheer her, but it was an uphill battle. Christmas lunch was a quiet affair.

Harry managed to get his hands on a goose from a friend in the black market. Mary knew it had cost him a lot of money.

'Harry,' she said, 'you and Audrey have been so good to me. I know how much this will have cost you. I want you to know I do appreciate it.'

Audrey was non-plussed when she noticed Harry's eyes moisten – lord oh lord, her hard-as-nails Harry had a soft side!

'It's no trouble, Mary,' he said. 'I've heard stories about you and for what it's worth I consider you as one of our daughters. I'm sorry for your loss. I just wish this bleedin' war would end.'

Betty was near to tears too but rallied. 'Okay, now. Enough of this sadness. It's Christmas, after nosh, we're gonna play parlour games and drink a glass of port to the King, that's what.' She held out her arms to her father on the right and Mary on the left. 'For the record, I'm the luckiest person alive to be with such lovely folks.'

Mary grabbed a smile.

Audrey had left the room and came in with a sponge cake with custard dripping all over it, topped with a sprig of holly. 'Can't exactly set light to this with brandy or it'll bleedin' go up in flames.'

They burst out laughing.

After exchanging simple gifts, the mood lifted. That night, love and attention filled Mary with joy, briefly replacing her unhappiness, and she slept soundly.

January 1943 introduced itself by freezing everything in sight. Mary read in the newspapers that German air raids were less frequent, due in part to Hitler's folly of taking on the Russians and the brave work done by the RAF – but the weather also helped.

As she and Betty sat by the fire, Mary fiddled with a notebook and pencil, making entries every so often, then crossing them out.

'I was so happy,' she said, with an air of hopelessness.

'I know, luv.'

'There are so many unanswered questions. I loved him so much, and yet I didn't really know him. I mean, I knew nothing about his parents or his brothers and sisters. He never seemed to have many friends and was a bit of a loner on the squadron. I suppose it was because he said he had to work with hush-hush equipment on his Hurricane.'

Betty put down her sewing.

Mary continued. 'He cared a lot about fairness, equality, and the working man – crikey he was an expert on George Orwell. The only clue I have is that he had dealings with a dodgy chap in a raincoat. I saw him in the woods once.'

'Used to have a bloke like that down our street, but he got locked up for flashing.'

'Be serious. If only I could find him, I'd try and see what he knows about John.'

'Flippin' 'eck that's a bit of a tall order. Have you got an address?'

'No,' then she sat up straight. 'Maybe there's something in his letters, I managed to keep a number back from the military police.'

Mary jumped off the couch and the warm blanket fell to the floor. Minutes later she returned with a cardboard box. After searching though letters and all sorts of papers, she came upon the last book he received from the dodgy raincoated chap which had escaped the attention of the military police.

She gave a whoop of delight. 'Here it is. *A Story Without a Title* by Anton Chekhov.'

Mary carefully flipped through the pages. Nothing. She threw the book on to the table and folded her arms.

'Hang about, is there a book shop stamp or something?' said Betty, now part of the mystery seeking. She picked up the book and looked at the front – no joy. Then she turned to the back pages. She smiled broadly when she noticed a very faded and easily overlooked stamp mark at the back, R Harrowitz Bookseller, 23 Muswell Hill.

'Yay, Mary, that's not far away. Come on gel, get yer clogs on and let's track down Mr Dodgy Raincoat!'

It only took an hour to get to the bookshop. Mary and Betty stood in front of Mr Harrowitz, who sat behind a faded mahogany counter. He wore black trousers and waistcoat and a white collarless shirt. His lined face resembled cracked mud on a hot day, and he wore round wire spectacles below his bald pate.

He looked at the book. 'Ah, Chekhov's story about an abbot who loses his monks. Very funny. Yes, I sold it. Got a good price too.' He began to flick through it.

Mary got excited. 'We're looking for a rather gaunt looking chap, who always wears a raincoat, beige in colour. Do you know him?'

Harrowitz slowly raised his eyes. 'I do remember selling it to him. But I don't think I want to know him,' he said soberly.

'Can you tell me where to find him?'

Harrowitz leaned back in his rickety chair. 'Well now, I doubt it.'

'Why?'

'For why? I tell you. I saw him being arrested and taken away in a black sedan some months back.'

Mary was speechless.

'I would buy this book back from you, but it's been vandalised. Pages are missing, and silly dots are placed under many of the characters. What a mess. Here take it back. In fact, better still, I will sell you a new one - half price?'

Dismayed, Mary politely declined the offer; it's not easy walking into a brick wall. Betty guided her out of the shop after wishing Harrowitz farewell. The journey back to Turnpike Lane was silent.

'The only possible lead and he was flippin' well arrested - probably for black market stuff. Well, Betty, that's it, I'm done with it all. I've too much on my mind, I can't cope with anymore.'

Betty sympathised and helped Mary into a comfortable chair by the fire. Stress had taken its toll and she was quickly asleep.

Winter can be a cruel season at best, but for Mary she hardly noticed. Her bump was considerably bigger and uncomfortable, and she still had images of John's face before sleep shrouded her thoughts. But Spring was beckoning, and she looked forward to that. Today though, she was fuming. The local doctor was rude about her pregnancy and clearly not a fan of single mothers. However, all was well with the baby and that was all that counted. The nurse quietly followed her to the door.

'If you feel any pains or aches you cannot place then go to this address,' and she proffered a card. 'It'll be a lot cheaper than this chap, I can assure you. Good luck and take care.'

Mary thanked her. On the way home she remembered it was Hazel's birthday. She bought a card and a stamp at the local newsagent on Turnpike Lane, then wrote and posted it. March is dull enough without your sister forgetting your birthday.

She got back to Betty's house and Audrey greeted her.

'Hello, my dear, sit in the easy chair and Betty will make you a cup of tea.'

Mary was grateful, she felt tired and strangely irritable. Halfway through her second sip of tea she jerked convulsively. 'Ouch!' she said and held her hips. A slower grinding discomfort filled her stomach and it tightened.

Betty looked at her, knowingly.

Suddenly, Mary looked embarrassed and stared back at Betty's mum. 'I'm so sorry. I think I've just wee'd myself!'

Audrey put her hands to her hips. 'No, luvvie, you haven't – it's your waters breaking. Time to get you upstairs.'

Just then, Betty's sister Marje came in. 'What's up?'

'Thank goodness' you're here. It's 'er time. Betty, let's get her upstairs. I need plenty of towels from the airing cupboard. I'll boil hot water, and Marje, get off to Ma Gilbert at number 49. No time for fancy doctors or midwives, not that we can afford them. No matter, Ma Gilbert's brought half the street into this world, including you. Tell her to come quick. Okay, let's get on.'

The whole operation went ahead with military efficiency. Mary was quickly bathed and dressed in a large nightie open at the front, and Marje and her mum held her hands. Ma Gilbert, the most wizened looking lady in the land with, a cheery face and warm personality, dealt efficiently with the physical process as well as encouraging her every step of the way.

It was quick.

Then there he was, a healthy boy with his arms jerking left and right and eyes so dark – John's son. Mary looked about her as she and the baby were cleaned up. Then she drifted into an exhausted sleep.

A couple of hours later everyone was beaming and happy. Betty's dad had found the light ale and his ruddy face showed he had been toasting the baby's head for quite a while. The women vied for the chance to hold the baby. Sunlight reached through the cracks in the curtains highlighting the dust particles in the air, as if also wanting to touch the child. Mary woke up several times in the night and Audrey was always there to calm her and show her how to breast-feed the baby. Of all the places to give birth and with all the choices of people in the world to have with her, this was simply the best.

There was light knock at the door and Betty came in, holding two mugs of tea.

'Good morning, *mother*!'

Mary laughed, 'Good morning, yes, I suppose I am. Goodness, I'm ready for the tea. What time is it?'

'Just after ten o'clock. Oh, and we sent word to your parents that you had a baby boy and that all was well. Drink your tea. Have another kip and we can talk things over tonight. Meanwhile, the war goes on and they need my undoubted talents in accounts back at the unit. Not sure that double entry bookkeeping will see off Hitler's bombers, but you never know. See you later, luv.'

The door closed and Mary took in the silence - that was, until baby began to introduce his lungs to the world.

The days after the birth were full of joy and yet Mary couldn't get the dreadful feeling of the future out of her mind. Her parents sent a message that they would visit when they could. No congratulations. No flowers or card. Just that. She decided to call the baby Michael, and this was well received since there was a Michael in Betty's family who was tall and good looking and had been awarded a medal for his bravery fighting Rommel's men in the North African desert.

Harry held baby Michael and she noticed his whole countenance changed. Betty said that he had been the same with Marje's baby. An infant, also without a father, held onto by the family, loved and owned. Her throat tightened.

A letter arrived in the morning post for Mary and Betty peered over her shoulder.

'What's this, a letter from the Queen?'

Mary folded it carelessly and flopped it on the table.

'Funny old thing, almost. It was from my mother. It was short and sweet. She was glad the birth had gone well, and she and my father will visit this coming Friday.'

'Oh, that's nice, luv,' Betty replied trying to be supportive.

'Is it? I can almost script what they will be saying.'

She sat down at the kitchen table and sipped her tea in silence, idly recalling the expression, *beware the ides of March.*

It was Friday and Mary had trouble concentrating. No matter how much she told herself it would all be all right, there was a feeling of foreboding, a niggle deep inside her tummy that swirled and made her feel edgy. She was grateful that Betty had a day off work and was able to keep her company. Audrey was busying around pretending that the impending visit was not such a big deal.

The doorbell rang and all three jumped slightly. Mary was breast-feeding Michael and it startled her. She stopped and tidied herself.

'I'll put the kettle on,' said Betty's mum and she rushed to the kitchen to get out the best crockery Without a word, Betty's father got out of his chair by the fire and scuttled towards the kitchen, then out of the back door, hurriedly putting on his donkey jacket. Betty winked at Mary and went to the door.

Mary looked down the corridor and saw her mother and father standing in the doorway, erect, heads up and very well dressed. Her father removed his hat politely and she heard him say to Betty. 'Hello, is this where my daughter Mary is staying? We're her parents.'

Betty was polite. 'Yes, Mr and Mrs Henslow, I'm Betty Wilson. I met Mary when she first joined the WAAF, and we've been good friends ever since. Come on in, please.'

They followed her down the corridor.

'Darling,' said her father on seeing Mary, 'how are you?' He looked to one side and saw the baby, smiled, touched it on the nose lightly, but said nothing.

Mary watched, embarrassed, as her mother stood by the open fire, looking around the room as if inspecting it, her nose wrinkling occasionally. She looked at Mary. 'Darling, how are you indeed? It must have been an awful experience. If you were at home, we could've called in our doctor.'

Mary responded defiantly. 'There was no problem at all, mother. Ma Gilbert did an amazing job. I was in very good hands.'

'Ma?' Her mother looked startled.

'Oh yes, Ma Gilbert, she has delivered generations of babies in the local area. I can say with no doubt whatsoever that she really knows her stuff.'

Betty's mum came in just in time with a tray laden with a pot of tea, cups, and a plate of biscuits. 'Hello, I'm Betty's mum, call me Audrey. I've made tea and there are biscuits I got special. It's so nice to meet you. Mary told me all about you. You are being a famous writer and all.' She shuffled on one foot and then another as if running out of words. 'Please do sit down.'

Her father was gracious and raised his hands palms up, 'It would please me greatly if you would accept a couple of my books. I can see through your window that you and your husband are keen gardeners.'

Mary's mother wrinkled her nose at the tray. 'That's so kind of you, but we can't stay that long.' She sat awkwardly on the edge of a large chair, rather than in it.

Mary angrily stiffened, 'But long enough to sip a cup of tea and chat, I'm sure.'

Her father broke the ice. 'Lovely, Mrs ... er, Audrey. Digestive biscuits. My favourites.'

Audrey smiled nervously, poured the tea, and left to fuss about in the kitchen. Betty stayed.

They had hardly sipped the tea when Mary's mother introduced the matter that had been the main cause for the visit. 'Mary, the baby is quite beautiful, but...,' she looked unsteadily across at Betty who stood with her arms folded in the doorway, '...we must face the future.'

She had no respect for timing.

Her father looked awkward and fiddled with a handkerchief.

'We've outlined our concerns already to you the other day and I know that must have hurt you but needs must. Let me leave these papers with you to look over and consider. We did a fair bit of work on your behalf, your father and I,' she looked at her husband as if encouraging him to speak up, but he simply sniffed and drank a little tea. Undeterred, she carried on. 'The fact remains that we must all think about the baby's...'

Mary broke in, 'Michael!'

'...yes, of course, I'm sorry. Michael's best interest. These are challenging times and frankly even when the war finishes it's not going to get any easier.'

Mary caught her father wistfully looking at the baby.

'What are the papers?'

Her mother paused for a moment. 'Adoption papers. What to do and how to find the best people to look after your son.' Then she stood up abruptly. 'I know how distressing this must be for you, dear. I think that it is best if we leave you to read them and take time to make your decision. I promise you we have agonised over this, but only wanted to help,' adding in a tone, 'we just want what's best for you.'

Her father stood up and leaned over to kiss Mary lightly on the cheek. 'These are difficult times for all of us. But you are free to make up your own mind, of course. Let us know what you decide.'

Mary was silent.

They thanked Betty's mum effusively, even though they drank little tea and didn't touch the biscuits. Then they left the house like royalty exiting a canning factory after a tiresome state visit, she tightening her fur stole and with her nose in the air, and him looking urbane, walking with his hands held behind him. Betty and her mum stood back and looked awkward. The contrast could not have been greater.

The door closed. No one knew what to say.

It took three days for Mary to pluck up the courage to open the buff envelope sitting on the mantlepiece. The instructions were quite clear. She threw it onto the table, put her hands to her face and wept.

The Wilsons did their best to raise her spirits. Even Harry surprised everyone by producing a small bunch of flowers. He had grown fond of baby Michael.

Mary accepted the flowers and touched his shoulder in recognition of his kindness.

A week had passed since her parents' visit. Mary hardly noticed the time it took the bus to get to Fentiman Road. Nor did she hear the voices around her, she was so absorbed with the prospect of talking about the contents of the brown envelope in her bag. She wrestled with taking baby Michael but thought better of it; her mother's look of disinterest at their visit to Turnpike Lane said it all. Betty's mum, Audrey, was happy to babysit. Mary's milk had stopped, probably due to stress, so bottle-feeding made her absence easier.

Here she was again, standing outside the large, terraced home - memories of her last visit to announce her pregnancy and John posted missing at sea remained painfully scrawled onto her memory.

Mrs Knight opened the front door and gave her the best smile she could muster, it was etched with sympathy.

Mary's brother Tony was just leaving. 'Hi, sis', here for a summit meeting?'

'Yes, you could say that.' She looked at his cheery face, adding, 'and how are you?'

'Oh, good, as much as I can be of course. I'm trying to work out which one of us has disappointed them most.'

Gazing at him absently, she tried humour, 'You wanna fight for it.'

Tony saw her distress and said warmly, 'I'd never fight you my beautiful sister, ever.' He paused and theatrically put his hands up. 'Besides, I'd lose hands down!'

Mary thumped his shoulder and watched him walk away, then went inside.

Mrs Knight touched her arm. 'There's a pot of tea ready in your father's study.' Unable to find more words she scurried away. *Papa's study - how interesting. This places him, like it or not, at the centre of the summit meeting, whether he gets a word in edgeways is another thing.*

At the top of the stairs her father stood ready to welcome her. His elegance was not so much in evidence today. Every line in his face seemed to point downwards and his eyes looked weary.

'Darling, come on into the study, I'm so glad you came.'

'Hello Papa.' Mary walked over the threadbare carpet to the middle of the room. 'This is not going to be comfortable for either of us,' she added uneasily.

'I know, but we must all think very clearly,' he said, almost clumsily, as if making an excuse, or readying himself to discuss complicated holiday plans.

'Why don't you sit down, dear?'

'No, I'm too wound up, I want to stand, thank you.'

He sighed and fiddled with his cufflinks, looking absentmindedly around the room, almost as if expecting a lifeline of some sort to pluck him out of harm's way. There was none.

Mary's mother strode in and said brusquely, 'Mary, dear, lots to chat about. Let's have tea.'

Without waiting for an answer, she poured three cups of tea and added milk. Her father took one and Mary did not.

'Your grandson is doing well by the way.'

Her mother tightened her lips, oblivious at the attempt to gain acceptance, responsibility, or inclusion for the infant. 'That's uncalled for. This is difficult for all of us, and may I remind you that this is your responsibility, not ours. Let's get down to business. I gave you an envelope that contained adoption papers. Have you signed them?'

Mary flopped the envelope onto the table and her mother opened it. She looked irritated.

'No signature, Mary, that's not good.'

'It's so difficult, mother. So final. So clinical.'

'Mary, lots of girls...'

'I'm not *lots!*' Mary shouted.

Her mother continued determinedly, 'It will be good for the baby...'

'Michael,' said Mary sharply.

'Quite so, the...baby!'

The forms were placed in front of her, and a pen was pushed into her hand.

'I want you to sign the forms, now. Let's stop all this prevarication.'

Mary was unprepared for the onslaught. Her mother's voice hardened, and she outlined in brutal detail the challenges for illegitimate children and their mothers in society. Facts were harvested from every source possible to support her case. Hearsay and vignettes of awful outcomes were added to bolster her view, but it did no more than illustrate that the reasoning was formed from whatever negative information was to hand. She knitted it all together to form an unarguable case, but in the end, it was rather like a jumper with an odd collar and different length sleeves, the result was clumsy.

Papa's face clouded and Mary felt the bile rising in her stomach. The monologue went on and on, relentlessly. The result was that there was no oxygen left for anyone else.

Mary felt the room swirling. Words became discordant and tinny as her mind raced. *For the best...good for the baby...no money... no future...the only sensible option...*

She was helpless against the verbal onslaught and as the words enveloped her, she weakened. Mary looked down through blurry eyes, slowly picked up the pen and signed the forms.

The pen dropped to the table making an inkblot on the cloth.

Her mother's voice returned to normal as she attempted to justify the decision. 'Good. It's the right thing to do. Look, there's simply no room here and you could not expect those people, the Wilsons, to wedge you into their lives forever. What kind of future for you would that be? I've put money in this envelope for the Wilsons by way of recompense, please give it to them.'

Mary absentmindedly picked up the envelope and put it in her handbag, her hands were numb with tension. She felt as if she was in a vortex, spinning, with words still coming at her: *no money...nowhere to live...no job...*

She slowly sank to the floor and passed out. As she did so, she heard her mother say, 'Oh, for goodness' sake!'

Mrs Knight gently roused Mary who was curled up on the leather sofa in her father's study. She held a cup of tea and stroked her forehead.

'Good job your father caught you, you might've bonked your head.'

Mary sat up, 'What have I done?'

'I can't comment about that, Mary, I'm just a spinster, I've no experience. My concern is for you, dear. You need rest and recuperation. Go back to those lovely people who've shown you so much care.'

Mary realised the truth of it - *the people who really cared for her.*

'Where are my parents?'

'Oh, they're downstairs in the dining room shouting at each other. Your sisters have taken to their rooms with a supper tray, and perhaps a couple of tin helmets.'

Humour was lost on Mary's battered mind. Nevertheless, she gave a thin smile. 'It's a good time to go – I want it to be forever.'

Mrs Knight straightened up. 'Don't be too hasty, time heals and for what it's worth, the situation is very confusing. As usual, it's *how* the problem is solved and *how* the message is delivered that counts, and on that note, your mother failed all her charm-school examinations.'

Mary recognised the attempt at mediation, but it did nothing to quell her anxiety and deep unhappiness. She got up, hugged Mrs Knight and after gathering her coat left the house. Rather than get a bus straight away, she walked slowly to the Oval. The birds sang and rays of sunshine reached down through the clouds to her, as if trying to stroke her in sympathy.

She had to be strong.

Betty and Audrey did their best to pacify Mary, but for the most part chose not to discuss the subject. What was done, was done. There was no turning back.

'Tea up,' shouted Audrey up the stairs.

'Coming,' Mary turned and looked down at baby Michael and whispered, 'So sorry, darling. So sorry.'

Downstairs, she flopped onto the couch and reached into her handbag. 'I almost forgot, my mother gave me this to give you, *for your troubles.'*

Audrey frowned and Betty reached out and wordlessly intercepted the envelope. She opened it revealing several large value banknotes. They were very short of cash.

'No,' said Audrey, 'no bloody way. Sorry Mary, but no.'

Betty stood up and said curtly, 'I won't be long.' She quickly left the room and Mary felt awkward. After half an hour she returned, wearing a satisfied smile. 'Okay, all done. I gave the cash to Ma Gilbert. She often pays out of her own pocket for things for all the new babies she delivers. This will help her out. Howzat?'

Audrey smiled.

Mary's eyes welled with tears of embarrassment, and she gave Betty the thumbs up. Her mother's donation was gauche, but the Wilson's honesty and strength of character turned it into something good. She admired them so much.

All she had to do now was to see out the remaining weeks.

9

Mary shivered slightly as she stood in front of the metal-framed window of her room in the St Maria Convent in Lambeth, one hand on the cold brass handle and the other to her head. She looked across the pebbled quadrangle surrounded by red brick walls to the ornate iron gate. This was it. This was the place that baby Michael would be handed over to a nameless social worker. Permission to stay for two days prior to the handover had been given, supposedly to allow the baby to calm before its transfer. To calm? And what about her?

They, the social workers - *they,* the nuns - *they,* her family; they all knew what was best for her and baby. She gripped the handle tighter as baby Michael gurgled softly and a painful shard pierced her heart.

Oh, to just grab him and run, fast, away - far away. But looking out of the door of her room she saw that escape was impossible. Her room was at the end of a corridor and the was entrance blocked by a nun sitting at a desk. *They* had done all this before and covered all the angles.

Mary would remember her arrival at the convent forever, and the hard-bitten greeting from the Mother Superior whom she quickly dubbed *the harridan.*

'Mary Henslow?'

'Yes,' she murmured hesitatingly in response to the harsh tone, 'and baby Michael,' holding him close to her chest.

'Of course, dear. That's why you're here. Now then, do you know what to expect?'

'It was in the letter after I signed the paperwork with the social workers but, I...'

'Right, well let me remind you. You will stay here for two days. At an appointed time, a social worker will arrive and collect your baby for delivery to the chosen parents for adoption. It's all quite straightforward. I would appreciate as little fuss as possible to avoid disturbing the others who are also involved in similar processes.'

Mary remembered nodding, accepting the bald facts without question, numb and incapable of conversation with someone so flat. She hardly remembered walking into the bare room, with its badly decorated beige walls and a single curtainless window that let light flood in. A wooden cross above the iron bed and a statue of the Madonna on the opposite wall were the only decoration.

The harridan left and a little later a young novice crept into the room, looking furtively over her shoulder. 'Hello, I'm Sister Lucy,' she said, her voice almost a whisper. 'If you need someone to talk to, please don't hesitate to let me know. Just fold your towel into a triangle and place it at the foot of your bed, I'll be able to see it from the corridor. I can come back when the coast is clear. God bless.'

There was a sound of voices at the end of the corridor and the novice quickly left, pushing a trolley of bed linen ahead of her. She smiled over her shoulder – it was like a warm ray of sunshine, or a rare and beautiful plant in a weed patch.

The harridan strode back into the room.

'I forgot to say, you must remove all clothing and personal items from the baby before collection.' She dropped a cotton baby-dress onto the bed. 'That means no rings, necklets, and suchlike.'

Without emotion, she walked towards the door, turned, and said over her shoulder. 'There's a canteen here, of sorts. You may like to get a cup of tea and mix with the other poor unfortunates. Just remember, this is for the best for you and the child.'

Mary closed her eyes as she left, *poor unfortunates? Bringing a child into the world is – unfortunate?* Her head buzzed and she felt dizzy with stress – it was difficult to focus, to think – and not to cry.

The whole process was brutally normalised, so uncaring. She continued looking out of the misty window her hand still holding the brass handle. A car arrived, it skidded on the pebbled surface outside the front door. It was black, like the sort depicted in gangster movies, and looked like a giant beetle. A woman in an immaculately cut grey suit got out. Her dark hair was in a bun and her face business-like. She was greeted by the harridan.

Her heart beat faster.

She tried to put the impending process out of her mind and recalled the night before, when she had talked for hours with the novice, Lucy Ellis. Their conversation had been full of warmth and kindness.

'Are you alright? Oh, silly of me, of course you aren't!'

'That's okay, thank you for caring. No, I'm not actually. I feel as though I'm going out of my mind, but then I don't suppose I'm the only one feeling that way in this place.'

'You're not. I'm sorry that you've encountered such indifference, not all the nuns are so uncaring. I wanted to contact you. I know your story, Mary, it's heartrending, so tragic. Many of the other girls are just victims of a good night out, or put simply, the actions of men without conscience. It's the cruelty of society that's the biggest blow to self-esteem. One of the girls in the room next door was distraught the other day as she recalled her parents telling her she had brought shame on the family, and if I've heard it once I've heard it a thousand times: *you made yourself pregnant!*'

Mary shrugged her shoulders. 'Ah, as if it's a virgin birth. But it's all the same though, pregnant is pregnant.'

They sat in silence.

'So, what made you become a nun?'

Lucy touched her arm. 'Well, penance I suppose. You see I'm a strong Catholic, always have been. I got involved with an amazing, gentle man who was killed in the Irish Sea. Torpedoed in 1941. It broke me. I became an angry, grieving, different person. Then I found out I was pregnant. By which time I'd taken to drink. The long and short of it is that following some rather violent incidents which I don't want to recount, I avoided a custodial sentence because my lawyer outlined my contrition and explained that I wanted to take holy orders. That led to me having to give my baby away for adoption. The penalty of making a fool of myself I suppose.'

'Lucy, I'm sorry to intrude.'

'You didn't. Sharing this with you will, I hope, help you to realise that your sad situation is being played out across the country. You're not alone. As for me, I like the work I do and I'm at peace with myself.'

They talked for a long while and the weight of the occasion lifted a little – she was still emotional and upset, but not guilty, why should she be? This simple, caring hand of friendship had calmed her enough to allow her to sleep, emotionally exhausted though she was, the whole night through.

Mary was still clutching the window handle, when she saw the woman in the grey suit given a cream-coloured blanket by the *harridan,* before she disappeared below the door canopy.

She's coming. Be ready. *Be strong.*

Mary looked at baby Michael and he gurgled, her eyes welled with tears. Be strong.

Just then, the harridan appeared. 'Mary,' she said with a false, tight smile. 'I wonder if you'd be kind enough to come to the office to sign a couple of forms?'

Mary knew well enough that she had signed all the forms required. Discussions with young women in the canteen highlighted that this was a ruse to distract mothers and allow babies to be whisked away, avoiding any possible *fuss.* Several of the women were broken by this experience.

The grey-suited woman appeared, far away at the end of the corridor, her heels clicking slowly towards Mary's room.

'No, I think I'll stay!' she said, and straightened her body defiantly.

'I really think...'

'You may think what you like, I'm staying. No doubt you are happy with my mother's donation to the convent, but that doesn't give you power over me. I'm staying. I will hand over my child with dignity.'

As she finished the grey-suited woman reached the door and saw her. 'Oh, dear, I thought...'

Mary looked at her. 'You thought I wouldn't be here. Well, I am. So, let's get on with the business in hand with grace and not shuffling me off so that my baby is stolen rather than freely given.'

The nun grimaced and made a move towards her, 'I insist...'

The woman held out her arm to stop her. 'No, it's the right thing to do in this case.'

Mary bristled. 'In every case, not just mine. Now let's get on with it.'

She carefully dressed baby Michael in the cotton gown and wrapped him in the blanket that the social worker handed to her. When she kissed his forehead, she just wanted to run, fast, away from this hell – but it was not possible. Slowly, she held out her shaking arms and the social worker carefully took the bundle and strode away without looking back.

Mary watched her take every step down the corridor. When she was out of sight she waited and heard the car start up and drive away. Slowly, as her eyes filled with tears, she fell to her knees and grabbed the mattress with both hands, her face wetting the bed cover, her chest racked with sobs.

It was an hour later when the day staff had left the building that Lucy came in with a mug of tea. She knelt beside her. 'Take my advice, get your things together and leave this place, now, not tomorrow. Go to a place where you have good friends who will look after you.'

Mary looked up at Lucy through red eyes, took the mug and drank the tea gratefully. Lucy gave her directions to the nearest bus stop.

Two months passed and Mary lived within a cloud of misery. The Wilsons cared for her as best they could but felt helpless. Dark days get darker if you let them. Even a happy house can be just four cheerful walls with a bitter centre.

'Right, Mary, we're going to do something - you're too nice a person to continue to suffer like this. Besides, it's doin' my 'ead in!' said Betty.

Mary managed a rueful smile.

Betty followed it up by throwing a ball of red wool at her. Mary caught it and deftly threw it back and it bounced off Betty's head.

'Howzat?' Mary forced a smile.

'Now you've woken up, let me make a proposition,' Betty kept her gaze on Mary to achieve a successful outcome. 'I think we should go to our favourite pub, tonight, not tomorrow, tonight. What say to that?'

'Pub? You don't mean the Wattenden at Kenley?'

'Yeah.'

'No.'

'Why not?'

'Betty, there are just so many memories - I couldn't. Another place perhaps.'

Betty thought, *another place...that'll do!*

'Okay, let's go into the city. The cellar bars are great fun, there's jazz and American soldiers with money to burn.' She paused and then urged Mary on, 'That's it then, come on, let's get ready, chop, chop!'

Mary was ensnared and with nowhere to retreat, submitted to the ritual of choosing the right dress and selecting the best make up. She listened to Betty chattering excitedly – it wasn't annoying, rather, she saw it for what it was: her best mate doing all she could to raise her spirits.

An hour later they stood by the dining room table and opened their purses, piling the contents on the table. It didn't look good.

Audrey joined them. She looked up at the ceiling, shrugged, then reached for her handbag and brought out a battered purse, then flopped a few pound notes onto the meagre cash on the table.

'Take this, add it to them bottle tops. Have a good time. I don't need it. But don't tell Harry!'

'Mum, we can't...'

'You bloody can, and you will. I was keeping cash for a rainy day – it hasn't rained but this will at least bring out the sunshine. If it puts a smile on your face, Mary, it'll be worth it.'

Now there was no going back.

There was a reduction in bombing raids as the war wore on, but London now had to face up to destructive new threats, from V1 and V2 rockets that appeared out of nowhere. Despite that, it seemed that everyone had grown used to taking chances. Cellar bars were popular based on the skewed belief that they were as safe as shelters. Betty told her that the Americans liked them and that, like it or not, they liberated British girls with their openness, fun, and of course, their cash.

The evening air was cool as Mary and Betty changed buses to get to Trafalgar Square. As the journey continued Mary noticed how Betty looked excited and it rubbed off on her.

'Let's go to the Coal Hole on the Strand, it's my favourite, pub.'

Mary agreed and they arrived just as a group of sailors was leaving. One of them barged into Mary. 'Whoops, sorry, luv. You lookin' for a night out with a handsome bloke?'

'Yeah, but I can't see any,' she replied, knowing that a smart answer was the only way to avoid conversation with men who had had one too many drinks. The sailor looked crestfallen, and his mates laughed then dragged him away.

The pub was noisy and the upright piano in the corner, played by an old gentleman dressed in shirtsleeves and bright red trouser braces, could hardly be heard. Mary watched his gummy smile as young men brought him pints of beer to ensure his continued attention to the keys.

Her mood lifted with the sounds of laughter and music around her, but her ears could only take so much after the isolation and quiet of Turnpike Lane. Betty noticed her discomfort and stopped talking to an army sergeant who had his eyes on her.

'Wanna go somewhere else?'

'Do you mind?'

'No,' she whispered, 'it's okay, this bloke's got bad breath!'

Covent Garden was a little quieter and they laughed at the antics of a man on stilts hustling for beer money. It was hazardous - as he reached for money he nearly fell.

They stayed a while drinking beer at a kiosk and chatting to two American servicemen, then visited the nearby pubs, drinking no more than a half a beer in each - it was about taking in the atmosphere rather than consuming a lot of ale.

Betty looked at her watch and frowned. 'It's been fun, but it's late now and I suppose we'd better go. I'm not a lady of leisure like you, darlin'.'

Mary agreed but felt strangely out of her depressed state and wanted just one more drink at Covent Garden market. They had thirty minutes before the last bus and decided fit in a couple of swift halves. As they walked along Floral Street a large black sedan drove past, it skidded to a halt then reversed back towards them. A passenger window was wound down and the cheerful face of Giles Masterson emerged.

'I thought it was you, how wonderful, Mary, how are you?' He smiled broadly.

Mary's face lit up. 'Giles, how lovely to see you. I'm okay, and you?'

'Well, I'll tell you if you let me. Come for a drink.'

'Oh, I can't, I'm with my friend and we were about to get the last bus home.'

Betty was quick off the mark. 'Hello, Giles. I'm Betty Wilson and don't you let this lady go. Mary, I'm off to the bus and you are staying with this good-looking feller. Giles, if you take her out then you must get her back to Turnpike Lane – if not she comes with me. Got it!'

Giles laughed aloud, 'Betty, you'd make a brilliant sergeant major. I agree and promise to take good care of Mary.'

Mary had no choice. The decision was made for her – and she was happy with that. She got in the back of the car and Giles gave the driver directions to a nearby bar.

Betty stood back and gave a hopeful wave as the car drove away.

Mary listened to Giles chatter about North Africa and his posting back to Britain, and how he enjoyed his new job, although he didn't elaborate on it. It was almost as if she was being rescued from oblivion. He was still as handsome and charming as ever. The bar was a private club and although quite plain it was comfortable and candlelit. Being with him felt like old times, except that they were new times and she felt enormously guilty.

'Giles,' she said, as he paused and took a sip of wine, 'I need to explain things you will unaware of.'

'Cripes, you're not going to tell me you're a lady of the night, are you?' he said with customary humour.

'Silly man. Be serious. Look, you visited Fentiman Road and left a note. I still have it. What you don't know is that my mother didn't give it to me. I received it three weeks later from the housekeeper. In it you explained that my mother had said I'd left London.

That wasn't true. I cannot explain her motives, but I was truly gutted.'

Giles frowned. 'Oh dear. What an awful thing to do.'

'Yes, and I found out just as I was about to join up. It's a long story, but the model of family life that I held in my mind didn't quite match reality. So, my WAAF experience was down to you, sir.' She sipped her wine and continued. 'The fact is, Giles,' she paused for a second and ran her finger around the rim of her glass, 'I met a sergeant pilot, fell in love and he was lost over the North Sea. I had his baby and the terrible wretch you see before you carries the guilt of having it adopted.'

'That's quite a burden, Mary, and one that you don't deserve. I'm so sorry for you.' He reached for her hands and looked straight at her. 'Now then, I too have something to say. I have carried a torch for you all the time. Except that I nearly got married.'

Mary winced and was surprised that she felt disappointed. 'Oh,' she said, resignedly, 'what was she like?'

'Well, she was pretty enough for her type, intelligent but picked her nose.'

'Eh?'

'We were good together, but it would never have worked out. Her mother objected and my commanding officer just didn't like her. That's the way it goes.'

Mary sat back confused.

'She's a chimpanzee at the zoo. You'd really like her.'

Mary burst out laughing and couldn't stop. The reservoir of tension spilled out of her like water from an overturned jug. She regained her breath and held his hands tightly. 'Same old Giles, release unhappiness with a joke. You are still a lovely bloke. Thank you.'

'My pleasure, but just do me one favour.'

'What?'

'Don't pick your nose here, it's very posh.'

Mary flapped her napkin at him, and they laughed. Giles ordered more drinks then spent the rest of the time explaining various events in their lives. All the agony that cleaved to her loosened and fell away with each reminiscence, she felt invigorated. Time flew by and dawn approached. She was impressed that he had a car on standby but didn't question it - why should she? It was a comfortable lift home. They were about to go when Giles took her hand in his.

'Mary, you've been through such painful times. My heart goes out to you. Speaking of hearts, I really want to see you again, but I know how much you must miss your man, John, and I don't want to rush things. Can we meet again? No pressure, just to enjoy each other's company, as we always did. I do appreciate that it's still a bit early and things are raw. Let's just have fun.'

Mary thought that was the most perfect thing to say. Recognition of love lost and the offer of a measure of happier times. It was just what she needed.

Betty heard Mary return in the early hours but had to leave early to get to work. Back home later in the evening she sat across from a tired looking Mary.

'Well, go on then, tell me. What happened?'

'Nothing *happened* we just talked all night long, about so many things and had a lot of laughs. I felt so good. I told him about John, the baby, and his letter I never received.'

'Oh, yeah, I remember you told me about that. Did he forgive you?'

'There was nothing to forgive, he simply skated over it. Actually...'

'Here we go with your, *actually, actually....*'

'As I was saying, actually, he said he had continued to carry a torch for me.'

'Bullseye!'

Audrey looked up from her knitting, inconspicuous yet ever-present chair in the corner. 'Oh, Mary, that's so lovely. Is he a nice feller?'

'Yes, Audrey. He was my first male friend as it happens. He's thoughtful, steady, and uncomplicated. I can't believe my luck, meeting him again. He gave me two pieces of advice that I am going to take.'

'What was that?'

'Firstly, to re-join the WAAF. He says that would give me a sense of purpose and focus my mind on anything but the sad events to date. I'll make the arrangements tomorrow. He has contacts and will try and get me posted back to Kenley so I can keep visiting you all and it's relatively close to home.'

Betty clapped her hands, 'Mary, that's great, the old team back together again.'

'Then, he suggested I smooth things over with my parents. His view is that my mother is in a bad place and botched her relationship with me, then double-botched her handling of the adoption, but from her perspective thought she was doing the right thing. I can't say that I agreed much with that, but I'll give it a go.'

'I'm so glad. My mate Mary's back.'

Mary smiled and touched her shoulder. 'And your mate Mary is seeing Giles again tomorrow, how about that?'

Betty and Audrey shouted, *Wahey!* in unison and they all hugged.

Mary's eyes misted over.

Giles masterfully managed the weeks that followed, and they went to pubs, restaurants, and dances. No questions. No pressure. No rush. Mary's mood was lifted whenever he recognised her infrequent low times and nudged her gently back to life.

True to his word, he also helped her with the administration of re-enlistment and promised to try and get her into signals work, which he said he was loosely connected with. All that remained was for Mary to contact her parents. So, she wrote them a note and gave a date that she would visit. This would be immediately prior to her re-joining the WAAF.

She knew that it wouldn't be at all easy.

It took a lot of courage to return to Fentiman Road, her mother's indifference to her plight wounded her. Her arrival was tense, and as she expected there was no recognition of her attempt at rapprochement. The next morning, her mother made it clear that she was quite busy with charity work and Mary might want to consider going back to Turnpike Lane. Her father chewed his toast and looked disappointed but was too loyal to take issue with it. He got up and silently left the room, then later stood in the doorway looking at her.

'My dear, I'm off out to see my agent, we can have a chat later if you want?'

'I'd like that, Papa,' she replied wearily.

He turned and left silently.

An hour later, Mary wandered into her father's study. She set out to replace the small brass key around Brer Rabbit's neck, this time she took more care not to fall off the stool. The walls and bookcases caught and sucked in what little light came in through the window which explained why her father almost always used a desk light on to read or write by. Her memories of him sitting in the thin shafts of light, smoking his favourite cigarettes, and writing furiously used to fascinate her.

Now, Mary sat on the sofa staring blankly at the neatly bound books of poems that lay on a large oak coffee table, all in Papa's neat copperplate writing. Her eyes brimmed with tears. One of the books lay open and Mary had to resist wanting to tear the pages out and throw them on the fire.

The poems that upset her appeared under the heading: 'Waxmoth'. She looked up the meaning in a dictionary. It made awkward reading. The verses in this part of the volume in front of her were crafted, not borrowed. They were his, not second hand, heard in a pub or read elsewhere - his! No matter how she tried to make excuses or look for reasons, there were none; the work was truly odious.

The front door slammed, and her heart began to beat fast. What should she say? What should she do? This time she certainly wouldn't hide her feelings.

Heavy footsteps trod up the carpeted stairs – the sound seemed to go on forever. She heard them come along the landing and they finally stopped outside the study. She looked up and saw her father in the doorway, tall, straight, and smartly dressed as always in a tweed double breasted suit. His chiselled features frowned slightly as he looked at her and the open books on the table.

'My poppet, what are you doing with those? They're not ready to go to the publishers yet.'

'Perhaps they never will be, Papa.'

'What do you mean, dear?'

He sat down heavily beside her on the sofa.

Mary sniffed back the tears, then said, hesitantly, 'Most of the poems are very you. Old-fashioned, some funny, some religious...'

'And?'

'Waxmoth!'

'Ah. Waxmoth,' he repeated slowly, and then sighed.

'Why write such awful stuff, it couldn't have been for fun because they exhorted Jews to go home, accused them of institutional theft, and of being, well, bloodsuckers in society, worse, dirty human beings. The Waxmoth is, I find out, a creature that lays its eggs in a beehive where they eat their way through the store of food finally ruining the colony. Beehives have long been a worldly symbol of a society. So, I can only assume that you chose the title Waxmoth as an allusion to Jews being a plague on society. It doesn't take long to conclude, Papa, that you're an anti-Semite. Why, why?'

'You don't understand, it's just one of those things,' he said emptily.

Mary broke in, her voice raised. 'Papa, Jews are being systematically killed by the Nazis, it was in the Daily Telegraph only last month. But even before that they have been horrendously treated in Germany throughout the last decade. What about Kristallnacht, and having their rights taken away and made to wear a Jewish star that earned them mistreatment in the street. Now the terrible truth is out about the concentration camps.'

'If it's true...!'

Exasperated, she blurted, 'Papa, you simply cannot ignore the facts.'

'Calm down for goodness's sake, lower your voice or your mother will be agitated. Listen, after the Great War we were, well...we were broken. Your mother and I had to live in a small flat. Worse was to come, in 1930 I was made bankrupt.' He looked crestfallen. 'I hated that.'

Mary felt his fear of penury and wondered what was coming next. She sat back, ready to listen. 'Go on.'

'The Great Depression lost the wealth of many families in the USA and here in England. Now listen to me. At the end of the last war, I talked to a lot of German officers, good intelligent men, and they were absolutely convinced, and had proof, that the Jews had ruined their country, stolen the wealth and weakened their society through sheer greed and duplicity. In various clubs I now belong to I've heard things that reinforced my views. Years after the Stock Market crashed there is considerable evidence that Jewish businessmen got out in time and made money from foreclosures and loans. I was crushed, Mary, crushed.'

He was shaking with anger and his face was flushed.

'And based on this hearsay you think they should all be driven out of England, or murdered?'

'No,' he shouted and put his hands to his head, 'not at all. But they should be encouraged to go. To get out. The foreign secretary Arthur Balfour said in 1917, on behalf of His Majesty I might add, that a Middle East state should be created for them and named Israel. That'll do for me. But, oh no, it's not popular with liberal politicians or the Jews so they stayed and embedded themselves in our society, sucking the lifeblood out of us.'

He stood up and his coat fell to the floor. His face was creased with emotion.

'Look, I acknowledge that they've had a raw deal at times in Europe, pogroms, and the like. Well, the Middle East solution would've been the right thing to do. You're young, you just don't understand. For heaven's sake, English life is under threat from so many directions, as we sleep-walk into an increasingly over-liberalisation of society, inseminated with the weakness of looking the other way as our financial institutions are hijacked and our values degraded by socialism.'

He put one hand on his hip, and the other to his head. 'The war gets in the way, communism get in the way, Jews get in the way, the life we all enjoy is trampled, ruined ... Pah!'

Mary saw that he looked confused as well as angry. Or was she hanging on to a thin strand of love and respect? She felt so terribly torn. John King's bad-tempered words about Papa's flaws hovered at the back of her mind.

'No, Papa, life gets in the way. I've read enough to know that. As for those poems, I am so very disappointed. I dearly love you, but today I don't like you.'

Her father let out a painful half-cry and stormed out of the study, and down the stairs.

The front door slammed.

Mary rested her chin on the windowsill of her bedroom. Her body was as taut as a drumskin, and her head throbbed with the tension after her confrontation with Papa. She felt forlorn and wondered: *how much more hurt must I suffer?*

The beauty and joy of loving can be punctured when people in your heart let you down. She reflected on the futility of asking endless questions as to why they do what they do or say what they say. It was a though only 'self' mattered.

Oh, Papa, are we all just walk-on actors in your theatrical world?

She smiled ruefully at her analogy. Poor papa. His production suffered from changing audience tastes and poor direction. He was unable to adapt.

'Enough,' she spluttered and went to the bathroom.

Her reflection in the mirror showed puffy eyes still wet with tears and she felt emotionally beaten - she held her head high, stared at her image and began to well up inside. After deep breaths, her expression changed to one of determination.

'I'm not beaten,' she said forcefully. 'I saved a WAAF. I saved a baby. I can ride a bloody motorbike.' As she said this, the image of baby Michael flashed into her mind and her heartbeat quickened and she had to breath hard. 'And it was not my fault. I had to give him away. I refuse to suffer any longer.'

The basic facts of her family life were simple. She tried so hard to make connections with them, connections that meant something, not just the perfunctory passing of the time of day or a casual interrogation of one decision or another. They didn't reciprocate in any way. It was a family where each of them kept to themselves. The ugly truth was that family values and habits are learned. Her mother's conversation was stilted and laden with resentment and innuendo of things unknown, exerting a kind of emotional blackmail. Her father hovered without control and appeared perpetually vacant.

Mary tightened her hands so hard they shook. *Oh. Papa, how I worshipped you.* She naively assumed that love was all that was important, but it was not. It was clear to her that all relationships are multi-dimensional; you can have love, but it must never shroud reality. Reality has a habit of biting when the stakes are down. Mary had been bitten, hard, and the emotional scars hurt and wouldn't go away.

Her mind was filled with so many questions. How could her Papa, whom she adored so much, flirt with fascism? Okay, it was only a flirt, and he didn't follow it up, but his stubbornness made him hang on to aspects of this evil ideology, unable to admit he was wrong. How could he write such vile, antisemitic prose and pass it off as, 'just one of those things'. Where did he get this world view?

Mary had to face the uncomfortable fact that her picture of his character had been childishly superficial and lacking in depth - it was constructed the way a loving daughter wanted it to be instead of how it really was.

Now the father-daughter relationship cracked because it morphed into a 'two-adult' position, where there was an entitlement to ask questions and know more, however uncomfortable that might be. The trouble was, she wanted the perfect father, and he wanted a family that showed unquestioning, unconditional respect - he was a Henslow, and the assumption was that the name alone demanded loyalty. He was from an age of male supremacy, but times had drastically changed for him and others in the antediluvian upper middle class, mired in the mush of old Britain.

Now it was all about trying to understand him more. But she was so weary. Why did everything have to be such a trial? God knows, she knew little enough about the man who was the father of her child, lost in the cold North Sea, leaving nothing but a flimsy shadow of himself for her to hang on to. Now Papa!

She ran her hands through her hair – did she even know herself?

Early next morning Mary awoke fully clothed, lying on top of her bed. Her face was sticky from a tearful night. She decided to get up, pack and leave before the household roused itself. There had been enough emotion bouncing around and she did not want to endure any more. It was time to go.

The front door closed with a quiet click and Mary looked back over her shoulder at the house, with its Victorian façade and nicely tended window boxes. She felt so sad. Luckily, a taxi was passing, and she quickly ran to the kerb and directed it to the Oval underground station. The journey was quiet, almost as if the world was avoiding her, but she was grateful for that.

There was one day spare before her entry back into the WAAF, which she had arranged weeks before visiting her family. She wanted to catch up with Betty, but more importantly, needed to talk about her woes and there was no one better.

Betty screeched, 'Blimey, Mary, so you're back to Kenley? You and me again together, that's a real bounce.'

Mary raised her hands. 'Hold on now, I'm destined for signals training first at a place called RAF Yatesbury in Wiltshire and who knows what afterwards. So, don't raise your hopes. But, yes, it'll be good when we can meet up regularly. Besides, am I right, did your mum mention you have a feller in tow?'

Betty looked coy. 'Yeah, he's a good-looking guy. Jim's his name. He works in pay accounts. That means he can deal with the household bills!'

'Hmm, sounds pretty permanent, Betty.'

'It will bleedin' be if I have any say,' she replied mischievously.

They spent the day catching up on their lives and Mary explained what had gone on with her father. She shed tears and Betty made a pot of tea.

'Sounds like getting back into uniform is just what you need,' Betty said, placing a cup of hot tea in front of her. 'Your Giles was right.'

That night Betty's mum came home from her hospital job, and they enjoyed a meal together. After Audrey had gone to bed, Betty sat on the large soft couch with Mary, who looked lost. She wanted so much for her friend but was powerless to help. They laughed and she did her best to bolster Mary as only good friends do, but wondered just how much more she could take.

They fell asleep together on the couch as the embers to the fire slowly died.

The next day, Mary set off to re-enlist in the WAAF, desperately determined to gain traction on a life that was slipping away from her.

10

The metal bed squeaked as its springs argued with the frame and Mary clutched the edge of the green pastel striped counterpane with her fingers to calm her anxiety. It had been a wrench to leave the warmth and kindness of Turnpike Lane. She recognised the sweet smell of military floor polish, the familiarity of it was comforting. Her return into service in the WAAF had been uncomplicated and she was delighted to be back at RAF Kenley. The induction process involving administration and the issue of new uniforms at RAF Innsworth, near Gloucester, had been very impersonal. It was all old hat.

Kenley wasn't quite the same, although the girls were pleasant, all her old contacts had been posted away, so there was no connection. She wondered whether she had done the right thing after all. Never expect things to remain the same forever.

As she emptied her handbag to clear out the rubbish, she came across the sheet of paper with pencil scribbled verse on it that she hadn't put back in the secret drawer in Papa's study all those weeks ago. Glancing at the words she frowned, how much more was she going to find out about him?

The signals course over the last eight weeks had been intense but she enjoyed it because it made her focus hard in a short time frame and she was able to put her emotional scars to one side – not gone forever, just to one side. The training involved setting radios to various frequencies and accurately recording the transmissions. Learning Morse code was not difficult, but she opted not to enter the lengthy German classes - she just wanted to get to work.

She took a deep breath, stood up abruptly and folded a brown envelope with her name rank and number on it, and placed it in her handbag. It contained her joining instructions indicating that she should proceed to Perth, Scotland, to temporarily join a signals unit, then return to RAF Kenley.

This had come at just the right time. Before the course at RAF Yatesbury, she had an uncomfortable feeling of being right on the edge and hoped that a change of scenery would help her survive. All that remained now was to get on the train at Kings Cross station and travel to Perth from where she would be collected by military transport and taken to a secret intercept site up in the nearby hills of Kinnoull. She didn't know what to expect and didn't really care - it was away from London, which was all what she wanted. New job, new life, and new place.

The railway station was crowded and noisy - it was chaos, even with the presence of military rail transport personnel directing everyone. Servicemen and women scurried around with their kitbags, helmets and gas masks clanging against their sides. Swirling smoke and steam hovered over the platforms making it difficult to locate the right train, but Mary could just make out on her right a large sign with the word Perth on it next to an engine embellished with faded letters, LNER. The light wooden carriages with their white tops made them look as though they were destined for a Sunday outing, rather than to transport troops northwards. Suddenly, there was a loud deep steam whistle from the train.

'Get a move on,' shouted the harassed train guard, 'we're off in two minutes.' For good measure he held his whistle up high before putting it to his lips and blowing hard, as if in competition with the iron engine.

The last few passengers scrambled, overburdened with kitbags and gas masks, into the carriages as the engine built up pressure, sending more clouds of steam from its bowels, giving notice of its imminent departure. Mary was pleased it was a large carriage with a central aisle with seats either side, and not one with separate eight person compartments – the memory of her Devon to London journey was still raw. She found a vacant seat and heard the doors slamming shut. Soldiers shouted goodbyes through the windows, waving, and blowing air kisses. Cases were hoisted and rammed onto racks above the seats, balanced precariously, threatening to spill over the edge. Mary squeezed into the seat and sat back, relieved to be off her feet. The smell of leather and smoke tickled her nostrils. It was all so noisy – all so absorbing; thoughts of baby Michael receded – a bit.

'This seat taken, luv?'

She looked up. The voice was soft and with a musical edge to it and the soldier pointed to a seat across from her, the other two being taken.

'No, not at all,' she replied absentmindedly.

The two other passengers by the window lolled against the side of the carriage and looked as though they were asleep despite the clatter around them. It would be a long journey and sleep would shorten the boredom.

'Thanks. Looks like it's the last one left, lucky me.' He sat down heavily after lifting his large kitbag onto the already overcrowded rack, then reached into a knapsack and brought out a book and a packet of Du Maurier cigarettes. 'Want one?'

Mary regarded him warily, mindful of her experience, en route to London from Devon, but he looked pleasant enough. He had a single pip on his shoulder indicating that he was a junior officer.

'Thank you, most kind.'

'I've just got back from Egypt. I'm not sure what was the scariest, being bombed by the Italians just before they surrendered or wondering whether a U-boat would catch me on the way home. But here I am, thank goodness. I'm Newcastle bound to see my wife and young daughter. I canna wait.'

Mary felt a sudden stab of sadness. She held her hands tight together and forced herself to pay attention to the man in front of her.

'How old is she?'

'Two years old, her name's Jacqui and she's quite a little rascal I'm told. The name's Alec, by the way.'

'Oh, sorry, of course. Mary Henslow. Exalted rank of leading aircraftswoman.'

He was pleasant company and a good conversationalist. His easy manner made her feel comfortable, and they talked for a long time about the war, rationing and how Mr Churchill's fine speeches lifted morale.

'What's your regiment?'

'Well, I'm not in a regiment as such, I'm supposed to be an education officer, but they keep finding other things for me to do. The army taught me German, and I spend my time listening,' he theatrically turned his head left and right, 'and interviewing and processing POW. Do you know what? The enemy are just like us, they don't even want to be where they are and cannot wait for it all to be over. Hard to believe, isn't it?'

'Yes, it is. I suppose we only see one side of the coin, mad Adolf cartoons and bombs everywhere.'

'Chin up, now the Yanks are with us we've got so much more clout. It can't be long.'

The journey that morning to St Pancras station had tired her out and there were many hours ahead. Her eyes were heavy.

'Look, Alec, I'm enjoying chatting, I promise you, but I really am so tired, I need to have a nap.'

'Here, use my coat as a pillow,' he handed her his folded greatcoat.

'Thanks so much, that's very kind of you.'

Mary snuggled down and was soon asleep.

The repetitive sound of the train's engine kept Mary in a deep sleep for over half an hour. Now, she began to stir. Her eyes opened slowly, and she looked around the carriage. It was warm and quiet, and smelled of people and cigarettes. The passengers were snoozing, apart from Alec. He was deeply engrossed in a book.

Unobserved, she took the opportunity to watch him as he gently turned the pages. He was not a handsome man; rather, he had pleasant features, the sort that befriends you without you even asking. He was tanned, probably because of his time in Egypt, and his frame was slim and neat. She saw his well-manicured fingernails peeking round the book cover.

Mary caught sight of the book title, *Gone with the Wind*, and was surprised to see it being read by a man. At that moment he looked up from his reading. Mary smiled back at him, sat up and handed back his coat.

'Thank you, the nap was just what I needed. I couldn't help noticing that you're reading, *Gone with the Wind.* I read that when it was first published before the war. It's a great book, I just like how it portrays Scarlett O'Hara's bravery and the descriptions of the devastation in the south. The film's good too, have you seen it?'

'Unfortunately, no, I've been away a long time, but everybody has been going on about it, especially my sister who saw the film a couple of years back at the cinema in Leicester Square, so I thought I might as well read the book.'

'Are you enjoying it?'

He paused and flapped the book onto the table. 'Well, I'm only halfway through it, but I'm not certain if *enjoying* is the right word. I have to say, so far, things bother me about it.'

'Really, what is it that bothers you?'

'Where shall I start? It focuses too much on the privileged society in the American south, with syrupy excuses from the supposedly hard-done-by Confederates having to give up their exploitation of human beings to keep them rich. It's almost as if we're supposed to feel sorry for them. Frankly, I can wait to see the plantation house, what's it called?'

'Tara.'

'Aye, that's it, Tara. Anyway, I can't wait to see if it gets burned down and the selfish, duplicitous Scarlett brought low.'

Mary winced. She hadn't even noticed that thread, but thought his angle was a little skewed.

'Come on, Alec, I grant you Scarlett is selfish, spoiled and does cheat on her best friend, but when the chips are down, you'll see that she gets her hands dirty and helps to maintain the farm in challenging circumstances after the war.'

'That's true enough, but it portrays racist exploitation and particularly class issues. I'm familiar enough with stories from my family, and ex-school mates who've spent their lives in the coalmines. Now there's a history of exploitation for you.'

'Yes, but this book is about the cruelty and greed of the American Civil War, action, romance, the dashing but flawed hero, Rhett Butler. It has it all.'

'Maybe, but it's put in such a romanticised way the reader is encouraged to overlook key issues, like equality and civil rights.'

'Okay, you have a point, but the book is a tour de force depicting a world that is changing around her. It was sad, wasn't it? I mean, when you are used to a certain way of living it's challenging to have to give it all up. In her case she's a fine example of someone who bravely confronts the psychological and moral issues that face her.'

'Well, that's true enough,' he said politely. His expression made her think that he wanted to say more, it was written in his eyes - and he did. 'I suppose the Tsar of Russia said that too.'

'Are you teasing me, Alec?'

'No, but - and don't take this the wrong way - your accent leads me to assume that perhaps you haven't had to wonder where the next crust comes from. Most people who want change, want it to elevate their lives.'

Mary softened, 'I do sympathise with the plight of working people, I really do. Just because I haven't lived it doesn't mean I don't understand the effect of poverty.'

'Maybe, but sympathy doesn't put bread on the table. Listen, I'm not forcing my ideology on you, really, I'm not. But when this is all over, there will be one great shake up of British politics, you wait and see.'

'Revolution?'

'No, lass, no. I'd never want to see that, ever. I'm a socialist but not a rabid communist. Just plain honesty, to the people of this country, and, well, an end to class structures. It destroys society. That's my view anyway. Have another.'

He offered his packet of cigarettes and, raising one eyebrow, impishly quoted a well-known line from the book, '*Frankly my dear, I just don't give a damn.*'

Mary took the cigarette, and not to be outdone, leaned forward, and said with a slow American drawl, '*Thank you, Rhett, don't mind if I do!*'

They both laughed and the subject was closed, there was no need for more discussion. She sat back and began to wonder about a lot of things. Looking around she saw the smiling faces of her fellow passengers as they chatted or played cards. There was so much she didn't understand and yet so much she wanted to.

Alec reached into his knapsack and took out a flask and poured tea into an aluminium mug. 'Get that down you. Sorry no quality biscuits, but I have got two of these.' He winked and pulled out two KitKat bars.

'Oh, Alec. You hero, but shouldn't you keep them for your little girl?'

He looked straight at her and leaned back in his seat. 'Mary flippin' Henslow, you are so unselfish. Most people on this train would've grabbed the chocolate without a thought, but you considered a little girl you've never met.'

She feigned humility and waved him away.

He touched her wrist briefly, 'I'll be straight with you, bonnie lass. The man that gets your hand is gonna be a very lucky feller.'

Mary laughed – then tucked into the KitKat.

The passengers were quietly snoozing as the train travelled at high speed along the north Yorkshire coast, having taken on coal and water at York. The countryside looked outstanding with dry stone walls of different sizes parcelling brown smudged hills that rose and fell along the horizon and smoke rising lazily from farm cottages. Occasionally they skirted the rugged Yorkshire coastline, and the sight of the waves and vast seascape infused her senses with dramatic beauty – it was so different and reinforced her sense that she was entering a period of change. The sound of the wheels on the track was hypnotic with the clunking rhythm over the fishplates that held the sleepers together.

Suddenly, there was a loud screeching, and the train began to skid along the track, sparks flying as high as the carriage windows in places, as it tried to stop. Everyone sat up. As Mary gathered her senses, she heard a soldier cry out, 'Jesus, it's a Jerry fighter coming towards us, get down, now!'

She looked out of the window and her eyes nearly popped out of her head. A German fighter plane was being chased by two spitfires and was headed straight for the train. Fear filled her body. Orange flames stuttered from the wings and bullets hit the side of the carriage, ripping the metal bodywork like paper, and smashing the windows into hundreds of shards of glass. She fell to the floor and heard the aircraft whizz overhead.

There was a strange silence. Passengers began to move about slowly and women screamed hysterically at the sight of two corpses crumpled over the arms of their seats, heads lolling to one side. She had never seen anything like this in her life, the blood, gore, bodies, and debris everywhere. It was truly horrific, and she started to shake.

A group of soldiers scrambled out of the train and stood waving their fists at the now-departing German fighter. 'Cowardly bastard,' they shouted and turned towards the pursuing Spitfires. 'Go on boys, get him.'

A soldier yelled urgently. 'Get out, get out, quick, there may be more of 'em coming.'

There was an oily, steamy, acrid smell in the air.

Still shaking, Mary scrambled to her feet, glass crunching underfoot and looked towards Alec's seat.

'That was bloody close, Alec. Alec?'

There was no one there. Horrified, she looked left and right then saw a trail of thick red blood on the floor coming from where he had been sitting.

'Oh God, no, please no!'

The slimy red trail led to the aisle where Alec lay writhing in pain. He had a large hole in his thigh and blood was flowing fast.

'Someone, help me. Now. Quickly,' she screamed.

A large man with sergeant's stripes pushed his way towards her through frightened passengers anxious to get out of the carriage. 'Okay, luv, let's get 'im straight.'

They both pulled Alec off the floor and manoeuvred him on to a long seat.

Mary put her face close to his. 'Keep going Alec, for little Jacqui, keep going.' She turned to the sergeant, 'We need a tourniquet.'

The sergeant held up his handkerchief.

'That's no bloody good,' she barked.

Without further thought Mary raised her skirt high and undid her left stocking from its suspender - with her personal allowance and pay she was not one for gravy browning and eyeliner lines on her legs. She quickly wrapped it around Alec's thigh and used a pen to help twist it tight.

The bleeding slowly stopped. Remembering her first aid she secured the tourniquet and used blood to write a time it was tightened on his forehead; tourniquets kept tight for too long lead to severe problems.

Alec winced with the pain then settled and looked at her. He gave her a wry smile. 'Woe is me, a red head shows me her thigh, what will I tell the missus?'

'Just hang in there, Geordie man. Hang in there, then you can tell her all you like.'

Apart from the sound of wreckage being cleared to free survivors and the hissing of escaping steam, it was eerily quiet, with people now working in an orderly, helpful, and disciplined way to clear the carriage. There was no sign of any more enemy fighters.

The sergeant went to get sweet tea from somewhere and Mary covered Alec with a discarded greatcoat to prevent shock setting in. She kept Alec talking, chattering about everything and nothing to keep him conscious.

An ambulance crew arrived forty minutes later from a local army base. A large beefy medic was heard coming through the carriage.

'Where's the blood case?'

'Over here, be quick, please,' Mary shouted.

The medic looked at Alec and immediately gave him morphine. 'Who did the tourniquet, you?' he nodded to Mary.

'Yes,' she said shakily.

'Then know this aircraftswoman, you probably saved his life. Well, done.'

He noted the time lapse from the blood figures on Alec's forehead and looked at his watch, then slowly let a little blood out before retightening the stocking.

'Stretcher,' he yelled, 'and bloody quick about it.'

Alec was carefully stretchered and taken to the ambulance. Mary scribbled her name and address on a piece of paper and thrust it into his battledress pocket, 'Let me know you're okay, Geordie man. Good luck.

Give little Jacqui a big kiss, hold on to that thought now.'

Alec looked up, in pain, but smiled and gave her a thumbs-up.

The chaos was eventually sorted out and the stricken carriage was literally bulldozed off the line to allow the remainder of the train to be coupled and resume its journey. It all happened within a window of just two hours. A dull silence replaced the chatter and laughter of the morning, as it proceeded slowly on to Scotland.

The train pulled into Perth station and shuddered to a halt. The passengers eagerly exited the carriages, wanting to leave the memory of the carnage behind them.

'Aircraftswoman Henslow, are you alright?' said a friendly sergeant as he pushed through the crowded platform. 'I was told to look for a red-head and I guess it's you?'

'Correct on all counts, sarge. You obviously heard about the attack on the train?'

'Yes, I did. Apparently, it was a Messerschmitt 109 that got detached from escorting a bombing run over Scarborough. He was being chased by spitfires and knew he was in for it when he decided to offload his cannons on the train. If it's any consolation the fighter boys took him out.'

'Not much,' said Mary, 'two dead and several injured. Can we just go? I'm so tired.'

'Yes, of course.' He took her kitbag and guided her to a jeep.

After about forty minutes of negotiating slippery narrow roads, through the mist and rain, Mary arrived at a radio site above the city at a place called Kinnoull Hill. All the buildings were camouflaged, and she caught sight of a tower out of the corner of her eye. She was taken to a canteen, given tea and a fried egg sandwich then ordered to bed.

Her quarters looked comfortable enough. It was a four-person room with large and small locker and bed with a very hard mattress for each person. She fell onto the bed, exhausted, and slept soundly for the next five hours.

The first few weeks at the signals site were interesting enough to keep Mary busy - so much so that she was almost able to block out recent events. Almost, but not completely, because the pain of baby Michael's adoption stubbornly lingered, and if she allowed herself to be enticed into reviewing her decision her mind raced left and right at a dizzying pace. It still hurt so much.

Signals work was interesting, if a little monotonous. Thankfully, it was easy to slip into a shift pattern and let life carry her on, day by day. She looked aimlessly out of the window and saw that the wind was blustery and dark clouds threatened on the horizon. Despite that, perhaps fresh air would blow away a constant feeling of edginess.

'Sarge?'

Sergeant Dobbins, the NCO in charge of the signals section, looked up.

'Yeah, wassup?'

'Nothing serious, I just thought I'd go for a walk. Okay with you?'

'Why on earth would you want to do that, it's gonna urinate down in an hour or so. Doesn't a warm billet and hot tea do anything for you?'

'Frankly, no. I'll grab this gabardine if you don't mind. See you all later.'

The operators looked up from their receivers and bantered: 'Don't get your vest wet,' and, 'Turn left at Skye.'

Sergeant Dobbins watched Mary gather her things and tapped his pencil on the table - he didn't remember saying 'yes.'

As she shut the door firmly, she felt the wind push against it and looked at the sky. It was mid-afternoon and autumn nights darken early. No matter. She would stride out and then turn around when it was sensible to do so. Besides, although dark inland it looked clearer across the sound and out to sea; perhaps the weather would improve.

The trail along the edge of the hill leading up to the mount was uneven but easily traversed and she strode on happy with the rhythm of her boots on the stony ground, the wind whistling in her ears. It was as if it blew away her cares.

Mary concentrated on the path so hard that she failed to notice the worsening conditions as dark clouds crawled low over the hills and stealthily spilled around the coastline. Pushing on regardless, unwisely led her to walk farther than she should as she sought a metalled road. Big raindrops driven by a strong wind, stung her face. Stumbling on, she was blinded by tears.

A less determined person would've sought a tree or wall for shelter.

Suddenly there was a flash of lightning, so close that the thunder followed almost immediately. It was dazzlingly bright. She jerked sideways in surprise and her foot stood on a large round rock, it slipped off and her ankle twisted, wrenching the ligament. She yelped in pain, lost her balance, and slid down a wet muddy slope towards the edge of the ridge overlooking rocky bays with crashing waves below. Her fingers dug into the soil leaving long lines gauged in the mud as she slid downward.

When she came to a halt, her face brushed against the soil, and she smelled the sulphur. She knew she had to stay as still as possible, to avoid a sudden loss of grip on the muddy surface. How long could she hold on? Crying for help would be useless in the wind but hanging by her fingers for a long time was perilous, every time she moved her feet slipped and the shock went through her body. The sea was breaking violently on the rocks below her. She felt truly helpless.

After ten minutes her determination was beginning to diminish. Her fingers hurt and her grip was weakening - would this storm never stop? Her thoughts became dark, life was such a struggle perhaps she should simply let go. A second later as she angrily rejected this and shouted, 'No, I'll never give up!' As if in response, she heard the unmistakable sound of a dog bark. Looking up, she saw a black and white collie with its paws on the edge of the slope, looking down at her. It was only twenty feet away but might as well have been a mile. As she wondered what to do next a figure of a man in a cape, wearing a flat hat and holding a stout walking stick arrived at the edge.

'Oh, lassie, what are you doing?'

'Well, sir, don't ask!'

The man quickly reached into his haversack and pulled out a length of rope and two small objects with three curved and spiked ends that looked like grappling irons. He stuck them into the ground and wound the rope into two bow-line loops, testing them several times with his stout arms.

'Now then, don't move an inch, not a single inch, do you hear?'

'I hear you, but please be quick,' she screamed, 'my fingers really hurt, and I can't hold on much longer.'

The man wrapped the rope around the anchors and put his body into one loop, with his left hand holding the second loop, and the other gripping the surplus line; he leaned backwards away from the slope. Mary saw his bulky body come up close as he let out the line with his right hand. He deftly put the second loop around her head and addressed her softly but with purpose.

'Now then. Take it easy, very easy, do exactly as I say. Lean very flat against the slope and slowly free your left arm, I'll steady you.' She did as she was told, and he held her against the surface. 'That's it, put your left arm through the loop. When you've done, hold on to the rope with your left hand and let's repeat it with the right arm, until both your shoulders are fully in the loop.'

Mary followed his instructions. When she moved her right arm, she felt her feet slip, but the man simply pressed her body to the slope, and she held fast. Slowly he dug his heels into the muddy edge and walked steadily up the slope, inch by inch, pulling in the loose end of the rope as he walked whilst holding Mary close. He was immensely strong. Soon they were almost at the top and by this time nearly upright. To her enormous relief, she finally limped over the edge and onto the path and sat down heavily.

The man looked at her. 'You okay?'

'Yes, of course,' she replied curtly, and then her eyes filled with tears. 'My ankle is hurt and so is my pride, not for the first time this year I might add. I think it's a bloody theme for me these days.'

She sobbed - this was one slippery slope too many.

Mary's head was ringing as deep sleep held her in its clutches. She awoke and became aware of the warmth in the air that enveloped her. It was so soft that she momentarily forgot what had gone on before and surrendered to the snug feeling of well-being. As she moved her ankle, a sharp pain pulled her out of her comfortable bubble.

She opened her eyes and looked around her. It was like a fairy tale. Before her was an open fire, alongside an old-fashioned cooking range on top of which was a large crusty pie. To one side a black and white collie lay, basking in the warmth from the glowing red embers of the fire basket. The walls of the room were bare granite stone adorned with pictures, photographs, brasses, and ornaments.

Mary sat up and tried to move her leg but noticed that it was stretched out to a stool and her ankle was wrapped in an elastic bandage. Now she was awake it throbbed like crazy, sending shafts of pain up along her calf. To one side she saw a woman dressed in a blue gingham gown with a woollen shawl wrapped around her shoulders sitting in a chair, carefully knitting. She looked up at Mary and smiled.

As Mary moved the blanket, she noticed that she was only wearing underwear. She grabbed the cover and held it tight to her.

'Don't be distressed, dear. I got you out of your wet outer clothes – they're drying over there by the fire.' She pointed to a clothes horse. 'Alistair was out of the room. Besides, he's too shy for such things. Now then, would you like a cup of tea?'

Reassured of her modesty, Mary spluttered, 'Oh, yes please, I'm parched.'

'Right then, I'll put the kettle on. Then I'll tell you what's going on. My name's Margaret by the way.'

'Mary Henslow. Thank you so much, Margaret.'

Margaret slapped the top on the kettle after filling it and put it onto the range. 'No need for thanks. You were in need and we're glad to be able to help, simple as that.'

Minutes later she heard hot water spluttering as it was poured into a large teapot, then there was the clinking of a spoon stirring the brew. Margaret approached her smiling.

'Here we go,' she said, offering a mug of tea, 'hot and wet. Do you take sugar?'

'No, thanks. Rationing weened me off the sweet stuff.'

'Aye, it's a bad thing this war. Alistair was thirteen years old when the Great War started and thankfully it stopped just as he was called up. When this one broke out he was well into his forties and has a touch of bronchitis. So, it was hospital work for him. He works in Perth General. I'm not ashamed to say that I am grateful for that. There's too much sadness in the world and I don't want to be subjected to that.'

'Yes, there is. Hopefully, it will not be long now. The allies are doing great things in North Africa and soon the Americans will help us chase Jerry out of Italy. Then who knows?'

'Maybe so, Mary. I canna wait. Now then. You were very lucky young lady, what possessed you to walk in a storm, especially up on the ridge?' She sipped her tea noisily.

Mary instinctively prepared for a telling off.

'You've Shelly to thank,' Margaret continued. 'She followed a scent then barked until Alistair arrived. Alistair's a strong man and was able to get you back up the ridge. The rest you probably remember.'

'I'm so grateful.' She turned to the collie, 'and to you, Shelly.'

Shelly wagged her tale as if understanding the attention but was reluctant to leave the warm hearth.

'As I said, we're glad to help. Couldn't have you floating out to sea, could we?' Margaret laughed softly and moved her hands in a wavy motion.

Margaret was putting the tea cups in the sink when a vehicle drew up outside the cottage and Mary heard the doors slam and the crunch of feet walking along the pathway. The knock at the door was aggressive and Margaret frowned as she answered it.

In the open doorway stood uniformed Sergeant Dobbins. 'Good morning. Your husband informs us that you are kindly looking after one of our airwomen?'

Margaret straightened. 'Yes, sergeant, and for the record I'd prefer it if you'd leave it to the Germans to knock my door down, thank you.'

'Oh, so sorry,' he replied, chastened.

She ushered Sergeant Dobbins and an accompanying corporal into the cottage. He looked straight at Mary. 'Well now, young Henslow, we were really worried about you. What have you been up to?'

Mary explained and Dobbins stroked his chin.

'This lady's husband told me as much. So, the ankle's badly swollen, is it?'

'Yes, very much so.'

Dobbins looked thoughtful. 'Look, we have enough operational staff and frankly the sick bay is full of folks injured after a recent bombing raid on Perth, so there's no point in rushing back to the base. Besides, I think you could do with a rest after all you experienced on the train journey up here. I don't think we properly took that into account, so take a week off. When you're fit to return, we'll come and pick you up.'

He turned to Margaret. 'Thanks for looking after one of ours, please accept this box of goods in return for your kindness.'

A box of rations from the base was placed gently on the kitchen table and Margaret nodded her grateful acceptance. Dobbins and the corporal left the cottage and as the vehicle drove away, Margaret began removing some of the tins. 'Oooh, bully beef, I do like that!'

She turned to Mary and smiled. 'Well, that's it settled then. We've a small downstairs bedroom and I'll make it up for you.'

Mary was speechless and gradually surrendered to the friendliness and warmth; what joy, to be helped unconditionally and to have decisions made for her. Now she was about to stay a while in this warm and friendly environment, she felt every part of her body relax. Margaret got up and walked towards her.

'Now put your head back one more time.' She took the empty mug from Mary's hand and touched her eyelids. 'Nod off again.'

Mary duly obliged.

The smell of cooked pastry teased Mary out of her slumber and sitting up she saw that the table had been laid for supper.

Margaret approached her. 'Let's get you into something respectable before we frighten the man of the house, shall we?'

Mary allowed herself to be wrapped in a large candlewick dressing gown. Shortly afterwards Alistair burst in through the door closely followed by the wind and rain - he had to fight to close it again. He secured the latch, turned, and addressed Mary with a fatherly smile.

'Now then, lassie, how are you doing?'

'Thanks to you lovely wife, Margaret, I'm doing very well indeed. I cannot thank you both enough.'

They settled and chatted idly over rabbit pie and fresh vegetables. Mary hung on their every word. It was all so – ordinary. The conversation ranged from politics to music and the weather. There were no disagreements or positions being taken. When they did not see eye-to-eye on a topic, they exited gracefully and with playfulness. There were just no big issues. She could have listened to them talk all night long, it was just like she used to with John. It softened her quest for independence, and she momentarily yearned for the comfort of a loving home-life with a partner.

Eventually, her eyes began to feel heavy, and she retired to bed in the small side room. Margaret gave her a hot water bottle and even tucked her in. Mary wondered whether there would be a goodnight story too!

The early morning sunshine probed through the kitchen window and touched the wooden breakfast table. Mary was given the only piece of bacon, despite her protestations, but Alistair explained that he was an 'egg man' and knew a farmer who kept hens, so they had plenty. She also learned to eat porridge with salt, and it wasn't so bad.

Soon, Alistair was off on his cycle to the hospital for another shift. Mary was able to stand on her injured ankle and pleased Margaret by washing up the pots. Margaret tidied the kitchen, stoked the fire, and told Mary to sit down, and she would bring a pot of tea. When they were both comfortable, she gazed at Mary.

'I hope you don't mind, dear, but in my family, we have a kind of sixth sense. Look, I've watched you and you seem in another world as if all is not well with you. My guess is that you were not just walking the other night, perhaps you were trying to hide in the weather.'

Mary was feeling strong, and Margaret's frankness didn't disconcert her. Nevertheless, she momentarily put her hands to her face, then removed them and breathed deeply.

'You got it in one, Margaret. In short, I fell in love with a pilot, got pregnant and he was lost over the North Sea. I had the baby and to my eternal shame, and I mean eternal, I had him adopted. My parents pressured me by going on about the difficulties of a single parent compared with a stable established family. But the hole in my heart simply will not close. Was I right, or was I wrong? Too late now I suppose. So many, what if's - I feel adrift in a sea of guilt.'

'Ah. That's difficult for you. I can see that.'

They sat in silence, then Margert spoke again. 'You've been honest, so shall I be. Alistair and I fell in love in our late teens and we, well how shall I put it politely - we didn't wait. I got pregnant. My mother knew what to do and contrived for me to visit a sick relative for a long while in Glasgow. Whilst there I had an abortion. I returned and Alistair never knew.'

'Oh dear, but you don't need to...'

'Yes, I do. You see, you and I, together, it's good for both of us to talk, isn't it? Anyway, Alistair and I got married a year or so later. Since then, I've not been able to conceive a baby - perhaps it's God's curse? Alistair has been so good about it and never pressured me. He's truly a good man. That's why I knew I couldn't let him down by holding on to the misery. I had to be strong and put it all behind me so that it didn't poison our love. Alistair's my focus, my reason for being, he's everything to me. My guilt should not get in the way of that, right enough. It's my issue, not his.'

She sipped her tea. 'And do you know what? That very focus keeps me from destroying myself. The way I see it is that memories are footprints we leave in our lives and without them we look back and see nothing that will allow us to learn from. But we must also avoid other people's marks in the ground, enticing us to follow mindlessly. That voice in our head is as slippery as a stream and unreliable as a rat – so don't listen to it, Mary.'

Mary considered her words carefully and felt as though she had been given a lifeline. 'You're so right, Margaret. I've lost my baby to another family, not dead but in the right hands and hopefully he'll have a good life. I hope to find another man, a good man, and when I do, I'll tell him everything. If he understands then he'll be the man for me.'

Margaret put her hands together and smiled broadly, 'Aye, that he will. So, what's more important, Mary, is the *now.* A book written on regrets is not worth reading. Now then, hold out your hands – I want to roll some balls of wool.'

So, there it is, thought Mary, *from misery to balls of wool!*

The days at the cottage passed far too quickly for Mary. She was in thrall of Alistair and Margaret's common sense, honesty, and love for each other. One day, when

Margaret was away for a nap, she was tempted to confide in Alistair that she and her mother didn't get on.

She watched him pull slowly on his pipe, and as he blew the smoke out, he said in a matter-of-fact way, 'Who says you have to?' His straightforward assessment shattered the brittle veneer of the problem.

Mary put her head back as she regarded his sage advice and smiled in acceptance. She gave him one more challenge. 'Another thing. I got angry with my father about poems he'd written. I don't want to go into the nature of them, it hurts too much. It' just that I felt I didn't know him at all. Then I found this scribbled verse that he wrote. I know I shouldn't have kept it and feel rotten about doing so. It's like putting your ear to the door and hearing something you don't like.'

She unfolded the paper and gave it to Alistair. He read it to himself.

Lord and Master

I hold that a morganatic wife is good,
I know that this will get a sorry shock.
But men are men, and be it understood,
like winds they veer and change the weathercock.
So long as duties they attend and perform,
what matter if this love hath wide embrace.
Good skippers fear not blast of rainy storm,
when harbours, more than one, give welcome place.

He stopped, raised his eyebrows.

'Oh, my dear. I wonder if you're not looking at everything you can find, almost as if he's let you down and you need further corroboration to damn him. He's your father, remember that. Remember too that he's just a man like the rest of us. In fact, his words remind me of our famous bard, Robbie Burns, who was a renowned womaniser and excused it by saying famously, *a man's a man for all that.* Your father's poem might also have been wishful thinking from a man in his later years – context is all, my dear.'

Mary reached and touched his hand. She felt as though a cool breeze of fresh air had enveloped her and her uncertainties slipped away. That was it. Let things go, keep life simple. Just being with these two, talking about everyday things and listening to their experiences and common sense was sheer therapy.

All too soon, Mary's ankle healed properly, and she was packed and ready to head back up to the radio site. She said her goodbyes and after a lot of hugs watched from the back of the jeep as it bumped its way up the hill. Mary didn't take her eyes off them until they were out of sight.

'Ah, the wounded lady returns,' Sergeant Dobbins said loudly as Mary came into the crew room. 'How are you?'

'Okay, in more ways than one, thanks sarge. And thanks for the break and getting my gear down to me. I really appreciate it. I think the air attack on the train really took it out of me and put me in a bad place.'

'Good. So now it's back to work. Ease yourself in slowly. Sit with Alice on Racal Receiver number two.

You're the morse-jockey and she's on voice interpreter. Get searching the airwaves. Second thoughts, there is an important priority,' he paused and smiled, 'teas all round!'

There was a loud cheer from the operators and Mary bowed and submitted to the banter and tea-making duty.

The work continued to be interesting, though boring at times, but as with all things secret there are moments of interest. Only a month or so ago a young German operator close to the Russian front let it slip that it was his girlfriend's birthday. This fact helped to crack an important code - something simple and small led to something big. In the meantime, she dealt with endless coded groups of letters and figures. She was an operative, without much responsibility, and concluded that for now she had achieved as much independence as was possible.

As she was making tea, Sergeant Dobbins caught up with her and introduced her to a new WAAF called Rachel. Mary was assigned to take her around and show her the ropes.

Earlier he had taken her to once side. 'Young Rachel is Belgian and went through a tough time at the beginning of the war. She and her family came across the channel in 1940 to escape the Germans, along with thousands of others. But when the Belgian King surrendered before Dunkirk, the public mood in London changed and they suffered quite a bit of intimidation. So, keep an eye out for her, will you?'

Mary readily agreed, but as it turned out Rachel was resilient, and they had a lot in common. Over the coming days they talked a lot and became good friends. One night, they got talking about family issues. Rachel leaned back in the wooden canteen chair.

'You know, from what you tell me about your family, especially that Aunt Agatha, they are a pretty detached lot of people, despite their good connections and obvious talents.'

'Yes, and it's taken me time to face up to that. Can I confide in you?'

'Yes, of course.'

'But it's difficult. You see, I noticed the six-sided star on your neck-chain, I think you're Jewish, am I right?'

'Yes, Mary. Does that bother you?'

'No, not at all. It's just that...' she faltered. 'Oh, dear, I feel awful. Let me explain. My father is a well-known author and poet. I found couple of handwritten volumes of poetry ready for publication in his study. They were obviously delayed because of the war. Well, in a section titled, Waxmoth, is a collection of awful antisemitic poetry. When I read it, I was so angry with him. We argued. I don't think we recovered before I set off to re-join the WAAF and it upsets me.'

Rachel frowned and spoke softly. 'The one thing I've learned about being Jewish is that for us, mistreatment goes with the religion. Don't ask me why, Europe is riven with hatred for us. It's all part of history, where despots or just plain evil people have blamed Jews for everything from poor harvests and the plague to financial treachery, to deflect their own actions or create a situation they can profit from. But I think that your dad is just caught up in a social loop handed down by others around him, where language and myths perpetuate, unquestioned and unamended, leaving Jews conveniently side-lined.'

She added graciously, 'Someday, he will change and look at people for what they are, not through religious bigotry or a class microscope.'

Reaching into her handbag she brought out a small picture card showing a dove with an olive branch in its mouth. 'This is an important image for us Jews, it means 'peace,' give it to him from me with warm wishes. A Jew he doesn't know who wishes him well.'

Mary took it and held Rachel's soft kind hand. She had experienced so much in such a short space of time. She had said farewell to naivety.

The train journey home was uneventful, not at all like the trip up to Scotland. It had been such an illuminating time for her - her Scottish hosts, Alistair and Margaret, the rumbustious Sergeant Dobbins and gentle Rachel. She had experienced such immense understanding and empathy from them all.

The Railway Transport Officer at Kings Cross station organised a vehicle to take several military personnel back to various bases, and Mary arrived back at RAF Kenley quite late. She felt the starched sheets cool on her body as she hunkered down to sleep. A short break offered by a forty-eight-hour pass was welcome and she planned to visit Fentiman Road.

11

Mrs Knight opened the front door to the house in Fentiman Road a long while after Mary had knocked. She looked tired and exhausted, and so much older. Her face instantly burst into a smile at the sight of her in her WAAF uniform.

'Mary, my sweet girl, how good to see you. Come on in. You look so smart. It's been too long.'

Mary stepped inside, took off her coat and hung it up, as though she were a day guest. Mrs Knight looked around furtively and her voice lowered, 'It's not my place dear, but it's your father. He's not well. He just doesn't look right, his skin is, well, kind of pallid and he moves very slowly. I think it's those bloody fags he smokes. He coughs like a steam-train.' She stopped and looked thoughtful. 'Sorry, I don't want to worry you, dear.'

'Not at all, Mrs Knight. Best to be forewarned. I'll pop upstairs and see him. Oh, before I forget, here's something small by way of Christmas present. I hope you like it.'

Mrs Knight's face beamed.

The stairs creaked as they always did and it evoked memories of years gone by, the way that sounds, smells and images do. As she walked along the first-floor corridor. Cigarette smoke tickled her nose and on reaching the door she looked through the smog and saw her father sitting in his captain's chair, his head in his hands. He sensed her presence and looked up. For a second, Mary saw something other than recognition in his eyes – she had never been able to read him – was it sadness, or regret?

He stood up unsteadily, holding the desk as he did. 'Darling, how lovely to see you. I missed you.'

She went over to him and kissed his forehead. He put his hands either side of her face before bringing it down to his shoulder. 'Yes, so good,' he whispered and rubbed his cheek against her hair. Then he sat down as if conserving his energy.

Sitting on the edge of his desk Mary reached out and took his hand. 'My lovely Papa, I missed you too. How are you? You don't look too well.'

He tried to smile and kissed her hand, 'Lovely Papa? I was so afraid you hated me.'

She squeezed his hand hard. 'Oh, no, you silly man. That's definitely not the case. We are different people that's for sure and you did make me angry, but no, I could never, ever hate you. I'm sorry we argued, let's not do it again. It broke my heart.'

'Mine too. Neither of us can change what we are and for that matter I look at you and see someone who is very special – so much better than me. You've grown up, Mary.'

He looked wistful then changed the subject. 'Thank you for your letters. Scotland sounded interesting, though I might not have gone mountaineering like you did. I did go shooting with friends who owned a small castle near Grantown on Spey, very posh. But I didn't like it. The idea of shooting beautiful creatures never appealed to me. I used to deliberately miss – I think they noticed because I was never asked back.'

Mary was amused at the idea of her papa being a rebel. 'Well, Papa, the ugly fact is that I wasn't concentrating and slipped on a wet path, and nearly slid into the sea. I was saved by an amazing Scotsman, then I stayed with him and his wife to recuperate, They are the most wonderful couple, you would really love them. They were kind and relaxed, and...well, they talked so much sense.'

She reached into her handbag and brought out the picture of a dove with an olive branch in its mouth. 'I also met a girl in the signals office whilst I worked there. Her name is Rachel. She gave this to me to give to you.'

Her father took it and instantly recognised the significance. He pondered for a moment. 'I really am a very silly old man. Will you pass on my thanks, I will put it in a special place and look upon its message every day from now on.'

Just then, Mrs Knight appeared with a tray of tea and a small plate of plain biscuits, then left as quietly as she had arrived.

They talked about anything and everything: the progress of the war, how she was finding the WAAF and politics. When the subject of the Labour Party came up, along with Clement Atlee's name, her father was visibly ill at ease, and Mary let his outpourings float past her; she now had the wisdom to know that prejudice hard-wired without reason is impossible to question.

Her father suddenly looked sad, and he took her hand. 'Look, darling. I must tell you something. I'm not at all well, so much so that my doctor thinks that I may not last the year.'

Mary's heartbeat quickened, and she tried to keep her composure.

'Is he certain?'

'Oh, yes. It's a tumour on my lung and before you say it, yes, it's the smokes that have contributed to it. My fault. Like everything else in my hapless life.'

'Steady now, Papa, that's not true. You are clever and artistic, the author of gardening and poetry books and you enrich people's lives, especially mine. So, go easy on yourself.'

His face almost fractured with a smile, 'Well, that told me! Thank you. Look, my dear, don't be sad. None of us can last forever. Let's just enjoy the moments we have together.'

'Wise words, Papa, that's the spirit.'

The hours flew past, and Mary had to go, she couldn't afford to miss the last bus. She was reluctant to leave but knew that her mother would be home soon from her bridge match, and selfishly didn't want confrontation or icy silences to spoil the moments she had just enjoyed. She would be smothered with indifference. Worse, with this awful news, her mother would be sure to say something silly and she was in no mood to fight her.

It was a long walk to the bus stop, near Vauxhall Station. As she approached a row of sandbags evenly stacked against an office building, she stopped, put her head against them and tears flowed relentlessly. Her body shook. All the sadness fell out of her. She reflected on the past and the present. Her pilot, her baby, her anger at her father's antisemitic poetry. Now he was dying, and she felt so terribly sad that time was too short to put things right – but she would try.

Settling back into life at RAF Kenley in her new role in the signal's office felt awkward. In many ways she wished she was back in the medical centre, but they were now fully staffed after she had changed to signals duties. On reflection, even the medical centre might not have been better. She had matured, so much so that it was all now a bit of a bore. Whilst the antics of the girls around her were amusing, she was no longer part of the group. Betty was the exception, she was great fun and she and Mary were so in tune with each other.

Tonight, she was going out for a pre-Christmas dinner with Giles. His choice of restaurants was always impeccable, and she was careful not to tell her new comrades, as they would take it all the wrong way, reverse snobbery is as bad as its twin sister.

She walked through misty rain to her billet but stopped at the sound of a car horn. It was Giles. She hunched her shoulders against the cold.

He'll raise my spirits.

'Where did you get this beast,' she said, prodding the black Ford with her umbrella.

'It's courtesy of my boss. I told him I wanted to take out the nicest and most attractive woman in Britain and her offered me his car. What say to that?'

'It's a compliment from you, kind sir. Otherwise, a complete fib!'

'That's me undone. Hop in. You get changed into civvies. I have some papers to read, so I'll wait in the car. Take your time.'

The rain had thickened, and Mary was grateful for the ride. It took her no longer than forty-five minutes to get ready.

The restaurant was small and barely twenty minutes away, and benefited from local vegetables and game, which was not subject to rationing. Mary chose pheasant and Giles the rabbit.

'Ah, lapin...'

'Show off.'

'Nest-ce pas?'

'Stop it or I'll order champagne which I'll drink, and you'll pay for, young sir.'

Giles touched her hand, 'It's so nice being with you, Mary. You're strong, fun and if I may say, very attractive.'

'Giles, you are sweet. Thank you.' She paused and gazed at him.

It was about time.

Look, I cannot think of one date with you that I haven't enjoyed. It's been truly wonderful. There's only been one thing missing.'

'Oh, and what's that?'

'Lean over a moment,' she said. When he was closer to her, she put her hand behind his neck. His hands held the edge of the table in surprise, but by then her lips had joined his and she pressed his head harder against hers. The kiss lasted for a long time.

As they parted Mary saw him grinning like a schoolboy and to her embarrassment a table full of airmen nearby let out an enormous cheer. Ever pro-active, she stood up and bowed which earned more cheers.

'Mary Henslow, that was the best kiss I have ever had in my life.'

'Giles Masterson, it was my pleasure. I've wanted to kiss you like that for so long, I simply couldn't wait any longer. Only one thing left now.'

Giles raised an eyebrow, 'And what's that?'

'The food!'

Giles sat back and laughed – just as the pheasant and rabbit arrived.

The months passed and work grew more tedious. There was a lot of excitement in the air following the allied landing in Normandy. Sadly, it didn't stop the V1 and V2 rockets - Mary just wanted it all to end.

Frequent dates with Giles were such a blessing – she was beginning to look forward so much to just being with him. He had given her the strength she needed.

She visited her father as much as she could and was now on a mission. Was it too late to give him her love and support, and perhaps to get to know him more? Favourable shift patterns at the signals centre and an extremely supportive sergeant in charge helped her make the necessary plans. Today, she arrived at Fentiman Road and let herself in with a newly cut key. Mrs Knight saw her from the open kitchen door, wiped her hands on her apron tilted her head to one side and waved.

Her mother's voice from the landing was strident and yet sounded uncertain. 'Mary, will you come up to my study? I want to talk to you.'

Mary hung her coat up and climbed the stairs slowly, full of trepidation. *What now? Please don't make a fuss about anything.*

Her study was colourful with flowered wallpaper and green drapes. A beige chaise longue, with a button hanging loosely from the middle edge, nestled in the corner near a bookcase and coffee table. Her mother was by the window, in front of her small mahogany writing desk. She stood straight, her hands clasped in front of her, dressed in a light blue Berketex day-dress, with padded shoulders and a line of large white buttons from the broad collar down to her pinched waist. Despite the glamour, her face was waxen, punctuated only by two mascaraed eyes and red lipstick lips. Her eyes glistened slightly, and she couldn't hide her discomfort.

'Mother, you look awful, are you alright?'

Her mother seemed to look for strength before she spoke. 'Yes. It's just that things are difficult right now. Anyway, I know we don't get on, but it's time we talked about a few things. Your father's going to die, you're a realist and I'm sure you've worked that one out. I want to get things off my chest.'

'You don't have to...'

'I do. Don't argue. You always argue. Things are difficult enough.'

Mary relaxed, and patiently deferred to her mother's obvious stress.

'I can't talk like this to your siblings. Your brothers are young men, and frankly men don't talk about issues, they tend to prefer sweeping them under the carpet. As for your sisters, they're very sweet but quite superficial. You're different – you always have been.'

Mary wondered what would come next.

'All right, here it is. I was having an affair with your father years before he left his first wife. Under the circumstances I could have been named in the application for divorce. It was a most unpleasant experience for us both. Your father had fallen out of love with his wife, and she took it badly. He left her, left holy orders, and later joined the army just as the Great War started. After the war she conceded to a divorce, we had two children before our marriage in 1920, your brother Tony, and Daphne who sadly later died.'

Mary was speechless. She had never taken much notice of birthdates and her parents' anniversary. Her chest tightened as she recalled her parents' cruel attitude to her own pregnancy. She guessed that the difference was that at least her mother had a partner for the illegitimate children, whereas Mary did not.

But all the same...

'We were very much in love, he was a handsome, vibrant man and extremely attractive, and women threw themselves at him. He was an intolerable flirt. Mother nature's a beast, men keep their looks for a long time and we women have babies and must do our best to keep our shape.' She unconsciously moved her hands down her corseted midriff.

'That must have been so difficult for you.'

Her mother was more composed now and she punched the words out.

'Yes, it was. There was another upsetting incident, but I don't want to talk about that. It did rather change the landscape. After that, we agreed that he should continue his writing and because of the parlous state of our finances I assumed control. I think he was grateful for that, although he never actually said so, but then he always was slow to admit to his failings. He was a hopeless businessman, and I can tell you it took a long time to put things right.'

Mary reacted to the open door to her mother's life with her father and wanted to reach out, despite their relationship, to touch her, to hug her and give her support that only a daughter can, but there was a force field around her that was impenetrable.

'Mary, I don't want you to think badly about your father, I know only too well how special you are to him. And frankly,' she straightened, 'I've been rather challenged by it.'

'I wouldn't say...'

'Well, I would. You must be careful, Mary. You have always had a habit of seeing life through rose-tinted glasses. Frankly, he's no different from other men of his time. But know this, I have always loved him, it's just that our lives changed as the years passed. He's an incurable romantic and totally unrealistic. If I seemed non-committal about having to move you and your siblings around the relatives it was simply because we had no money, even less after your father was made bankrupt in 1930.'

Mary put on an expression that pretended not to know already.

'So there. You've had the lot. Know this: I hated farming you all out to relatives and I hated us being broke. But things gradually got better, his books sold, and our lives improved. Well, that's it, I've said my piece. I must go now. I have an appointment.'

'Can't we...?'

Her mother bridled. 'Can't we what? Sit and indulge in the vice of meaningless conversation and self-pity? There's nothing to say. I just thought you were old enough to have the big picture.'

With those last words she stubbed out her cigarette in a glass ashtray on the mantlepiece, straightened her dress and left the room.

The facts of her parents' life together had fallen on Mary like an avalanche of jigsaw puzzle pieces, most of which now formed a picture that she had never seen. Mary sat down heavily on a sofa. *What did it all mean? What kind of a naive dream-world have I been inhabiting?*

Today, she decided not to stay longer in the house and went back to her billet at RAF Kenley. Tonight, she wanted to be alone.

It was a long day in the signals centre, and with little to challenge her Mary was dogged by her mother's revelations. At the billet she found Betty packing a suitcase to take clothes home to Turnpike Lane. She sat down wearily on her bed and as her eyes misted told Betty all that she had learned.

'Blimey, poor you, another punch in the tummy.'

'You could say that.'

Betty stopped packing and sat on the bed next to her. 'Look old chum, I need to be straight with you. We've known each other for quite a time now. Now listen, what you just told me forms a picture of everyday life all along Turnpike Lane. That's what life's about. You've been farmed out so much you haven't seen or lived real life, Mary. You lived a – what did you call it – a jigsaw puzzle of events, but I must be honest and say that nothing you've told me is unusual. A pain in the bum, yes, but unusual – no, not at all. We just deal with things as best we can. I reckon being stuck with that aunt in Devon cramped your view of the world.'

Mary sniffed and looked at Betty. 'Can't say that I like this flipping *life* bit, I prefer my dreams!'

'Well, my friend, this ain't gonna be the last painful thing you hear in your long and healthy existence, I bet. Besides, you've got balls, Mary. I mean that. I just know that you will endure all that life throws at you, just don't let events knock you over. You deserve better than that.'

Mary hugged her friend. 'You in a hurry to leave?'

'No, why?'

'Let's go to the Wattenden Arms for a quickie?'

'I'd rather have a beer...!'

Mary squealed and hit her with a pillow.

The pub was crowded. There was jubilation at the news that the war was going in the allies' favour. The radio played jazz that suited the American servicemen and there was a lot of lively laughter. No one wanted to let the euphoria go.

'Two glasses of mild over 'ere,' Betty shouted.

A voice that Mary recognised shouted, 'I'll get those.'

It was her Giles. Just what she wanted. Without thinking she fell into his arms, and Betty winked knowingly at Giles and slowly left the pub – she would get the early bus after all.

'Hey, you feeling a little wan? Is your father still in a bad way?'

Mary nodded and looked up ate him. Giles was perceptive and held her tight with his left arm and with difficulty paid the barman using his right hand. When she pulled herself together, he grabbed the beers, and they went outside and sat on a bench.

She repeated her story.

'Oh, dear,' he paused, 'but look at it this way. Don't tell me you've never wondered why she behaved so badly? Well, let's just leaven the bread a bit. You see, it seems to me that she's had to put up with such a lot and like it or not she's managed to win through. Not without casualties though. But at least you know the background now. Perhaps it's time to let things go.'

Mary smiled at his common sense and hugged him. She looked into his blue eyes and found herself falling more in love with him. Could he ever replace John?

Mary carried on visiting her father during the weeks that followed her mother's openness. His bedroom was quite spartan, it had to be to contain the various trays, kidney bowls, liquids, and piles of towels. It had previously been a junk room, which was why the faded flock wallpaper had never been changed in years. But at least he had copies of all his books and was brought a copy of *The Daily Telegraph* every day. He was in awe at her tales, her bravery award, saving the baby and the aircraft attack on the train. His face radiated with pride as she spoke.

They played chess, discussed his latest poems and she felt as though they had bonded so well under the awful circumstances. She knew in her heart that it couldn't last, because at each visit he looked weaker and coughed so badly, he hid his handkerchief from her, but she noticed the blood. Once a tall, elegant man, he was now pale and thin. It seemed that only his tartan pyjamas held him together.

It was so odd. Papa was clearly dying and yet despite all the disappointments, Mary was able to sit with him and talk, without rancour or regret. She felt closer to him now more than ever before, and as they talked the more, she began to understand and have sympathy for him. It was a strange feeling, she was now not just a listener, but almost a conspirator.

He sat forward in his bed and moved his bishop. 'Check mate,' he said triumphantly.

'How do you do it? I didn't see that coming.'

Mary poured him another glass of port, he took it and winked at her. She began to box up the pieces.

'Given up, eh?'

'Yup, I know when I'm beaten.'

Papa reached out and touched her arm. 'I've learned a lot about you, my dear. Frankly, you're the kind of person who doesn't give up.'

Mary warmed to the compliment. Her eyes moistened very slightly as she looked at his face, his eyelids sagging away from the eye sockets revealing the red underside.

'Yes, I'll give you that, I have toughened up a lot. Life's journey is a funny old thing, isn't it?'

'Is that an oblique reference to me?' He tilted his head to one side.

Mary paused and reflected on the need to speak truthfully, especially now Papa was in God's waiting room. 'Papa, I've seen so much over the last few years since I joined the WAAF. I saw the way everyday people from all parts of the country viewed the world and how they dealt with their problems. Some people may be on a different social level, but the honesty and quality of their lives is beyond question. I put you on a pedestal, Papa, and yes, that pedestal has wobbled the more I know of you. I am now able to understand more about context, I mean the world around you what with the Great War and pressures like the Wall Street Crash. You are my father and I love you to bits – nothing will ever change. But know this, I will never, ever accept any kind of fascist or antisemitic ideology. So please never mention any of it to me again.'

'Nicely put, darling,' he looked at her admiringly. 'I wrote a poem about the devils and angels inside us all and the importance of banishing the former and yielding to the latter. I'm never sure I got the balance right.'

'Yes, I remember that one. I loved it.'

'Well, I've faced demons and sadly, when I was younger and less worldly-wise, I was seduced by hubris and I'm sorry to say, greed. I behaved badly and got divorced from my first wife. I was unfaithful several times, which was wrong of me. Then I left holy orders, and it was the Great War that gave me a sense of purpose.' He paused and Mary acted as if this was news to her. 'So, military life sorted us both out.'

He began to cough, and Mary fetched him a glass of water, which he gulped down noisily.

Composed, he put his hands to his face and added thoughtfully. 'It seems to me now, that I could only experience life through my eyes, and I see now that my lens was a tad flawed. I'm a bit of a chump really.'

He began coughing again and it lasted for a long time. Mary was worried. Then he stopped, exhausted, and weakened, and lay back on the bed.

Small tears crept down Mary's cheeks. She thought how strange it was that Papa with fallibilities was so much more understandable than a saint. He had led a chaotic and dysfunctional life; it's hard to climb out of a slippery trench once in it. Things were now so much clearer to her.

'But look at you now,' he whispered, his voice fading, 'my Bambi is now a full-grown deer.'

She smiled and held his warm hand tightly. He drifted off to sleep. Whilst he lay there, snoring lightly, she looked idly around, and her eyes fell on a paperweight that was on top of several letters - inset was a medallion that had a silver crescent moon engraved on it. There was no doubt that it was the one worn by the woman in the photograph she found in her father's cabinet. Shaking her head gently, she muttered, *a man's a man for all that.*

Mary dozed, and as she awoke realised that his hand was very much cooler. The home nurse was passing the door and she called her in.

The nurse pulled down his collar and felt the side of his neck with her fingers and then looked at Mary.

'I'm sorry, dear, but he's gone.'

Her mother's letter was short and to the point; how like her to be icily efficient at such a time. Her beloved Papa was dead. No time to get to know him better, no time to share her thoughts about the future, no time to introduce him to Giles. He would've liked Giles, as she did more and more each day. The letter outlined the date of the funeral and wake afterwards, and Mary put it into her diary.

The only bit of news that was in any way refreshing was a postcard she recently received from Alec, the officer she had helped on the train to Perth.

Dear Mary,

I am writing to tell you that I am now fully recovered, and all is well. I suppose I should be grateful to Jerry, my leg took a long time to mend, and it gave me lots of time to spend with my little girl.

Thanks for all you did for me.

Regards,

Alec

12

Mary was grateful that Giles agreed to drive her to the church in Boarhunt, Hampshire, where her father was to be buried. Her grandfather had been the rector there and her father served there prior to his ordination. Giles agreed to attend the funeral and wake, even though he had every reason not to want to be in the same room as her mother. He was such a gentleman.

They got out of the car, which Giles had parked some distance away, joking that it was ready for a quick getaway if the going got rough – it amused Mary and she thought that might even be true. They sat on the cemetery wall underneath a huge yew tree.

'I hate funerals,' said Giles, turning to look at her. 'You know what? When I flee this life, I'm going to do it in style. Perhaps I'll have one of those jazz bands like they do in New Orleans. The music will be gloriously happy and cheerful. Crying and frowning will be banned, jokes will be told and all the silly mistakes I ever made will be announced and forgotten. Because that's what should happen to mistakes. What do you think?'

Mary smiled enigmatically. 'Giles, you are a complete nut! So, who would you invite to the pre-heavenly soiree?'

He put his fingers to his lips and looked skyward with a theatrical expression, 'Oh, my wine merchant, my squash partner, and of course the three waitresses from the Ivanhoe Club in London...'

Before he could finish, she swatted him with her gloves, 'You rotter, the rest I can take but not the waitresses.'

This was the way it was with them both. Laughing, joking, and understanding each other's humour - just when she needed it most. Mary held the top of Giles' arm and put her head on his shoulder. As she looked up at him, the church bells rang, and she put the urge to kiss him to one side. They heard the chattering from several mourners making their way to the church.

'Spell broken, we'd better get a move on, I think we're late anyway,' she said resignedly.

They walked down the cobbled path, joined a line of people snaking towards the church and came to the vicar. He smiled a row of ice-white teeth, nodded, and welcomed them. No other words were exchanged, and Mary felt it was rather like a queue at the Labour Exchange. As they went inside, the hum of voices in the congregation, that sounded like a swarm of bees, enveloped them. The building had a familiar 'other worldly' smell about it, a little bit like upmarket mothballs. The church warden handed them the order of service, hymn-sheets, and a prayer book.

Mary took a deep breath and headed towards the front of the congregation where her mother was sitting; as her pace slowed, Giles gently took her arm and pressed her onwards. She whispered to him, 'Beast!'

Giles guided Mary to the pew immediately behind her mother, who turned and regarded them, her face taught and expressionless. Before she could speak

Giles took the moral high ground and held out his hand.

'Mrs Henslow, Giles Masterson. I'm so very sorry for your loss. I do so admire your husband's past military service in the Argyll and Sutherland Highlander Regiment, the soldiers were a fine bunch of men. I'm also sure that his horticultural expertise and love of poetry will be missed by many people.'

Mary glowed. Her mother softened, gave a thin smile, and then nodded appreciatively, before turning and rooting around in her handbag. Mary's brothers were sitting beyond her sisters to the left. Her brother Charles, whom she had not seen for a long time looked at Giles, nodded and gave a thumbs up. Good old Charles. He was the character of the family. His conversation always skated over family tensions. Younger sister Mavis couldn't hide a girlish grin, whilst Hazel looked distinctly jealous and hardly acknowledged her.

The vicar's comments were polite and comfortable, a kind of verbal noticeboard of her father's life and achievements. On display, today, but gone tomorrow, except for a precis in the local newspaper.

Mary reflected how sad it was that there was no humour, nothing of everyday substance in the words.

At the graveside they went through the ritual of throwing dirt onto the coffin. More prayers were said and quite a few tears were shed, it pleased Mary that he would be missed, and that people thought kindly of him, if only for a moment. As Mary sniffed back her own tears she looked up and saw a man, about her age, ten yards or so away from the congregation. She wondered who he was. When she looked back a moment later, he was gone.

Mary thought that it always seemed bizarre catching up with relatives on such sad occasions. So much needed to be said, remembered, or challenged, in such a short time. The conversation becomes stilted and polite, platitudes abound, and promises are made to 'catch up some time', which are nearly always forgotten. She was relieved to hear that Agatha was too ill to attend, though she felt in such a good place to be able to face her.

Giles was patient and charmed everyone. Her brothers liked him a lot. Sadly, they had to leave to get back to their respective units, but they left wanting to meet up with him again.

At last, her mother joined them. She stood with her elbows tight to her body holding her handbag immediately in front of her.

'I thought that I'd come and talk to you since you seem to have been ignoring me.'

'Not at all, mother. Look, I appreciated your openness the other day, I really did. I left knowing a lot more about you, your life with Papa...'

'Well, I...'

This time Mary was driving, '...let me finish. We are two different people. I am older now and the war has shaped me a lot. Despite everything, you are my mother. You brought me into the world and cared for me in childhood. I owe you a child's respect and I freely give it. Who am I to judge you, or Papa, you both lived in a different time, with different challenges.

Let's move on and resolve that one day we will drink coffee together without a barrier between us. There's no need to say more.'

Her mother looked taken aback but seemed to accept Mary's volley.

Mary added quizzically, 'by the way, I saw a man, about my age, in a raincoat, over by the large yew tree, but he doesn't seem to be here now. Did you see him, is he anyone we know?'

Her mother's eyes misted, she raised her chin and said quickly, and without emotion, 'he's your half-brother.' She straightened and looked over Mary's shoulder, as if this was just an ordinary piece of news and she needed to get on.

'Yes, we must make time to talk more, later perhaps.' Then she was gone. To another group. To a life without Papa.

Mary was stunned. Half-brother. So, this was the incident alluded to weeks ago. She recalled the photograph in Papa's secret drawer of a woman with a toddler. Betty had been correct, there's always something else – sometimes secrets just fall out of the cupboard when you least expect them to, as if energised by hibernation.

Giles drove her back to London. The light was getting dim but there were occasional flashes of orange in the sky. They didn't talk, but he rested his left hand on hers and squeezed it, wanting to comfort her but not knowing exactly how to.

Mary looked at him warmly and felt blessed that this man had been her rock for so long.

Several months passed and although sad at her father's death, Mary felt that she and her mother had both reached an understanding of each other. She resolved to one day seek out her half-brother and his mother. Perhaps she would discover even more about Papa.

It had been a long time since the Normandy landings and allies' surge towards Berlin. However, there was a sense of national impatience as well as hope following recent key victories against German forces, but more especially because today the Prime Minister was going to make an announcement and the atmosphere was electric. The Wattenden Arms public house was crowded with civilians and air force and army personnel from local units. The beer could not be pulled fast enough.

Mary and Betty excitedly enthused about what to do after the war, but their chatter was disturbed.

'Come on,' shouted a soldier, tapping at his wristwatch, 'put it on!'

He was supported by others, and the publican looked flustered as he struggled with the knobs on the wireless. The murmuring decreased as he turned up the volume and tuned the radio to the BBC Home Service. Hissing and crackling filled the air - then came the deep sound of Big Ben's chimes.

The pub went silent.

Winston Churchill's voice was clear and his message to the people was precise. 'Yesterday morning at 2.41 a.m. at General Eisenhower's headquarters, General Jodl a representative of the German High Command and Admiral Donitz the designated head of the German state, signed the act of unconditional surrender of all German land, sea, and air forces in Europe, to the allied expeditionary forces, and simultaneously to the Soviet High Command. Hostilities will end officially at one minute after midnight tonight, Tuesday 8 May, but in the interest of saving lives the ceasefire began yesterday to be sounded along all the fronts. The German war is therefore at an end. We may allow ourselves a brief period of rejoicing – today is victory in Europe day.'

Mary and Betty held on to each other tightly and tears welled in their eyes. Churchill's last words filled them with pride.

'Advance Britannia, long live the cause of freedom, God save the King.'

Almost immediately, shouts of joy broke out. Everyone hugged their neighbour, whether they knew them or not. Kisses were given freely, and the cheering continued, drowning out the rest of the broadcast.

Mary's chest pounded and she felt that this was one of the best days in her life.

It was all over.

There were also tears for those lost or damaged. But jubilation over-rode everything. For the rest of the day and into the night, relief and happiness gushed throughout the country and people sang and danced – and drank! It was to be a very long twenty-four hours.

It is quite surprising how quick bureaucracy can work when it wants to. Mary was issued with discharge papers from the WAAF towards the end of 1945 and readily accepted them. She was now out of work and to her great joy, free to make a new life. If life was a book, then she surmised that for her, this was the next chapter. It was all about resetting herself.

For now, it was such a strange time. The war had ended, and people had high expectations, yet rationing continued without an end in sight and jobs were scarce. There were also conflicting emotions: grief, sadness, happiness, hope, and anger. It was like attending a birthday party that had empty tables. In 1939 the British had experienced what was termed the 'phoney war', the long period before the deadly conflict arrived. Now it was as though there was a 'phoney peace', as expectations of a better time had yet to materialise out of the chaos of war.

The new Labour government provided large numbers of government offices to help ex-servicemen and women to assimilate back into civilian life, including payment of social security and help to find work. Despite that, Mary and Betty set up a small local group called Signpost, in the Haringey area, directing many of the bewildered returning soldiers and airmen to the appropriate authorities - it's fine having new agencies but quite another thing telling people which one to go to. For four months they had their work cut out, but after that, requests for help slowed significantly.

What next on the Mary Henslow agenda?

Giles had been uncharacteristically edgy recently, but never once did he take it out on her. It was probably the high volume of work entailed due to the chaotic aftermath of the war.

She was clearing out the makeshift office in the spare bedroom at Turnpike Lane, when Betty came in and flopped onto a large chair.

'I'm bushed, Mary. I think I'll finish early today.'

'Lightweight!'

Betty threw a ball of paper at her. 'Maybe, Lady H, but I'm gonna go downstairs and sit by the fire with a cup of tea, then eat fish and chips – and after that, I'll float away on gossamer wings...well, to bed that is!'

'Very poetic. You go, you deserve a break.'

'No rest for the wicked. I've got another mission.'

'What's that?'

'Mum looks after a couple of young Polish people. Well, the feller was beaten up by a mob of Moseley's old followers. There's still a lot of evil stuff going on out there Mary, Jew-baiting, hatred of immigrants. I'm sick of it, but I'm not gonna stand back and let it happen. So, me and my mates are setting up a social centre to welcome any foreigner who needs our help.'

'You're a gem, Betty.'

'No, I ain't, I'm a human being and I want to help those who need it.'

Betty blew her a playful kiss and left the room to a deserved night of rest.

After tidying away a bunch of papers, Mary slipped into a light navy-blue raincoat and picked up her handbag. It had been busy day and she needed fresh air and exercise. The door to the front of the house creaked in protest as she opened and closed it, and once outside she turned left and walked along the damp pavement. She made her way briskly away from Turnpike Lane towards Priory Park and watched the sun gently lowering itself towards the horizon, the bright orange backlight darkening the buildings in front of her. She would have to be quick to avoid the fading light.

As she passed the off-license, grumpy Mr Leonard came out with a crate of empty bottles. Uncharacteristically, he smiled at her.

'Allo,' he said cheerily. 'Thanks for all the advice you gave my daughter. 'Er man's never been the same since the end of the war, what with his disability and all, thanks to you there's some 'ope for a job, or money off the social. 'E ain't very bright and just needed to know where to go.'

'No problem, Mr Leonard,' she replied, 'you take care now.'

Mr Leonard being polite – there was a success.

How she wished that she could engage with her mother and describe how many ex-servicemen had been helped by Signpost, to navigate the minefield of form filling and engagement with government officials. She was proud of that – Papa would've been too.

Mary could never work out why it was that she sought approval and recognition from her mother; it was hard-wired into her, as was her earlier worship of her father. A vision of him crowded her mind. He was a man who had been lost in a changing world – weighed down by the chains of family history with its skewed social attitudes, two world wars and the devastating effect of the Wall Street Crash. But he would always be special to her no matter what.

Mary put errant thoughts to one side. Having saved some money, she was on the lookout for new opportunities. Her confidence was high, and everything seemed in balance and the future looked bright. She breathed in the cold late afternoon air and watched light snowflakes begin to fall.

As she walked along the pavement, she swung her arms and hummed Glen Miller's 'In the Mood' – that certainly fitted her temperament. She wiggled her hips without realising what she was doing, when suddenly there was a sound that she instantly recognised: it was the roar of a motorcycle. It came from behind her and swiftly moved past and into the distance, the sound gently dying the farther away it went.

Stopping momentarily to watch it pass, Mary resolved that as soon as she was settled, she would spend some of her savings on a new motorcycle; one that she owned and would never be taken away from her.

Once in the park, her pace slowed, and she looked through the white-speckled light of gently falling snowflakes to try and find the path. As she took in the natural beauty of the snow, the figure of a man wearing a long raincoat and a trilby hat emerged from the mist.

She watched, with a growing sense of unease as the man slowly come towards her and couldn't make sense of what she was seeing. He came closer, and it began to dawn on her that the familiar jaunty gait leaning slightly to the left, one shoulder lower than the other was familiar. It looked exactly like John King, but it couldn't be, he had been lost in action.

The man stopped in front of her, and she knew then that it was John. Her mind raced and her legs became like jelly so that she stumbled towards him, reaching out to touch him, as if to test the reality of what she was seeing. Without a word he supported her and moved to a nearby park bench, and they sat down, staring at each other - she was too scared to speak. He held her shaking hands and looked into her eyes.

Mary stuttered, 'My God, it's you. I can't believe it – I can't believe what I'm seeing. But...where've you been? The last time I saw you, you were heading off to the base, and then you just disappeared. No-one could tell me where you were, and now you're here – I don't understand.

John gripped her hands tighter. 'I know, and I'm sorry you had to go through all of that, but Mary, I'm here now, and that's all that counts.'

Mary was confused.

'All that counts. John don't brush over things. It's been so long, and I've heard nothing. Where have you been?'

John paused and looked awkward.

'It's an easy question,' she added desperately.

'Mary, I've dreamt of this moment for years. It's been a long time, but I've come for you – I've come to take you back with me.'

'Take me where? What are you saying? I'm confused.' Her voice rose and she felt guilty about sounding angry. Here they were, together again, yet something was wrong.

'Let me explain.'

Mary closed her eyes and breathed hard to calm herself. 'Please do. John, I should be happy, we should be happy, but something's not right.'

John straightened and looked at her directly.

'I know it's going to be an awful challenge, but please just listen. Believe me, Mary, I've been tortured about this for the last few years. You must understand,' he paused and took a large breath, 'sometimes what drives a man is bigger than anything else. I've seen so much cruelty and indifference in the world, and that's what made me the person I am. The terrible inequality in the West, its selfishness and the dreadful use of political expediency ignoring the needs of the common man. It drove me into a space I couldn't escape from. I had a mission. I wanted desperately to make a difference to people's lives. Then you came into my life.'

'John, where's this going?'

'I want to take you to the Soviet Union.'

Mary stood up abruptly. 'What? How? Why? Good grief, what's going on?' She put her hands to her face, now red and wet with tears. 'Is that where you've been all this time?'

'Dearest, you need to understand.'

'Understand!' Mary blurted. 'You're posted missing, I thought you were dead and grieved for you for 3 years. I had your baby and was forced to give him away for adoption.'

'A baby?'

'Yes, a boy. I called him Michael. Do you know what the adoption did to me? It ripped my heart out, that's what. Now you turn up out of nowhere. as if you've been away for a weekend and come out with an absurd proposal that we go to Russia.'

John was taken aback and searched for the right words.

Mary was gasping for breath, her chest heaving. Then emotion got the better of her and she flew at him, pounding her fists against his chest.

'How could you do this to me?'

John grabbed her hands. He tried to draw her into him, but she broke free and walked away, she didn't even want to touch him.

He looked away as if in a daze and in his own world. 'I have a child! Don't you see, Mary, we can get him back and go away together. Make a new life. I know you'll find it challenging, but the Soviet Union really is a place of hope and equality, not the pathetic charade that the United Kingdom has become, in hoc to the Americans. It has so much to offer.'

Mary was numb – *Soviet Union?* He wasn't even apologising and misguidedly thought that somehow, they could get their son back.

Mary cut him short and shouted, 'You really are a selfish bastard!'

John persisted. 'Stop it. Look, trust me, the more you get to understand the world about you, the more you will see how good it will be to set up a new and exciting life together, with our son. What we must do is...'

He stopped talking, startled, and looked left and right, before dropping his shoulders in hopeless dejection.

'Hell's teeth.'

Three men walked towards him from different directions. As they approached John, it looked as though he was going to make a run for it, then he resignedly put his hands into his pockets.

'John King,' said a voice Mary recognised instantly, 'I'm Captain Giles Masterson.'

'Nice to meet you, Giles. I'm sure that you are aware that I am a Soviet citizen and part of a trade mission here in London. We wouldn't want to upset the delicate entente cordiale now, would we?'

Mary sat back onto the park bench and the words sank in. *Citizen - Soviet Union?*

'Ah, yes, I'm aware of that. But you are also a deserter from the Royal Air Force. Let's just talk things over in a gentlemanly fashion, shall we?'

The two other men moved forward and handcuffed John's right wrist and led him away. He turned his head over his shoulder and shrugged.

'It would've been so good, Mary. So very good.'

Mary watched as he was escorted to a waiting black Ford sedan parked nearby with its lights on and engine running. As it drove away, she hunched her shoulder and sobbed.

Giles sat down next to her on the bench. He gave her time to gather herself, then put his hand on her arm and said, 'you deserve an explanation as to why I'm here.'

'I most certainly do,' she responded sharply.

He took a deep breath.

'I'll tell you as much as I can. I was seconded to MI5 when I got back from North Africa, I knew a bit of German and gained an experience interrogating POW. As part of the job, I inherited piles of case files and John King's was one of them. It was confusing because he suddenly deserted with his Hurricane aircraft to the NAZIs. The Air Ministry was extremely miffed because it was packed full of experimental equipment. It was a complete surprise because his clearance had been carefully scrutinised.'

Mary sniffed back more tears and shook her head. 'Deserted? That makes sense. After his disappearance, John's details were deleted from RAF Kenley's records and all his possessions were taken from our flat. On top of that, when I had the temerity to make enquiries, I was rudely stonewalled. Why on earth did he do it?'

Giles held her hands, which were now cold from the shock. He knew that there would be a lot for her to take in, but she had to have the full story.

'Who knows, it would've remained a closed case, but we received information towards the end of the war from a double agent that John was an undercover NKVD operative whilst serving in the RAF. His political masters knew the Germans were in a bad place after losing the battle for Kursk in the July of 1943, so they ordered him to desert and gain the trust of the NAZIs. Thereafter, he was to report on the German situation to give them a strategic edge. I must give him his due, he succeeded. Then he escaped to Moscow.'

'He's a communist?'

'Yes, he has a new name: Sergei Romanov,' Giles sighed, 'although I hate to admit it, the agent told us that he remained deeply in love with you. He talked endlessly about you and his wish that one day you would both be reunited. That's why he inveigled his way onto the trade mission to London. It was a simple deduction for MI5 that he would try and seek you out.'

'What will happen to him?'

'There will be subtle questions and threats, but we just want security holes plugged. If it can be shown that his motives were purely political and did not endanger our national interests during the war, then he might find himself back on a plane to Russia. We must be careful, because we are after all, supposed to be friends with Uncle Joe Stalin.'

Mary's face looked pinched, and she said, deliberately, 'Okay. So, our meeting in Covent Garden was not a coincidence, you used me!'

'No, not at all,' he replied urgently, 'that's not the case. It really was serendipity, I promise you.'

Mary got up, walked to the path, and stared at the horizon. The snow had stopped falling and the carpet of whiteness made it eerily quiet. Nothing was said.

Giles' face was ashen, and it looked as though Mary was about to walk away. He had to act quickly and stood up.

'I want you to know this, for sure, Mary. After we met on the train to London all those years ago, I just knew you were someone I could love. The fleeting time I spent with you before my posting was wonderful, and then we lost touch. But we met again, in London, and you explained that your mother meddled and sent me away, then kept my letter. My heart sang, and I put everything else out of my mind.'

'Except John King!'

The bald fact pierced his heart.

'Oh, God. Yes, except him. I couldn't believe it when I later saw the connection between you both and so wished that he had been in another officer's cache of case files. It was the inevitable pull between duty and love. Frankly, I just wanted the case to die, with him disappearing and marrying a large muscovite, and living on vodka and potatoes for the rest of his days. I would never have told you.'

Mary put her bag over her shoulder and brushed non-existent dust from her coat. She was deeply hurt, confused, and agitated. Looking back at Giles she saw his perplexed expression and he was searching for the right words.

He was tense but spoke slowly and determinedly. 'After we met again, I was overjoyed, but saw your distress. I wanted desperately to look after you. To hold you, love you and make everything all right. Work inevitably got in the way, so I arranged for you to be posted to Scotland. And back you came – a different person. It's been so difficult for me you must believe that.'

He ran his hands through his hair as he paused for breath.

'I respect you. I love you – I really do.'

He hesitated then looked at her imploringly.

'Mary, I know that this is not the best time or place. In any other situation there would be dinner, flowers, and music. But, oh goodness me...!' He hesitated and put his hand to his temple. 'Mary Henslow, will you do me the great honour of becoming my wife?'

Mary's heart skipped a beat.

In a short space of time she had walked, carefree, to Priory Park, happy that she was at last beginning to get some kind of purchase on life, coming to terms with her family and having experienced so much. Her world then exploded when confronted by her supposedly dead lover making outrageous suggestions about relocating to the Soviet Union. To top it all, her new lover, Giles, turned out to have known that John was a spy and was waiting to apprehend him. Now he wanted to marry her.

The highs and lows of the emotional rollercoaster she was on pulled her in different directions, and she felt out of control.

Could she be sure of Giles' feelings?

She looked at this genuine man caught up in a web of circumstances, not of his own making, professing such love for her. When she talked to Alistair and Margaret in their croft in Scotland she had said, *'...I hope to find another man, a good man and when I do, I will tell him everything. If he understands then he will be the man for me.'* Giles had already quarried a place in her heart, encouraging her to want a loving relationship and a normal home life.

Her anger melted, but deep down she felt taken for granted, too much had happened. It was difficult to let go of all the facts – she just had to be sure.

'Giles...' she paused.

His face twisted with apprehension.

'Thank you so much for what you just said, for your love, and I know you do care for me. For that matter, I feel the same about you, but...'

His face fell.

'Giles, I don't want to upset you, you don't deserve that. Frankly, I feel betrayed, and used. I need to sort myself out. You are a truly lovely man, I know that, and I do love you, really, I do. Please don't give up on me, just give me time.'

She cupped his head in her hands and kissed him gently, then walked slowly away into the darkness.

The End

Author's Notes

My mother's father, Thomas Geoffrey Wall Henslow, MA Cantab, was a clergyman, soldier and a horticultural journalist who wrote books on the subject, and a poet. The family line dates to the 1400s, one relative was Shakespeare's theatre manager in London, another was high in the administration of the royal naval dockyards, and John Stevens Henslow tutored Charles Darwin.

This story uses the template of my mother's life as well as details from her stories about her family and their antics. Like others, they went through tough times after the Wall Street crash. Although I use some family names, all the conversations and incidents are completely fictitious.

Her father was a mercurial character who joined the Argyll and Sutherland Regiment at the outbreak of the First World War, after leaving his first wife and holy orders. I knew little about him until I did some research. The poem, *Lord and Master,* which I include in the story was a pencil scribbled page I found in his collection. It is a somewhat skewed attitude to socially unequal marital relationships. I can only guess that he was a little selfish, an incorrigible flirt. Worse than that, he was antisemitic, judging by the awful poems he wrote in a journal titled, Waxmoth. I am so disappointed.

Mary spent a lot of time in Devon, because she suffered recurring illnesses like rheumatic and scarlet fever. She did ride a motorcycle (her picture is on the reverse of the book cover). She did join the WAAF.

The loss of her Sergeant Pilot lover caused her a lot of pain, and she was pressured by her parents to give up his baby for adoption. I met my half-brother, Michael, (now deceased) in the eighties - he was a lovely man and had all the Henslow looks that is for sure.

Mary's life was full of enormous challenges, but she was always a loving mother and courageous in her attempts to make ends meet, especially latterly, to support my disabled father. She spoke with a received accent and lived in a working-class environment having met and married my father who was ex-RAF and a builder and decorator - I was born at 71 Turnpike Lane, Hornsey, North London - hence my fond use of this location in the book.

This story follows Mary's journey from Devon to London, through her WAAF wartime service, facing and dealing with danger as well revelations about her family, bitter loss, and betrayal. It occasionally touches on unsavoury social attitudes and the atmosphere of imminent change in British society as it reset itself on its journey towards equality and the reduction of class-structures. I know it took a long time, but we need to look back to the 1940s to see just how ridiculous and unfair it was then. They were not the good old days at all.

Mum would not like this book because she adored her father. I respect her loyalty and hope that this is a suitable tribute to her courage and grit - she never gave up.

Lancelot Geoffrey Clarke
August 2022

Printed in Great Britain
by Amazon